L.M. Merrington is an Australian author and editor. Her other books include two Gothic mysteries, *Greythorne* and *The Iron Line*, and a steampunk romance novella, *Tea Dreams* (written as Elizabeth Wren). She lives in Queensland with her husband and daughter. Find her online at www.lmmerrington.com

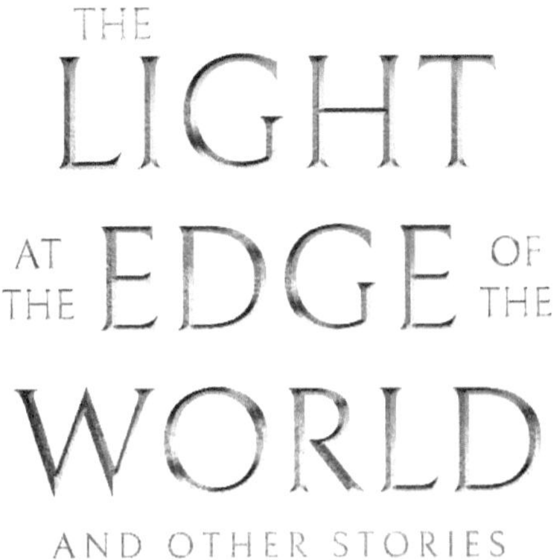

THE LIGHT AT THE EDGE OF THE WORLD

AND OTHER STORIES

L.M. MERRINGTON

A catalogue record for this book is available from the National Library of Australia

ISBN-13: 978-0-6489825-1-7

Edited by Maxine McArthur
Cover design by Deranged Doctor Design

For Anna

CONTENTS

The Light at the Edge of the World

A storm was brewing and the clock in the square was striking midsummer when Thorsten Mackinder arrived in the village of Finster. For several hours he'd been walking through a deepening twilight and, now that he was finally here, it was fully dark. A few candles, the only sign of life, guttered in the windows of the houses that overlooked the square. Thorsten hunched into his coat as thunder rumbled in the distance, his shoulders bending under the weight of his pack. It had been a long walk; the road through the forest into Finster was poor, for few people left, and even fewer came.

He reached into his coat and pulled out his pocketwatch, rubbing his thumb along the intricate filigree of its case. Its steady ticking was reassuring as he opened it and noted the time: a little after four—in the afternoon, he reminded himself. He wondered how one kept time straight in this village of endless night.

Thorsten had come to Finster on a whim and a rumour, as he was wont to do. Now, he crossed the square to the public fountain and sat on its edge, shrugging out of his pack. The only sound was the splashing of the fountain and the *thunk, thunk* of the village clock above him, its face dimly lit by a lantern to either side. Beneath the clock face, small wooden figures danced around a maypole under a summer sky, in a field splashed bright by the sun. Leaving his pack, Thorsten stood and peered at the clock with its three dials: the season, the day, and the hour. A small window in the hour face showed a tiny sun peeking through—the only indication that it was not currently deep night. Thorsten frowned to himself.

He jumped as the thud of a closing door rent the silence, and turned, instinctively reaching for his weapons. But his bow was slung on his pack, and his hand had barely grazed the hilt of his knife when he saw that the newcomer was a doughty, matronly woman in full skirts and an apron. Sensing no immediate threat, he let his hand drop.

The woman crossed the square towards him, squinting into the dimness as if unsure of what she was seeing. Thorsten supposed he must cut a peculiar figure, with his long, travel-stained coat, and his broad-brimmed black hat pulled low over his eyes. His dark hair was overly long, almost brushing his shoulders, and several weeks' worth of stubble lay scratchily on his chin. That was what life on the road did to you. He'd once owned a pair of seven-league boots that could cross entire counties in a single bound, which had meant much less time sleeping rough, but he'd given them away on impulse long ago. The ordinary leather ones he now wore were thinning at the soles, but they were so comfortable he was loath to part with them.

He stood tall and open as the woman approached him, although he remained mindful of the possibility of a trap.

You didn't last as many years on the road as he had by being dull-witted. She was about fifty, he guessed, with work-roughened hands, and arms muscled by manual labour.

"Where are you from, stranger?" she asked, peering at him. She wore spectacles as thick as the bottom of a glass, but they seemed to give her little relief.

"Here and there," Thorsten replied. It had been a long time since he'd lived in a place long enough to call it home.

"And what brings you to Finster?" She eyed his pack, the bow, his strange garments, clearly trying to work out what to make of him.

"Just passing through."

The woman laughed mirthlessly. "No one passes through Finster. One road in, one road out. But you already know that, don't you?"

"I do." In the pocket over his heart was a cryptic letter from his late mother, which had upended his world and brought him here. For someone apparently half-blind, the old woman didn't miss much. And from the glance she gave him, it was clear she knew there was more to the story than he was letting on.

"You'll be needing lodging for the night, then?"

Thorsten paused. His natural inclination was to set up camp in the woods, for people could be unpredictable and dangerous, and he disliked being shut inside with locks and bolts on doors and windows. But he had a job to do, and he needed the townsfolk's help to do it. And, he admitted, there was also the unmistakable allure of a hot meal and a feather-bed.

"I will. Would you be so kind as to direct me to the inn?"

"I'll do more than that," she said. "I'll take you there direct—I'm the proprietor, along with my husband, Frank. Ada Mottle's my name. Pleased to meet you." She stuck out a meaty hand, and Thorsten shook it.

Hoisting his pack, he followed Ada across the square to a neat wooden door, above which hung a sign, 'The Widow's Walk'. The lettering was capped by a picture of a woman, dressed in black, pacing despairingly along the rooftop of an old house on a cliff while the sea crashed and foamed below.

Inside, the inn was warm and cosy, lit by a multitude of lanterns. A fire roared in the grate, although the temperature outside was mild. It was too early for it to be truly busy, but one or two patrons were nursing drinks at the bar or sharing a game of chequers across the low tables. They looked up when Thorsten entered and stared without compunction, clearly amazed by the presence of a stranger in their midst. Thorsten shrugged it off; he was used to being a novelty.

"Don't you be minding them," Ada said as she fetched him a key, but her glance was wary. When Thorsten paid in advance for three nights, however—in gold pieces, no less—her demeanour softened slightly. "Up the stairs and to the right," she said, pointing to a narrow wooden staircase at the back of the taproom. "You've picked a good time to be visiting. It's our Festival of Light tomorrow night."

"Indeed?" Information on Finster was scarce in the outside world, and this was the first he'd heard of such a festival.

"Eh now, but here's me blathering on when you no doubt want to rest. There's water in your room for washing, and dinner starts at six o'clock."

Thorsten opened his mouth to ask more about the festival, but Ada had already turned away. Deciding to take her advice, he climbed the stairs to his room, which was small but clean. He flung his pack on the floor and sat on the bed to remove his boots, wondering.

HE'D ONLY MEANT TO rest for a moment, but when he woke, he immediately knew he'd slept for much longer. Raucous laughter drifted up the stairs from the tavern below, along with the occasional crash of breaking glass as someone stumbled against a table. It was clearly late enough for the patrons to be considerably inebriated. Thorsten's stomach rumbled, and he wondered if there was still the possibility of a meal. His thoughts felt thick and dull; he was no longer a young man, and travel took a harsher toll than it used to. Plenty of times he'd stayed in inns such as this one and had thought nothing of joining the party downstairs, making merry into the wee hours and, if necessary, cracking heads as well. But now the thought of it just made him weary.

He was pulling on his boots when there was a knock at the door. Instinctively he reached for his knife.

"Come in!"

The door opened awkwardly, revealing a girl of about fourteen bearing a tray.

"Aunt Ada said you must have been tired after your journey, so she asked me to bring you some supper," she said with apparent fearlessness.

Thorsten was unused to such hospitality. "I...Thank you...Miss...?"

"Darke. Eleanor Darke." She set the tray on the dresser then turned, but instead of leaving, she just stared at him as if he was the most curious thing she'd ever laid eyes on. Thorsten wondered if she was waiting for a tip, and slipped his hand into his pocket for a coin.

"Is it true you've come from *Outside*?" she asked suddenly.

"Well, yes."

"Tell me what it's like?"

"I...uh...well now, I don't really know. You've never left Finster?" Much as he loved solitude, Thorsten was intrigued by this waif.

She shook her head. "Only the Shadowless leave Finster."

"Shadowless?"

Eleanor eyed him for a moment, but didn't answer the question. "Have you come for the Festival?"

"Not intentionally, but I understand it's tomorrow night. Can you tell me about it?"

At this, she seemed to have second thoughts. "Well...I don't know if I should, what with you being an Outsider and all." But he could see the curiosity in her eyes.

"Tell you what, if you tell me about the Festival, I'll tell you about the Outside."

This seemed to sway her. Thorsten recognised the hunger for knowledge from his own youth.

"It's the Festival of Light. Every Midsummer's Eve we make pilgrimage to the Light. Those blessed with shadows return to Finster, but the Shadowless are cast out."

Thorsten frowned. "I'm afraid I don't understand."

"Shall I show you?"

He nodded. He had a feeling that this mysterious Light held the answers he sought.

"Come with me, then."

Thorsten stood up, and she grabbed his hand. Rather than leading him through the taproom, however, she took him down the back staircase and out behind the inn, into a dingy alley smelling of refuse. The cobbles were slick with damp; the storm must have passed while he slept.

"We're not meant to go there except at the Festival," she muttered. "Best if we're not seen."

"Why are you trusting me?" Thorsten asked as they crossed the square, where the clock face was now showing a crescent moon. He had been a stranger in plenty of places, but he'd rarely been accepted so readily.

Eleanor stared at him. "Because Finster is dying. Can't you feel it?"

He could feel it, of course: a slow withering away of the heartbeat of the world. It was part of what had brought him here in the first place. But he'd never encountered anyone else as attuned to life's rhythms as he was. There was clearly more to this girl than met the eye.

They slipped down another alleyway between buildings on the far side of the square, and shortly afterwards found themselves in the forest. The woods grew up against the village, thick and foreboding, but Eleanor seemed right at home. Her night vision was better than Thorsten's, and she moved as easily as if she were walking in broad daylight.

Presently, he noticed they were following a path. It was narrow but well-kept, with the surrounding foliage neatly trimmed. There were no lights to guide them, but every so often the way was marked by white rocks that glowed dimly through the darkness. He let Eleanor go ahead, following carefully in her footsteps as the path ascended a small hill.

After some time, the path began to widen, then opened onto a clearing in the woods. They had reached the summit of the hill, and atop it was the last thing Thorsten expected to see—a wrought-iron lamppost, glowing with a strange white light. It lit up the trees all around and he blinked, momentarily dazzled.

"Beautiful, isn't it?" Eleanor said, smiling. "This is the Light." He could hear the capital letter in her voice.

Thorsten regarded it. The ironwork was indeed beautiful, but he found the light itself harsh, its colour too white and stark compared to the gold of true sunlight. As he watched, it flickered for a moment, as if the bulb was almost burned out. "How did it come here?"

"Well," Eleanor said, "the stories say that, once upon a time, the outside world was in moral decay, and the Divine chose to protect the people of Finster by causing the forest to rise up and darkness to fall. The Light was left to remind us of the light of the Divine. When we approach the Light, we see our shadows growing out of our feet, and know that we are the Divine's chosen people: those who know both light and darkness. But sometimes those among us succumb to worldly desires, and are revealed on approaching the light to be Shadowless. So they must be cast out of Finster for the sake of the village's moral purity."

She laughed rather harshly, and Thorsten narrowed his eyes.

"Do you believe that?" he asked with genuine curiosity rather than judgement.

Eleanor glanced quickly over her shoulder. "We shouldn't be talking about this. I don't even know why you're here."

"Let's just say I help places like Finster solve their problems. I'm not going to report you, if that's what you're worried about."

She considered for a moment, then took a deep breath. "I used to believe it," she said. "But there's so much I don't understand. I see other things; things that make me think that perhaps there's another explanation."

She looked up at him, suddenly shy. "I think Finster is cursed," she whispered.

THE NEXT MORNING, THORSTEN woke to find that word of his arrival had spread quickly. He'd barely finished washing and dressing when there was a knock at the door. He opened it to find Ada Mottle.

"Beg your pardon, sir," she said, "but there's some folks downstairs who'd like to meet you."

"Of course." When she'd gone, he slipped his blades into his boots, just in case.

The guests turned out to be a blustery, red-cheeked man and his retinue. He wore a sombre black cloak and a wide-brimmed black hat, even indoors. Thorsten immediately pegged him as Finster's leader, and his suspicions were confirmed when Ada breathlessly introduced him as Markus Kettle, the village mayor. Thorsten had dealt with his type many times before, and he knew that the success or failure of his job would rest entirely on how well Kettle took to him.

"Welcome to Finster, sir," Markus Kettle said, once the necessary introductions had been made. "As I'm sure you know, we don't often receive strangers here. What brings you to our small pocket of the world?" It was a loaded question.

"I'd heard tell of Finster's...troubles," Thorsten said, trying to be diplomatic. "I have some skills that may be able to assist you. I'm a curse-breaker by trade."

"Troubles?" Kettle blustered. "Whatever do you mean?"

"Well..." He waved his arm at their surroundings; the inn, as always, glowed with cheerful lamplight, but outside the windows it was black as ink. "The darkness, sir. Finster's eternal night."

Kettle frowned. "I see there's been some misunderstanding, sir. Finster isn't in any trouble. Our darkness is a blessing, a reminder of our saving grace. It isn't a curse, nor something that needs to be cured."

"If I may beg your pardon, Mr Mayor, I've seen curses like this before, although none so wide-ranging or long-running. Sooner or later they become unstable and destroy everything they touch. Surely you yourself have noticed some small changes over the past little while?" He thought of Eleanor's certainty that the village was dying. He'd felt it himself as soon as he'd set foot in the darkened forest.

"Nonsense!" Kettle said. "You are an Outsider, sir, and so I forgive you your ignorance. But I bid you come to the Festival of Light tonight. There you'll see the abundant blessings granted us, which I have no doubt will put this ridiculous notion of a curse to rest."

Thorsten inclined his head. "As you wish, sir." He wasn't ready to give up yet, but things would clearly have to be taken gradually. The situation was more sensitive than he'd thought.

After the mayor left, Thorsten took the opportunity to ask Ada about Eleanor. He'd noticed the girl flitting here and there in the inn, wiping tables and ferrying glassware, but hadn't had the chance to speak to her.

"You're lucky to have your niece working with you," he said, taking a seat at the bar as Ada brought breakfast.

"I am, that. She's a good girl. I've looked after her since she was eight, and now she's almost grown."

"What happened to her parents?"

Ada's face clouded. "They...died." But there was something in her tone that suggested she wasn't being entirely truthful.

"They didn't die," Eleanor said abruptly. Thorsten flushed; he hadn't realised she was close enough to overhear.

"Now, love..." Ada began, but Eleanor cut her off.

"We owe them the truth, at least, Aunty," she said. Then she turned to Thorsten and lowered her voice. "They were Shadowless," she murmured.

"So they were cast out?"

Ada nodded sadly. "My own dear brother and his beautiful wife. I don't know where they are now. Theodore was a horologist, one of the masters of his craft. He built the clock in the square, and now that's the only thing left to remember him by." She snuffled, and Eleanor patted her hand comfortingly.

"It's heretical to say so, but I don't believe they were sinners," Eleanor said. "I don't know why they lost their shadows, but they were good people. It's just wrong." She frowned and went back to wiping tables.

"Theodore and Mary were dissenters," Ada murmured, low enough that Eleanor couldn't hear. "We've never told her—it's safer if she doesn't know. I can't prove that's why they were cast out, but...well, you never see Markus Kettle's supporters declared Shadowless." She sighed. "The poor lass took it hard, as you'd expect," she said. "We've done the best we could, but we'll never be her true parents."

"Why didn't she go with them?"

"The Shadowless must leave the village immediately. They aren't permitted to take anything—not belongings...nor family."

Thorsten started slightly at that. He'd seen some cruel things in his time, but this was something else. "Tell me, Mrs Mottle," he said, "when did Finster first become cloaked in darkness?"

"Eh now, that's a question," Ada said. "Well before my time. I'd say nigh on a hundred years ago. I remember my grandfather speaking about how there was still sunlight when he was just a boy, but the darkness came when he was about ten."

"And did anything important happen around that time? Any strangers in town, or some sort of falling-out?"

Ada leaned on the bar. "I can't quite recall. I believe there was some rift on the village council—at least, that's what my mother always told me, and she'd had it from her father who'd had it from his. There was a Mayor Kettle back then too—the current mayor's great-grandfather—and something happened, although I couldn't for the life of me tell you what it was. But now, come to think of it, we've always had a Kettle as mayor. Funny, I never considered that before."

"Thank you, Mrs Mottle. You've been a great help."

"Oh, not really, surely."

"More than you know. I hope I may accompany you to the Festival tonight."

Ada Mottle laughed. "Why, of course, and welcome." She looked at him archly. "Just mind you don't misplace your shadow."

AT SIX O'CLOCK, THE bells tolled to mark the start of the Festival of Light. Villagers congregated in the square, dressed in their best clothes. Thorsten joined them, conspicuous in his black coat among the sea of colour. Eleanor appeared beside him as the crowd began to move slowly towards the woods, but they didn't speak. The whole occasion had a sombre air.

Thorsten glanced towards the front of the crowd, where Markus Kettle was leading the procession. The mayor wore his official robes and walked with his head held high, lord of all he surveyed. Thorsten thought about what Ada had said—that Finster had always had a Kettle as mayor—and wondered. He was beginning to develop a theory.

"Does Markus Kettle have any children?" he whispered to Eleanor.

She shook her head. "No. I'm not even sure they ever tried for one. Why?"

Thorsten shrugged. "No reason."

"Shh!" someone behind them hissed.

They fell silent and Thorsten retreated into his thoughts. If Markus Kettle's ancestor had, for whatever reason, decided to pull Finster out of the world, it made sense that the power to maintain the curse fell from parent to child over the generations. And now, with the line about to be broken, the curse was collapsing. Thorsten had seen the aftermath of such things before: places or people who had been destroyed before he could reach them. The waning life-force that both he and Eleanor could sense was surely an indication that the end was nigh. If he was unable to convince the villagers to let him lift the curse, Finster would soon be no more.

They were now processing slowly along the forest path. As Markus Kettle passed the white stones, each glowed brightly with the same cold luminescence Thorsten had seen in the lamp, then died away. If the villagers thought this odd, no one showed it. They ascended the hill and formed a ring around the lamppost, although Thorsten noticed they were all careful to remain outside the circle of light.

"Friends and countrymen!" Kettle proclaimed. "We meet again at this most sacred place, to humble ourselves before the Divine and undertake the one true test of our faith!"

The crowd murmured; there were the occasional shouts of "Amen!" and "Hallelujah!".

"As your mayor and servant, I offer myself as the first pilgrim, to pay homage to the Light!"

Thorsten had the feeling that this was the way the ceremony always ran. Kettle turned his back on the crowd and stepped forward into the circle of light. Slowly, with measured steps, he walked towards the lamppost. When he reached it, he laid a hand on its wrought-iron frame and fell to one knee. His shadow, black and thick, stretched out behind him, and the crowd swelled with cries of praise. He took up a position beside the Light, standing straight as a sentinel.

Following their leader, the villagers formed a line that inched towards the sacred lamp. Thorsten and Eleanor found themselves shunted to the end. Each person filed past the Light, knelt to check their shadow, and continued back into the darkness at the edge of the forest. Thorsten couldn't help noticing that, with Kettle standing there beside the Light, the villagers were also inadvertendly bowing before him.

The line was about halfway through when suddenly a shout went up. "Shadowless! Shadowless!" Thorsten peered past those in front of him to where a woman, holding a child of about two, knelt before the lamppost. No shadow bled out behind her.

"Heretic!" cried someone in the crowd. The woman burst into tears as two burly men, whom Thorsten recognised as Kettle's hangers-on from the inn, hauled her to her feet.

"Banish her!" the chant went up, swelling as more people joined the chorus. Eleanor glanced at Thorsten in horror, pain in her eyes as she mouthed the words.

"No!" the woman screamed as one of the men wrenched the child from her arms. The little girl shrieked and cried, reaching for her mother, but the thugs hauled the woman to the far edge of the forest, and Thorsten saw with a chill that each of them carried a whip at his belt. "Walk!" Markus Kettle commanded, his tone lacking any of its previous warmth. "Be gone from this place, and never set foot here again!"

Sobbing, the woman stumbled down the hill, away from Finster, towards the outside world. Thorsten wondered if she would even make it, with no food, shelter or means of making a fire. And if she did, what then?

The child was still screaming. The man holding her shoved her at a woman in the crowd, and she hurried back down the path to the village. Thorsten laid a hand on Eleanor's shoulder; the girl was visibly trembling. As the little girl's wails died away, the crowd calmed down, and the line continued to file past the lamp as if nothing had happened.

As their turn approached, Eleanor became increasingly agitated, scuffing her feet restlessly and glancing around as if looking for an escape.

"What's wrong?" Thorsten whispered.

"I just know I'm going to be Shadowless."

"How do you know?"

She moved closer so they wouldn't be overheard. "That woman, Maybelle Keening—she's a friend of mine. We used to talk about...things. She didn't like the mayor. But none of his supporters have ever been declared Shadowless."

Thorsten said nothing, but wondered. It echoed what Ada had already told him; despite her aunt's efforts to protect her, Eleanor had clearly not remained ignorant of Finster's politics.

When their turn came, he pushed Eleanor behind him and strode towards the Light. He bent his knee, and was unsurprised when the cry went up: "Shadowless!" Lifting his eyes to the lamp, he noticed that Markus Kettle's hands were glowing. In the lamplight it was almost impossible to see except at close range, and only then if you were used to noticing small things out of the ordinary, as he was. Thorsten almost smiled at the simplicity of it: provide light from different angles and a shadow would disappear. He bowed his head again and waited for the mob to grab him, but they didn't come. Instead the mayor stepped into the circle.

"We have among us a stranger, the first time the Festival of Light has been witnessed by an Outsider!" Markus Kettle boomed, his voice carrying across the clearing. "In him you can see the corruption and wickedness that leads the Divine to curse him as Shadowless! In time he will return to the outside world, that den of sin, but we hope that when he does, he can proclaim Finster's purity far and wide!"

The crowd cheered, and Thorsten stood up, forcing himself to smile. Over the mayor's shoulder he could see Eleanor slinking away from the circle of light and melting back into the forest. His diversion had worked.

Thorsten followed the crowd back along the path towards the village but, glancing back, he saw that the mayor and a few other men had stayed behind. He bent down, pretending to fix his bootlace, then slowly slipped off the path and into the woods. He doubled back towards the Light and crouched in the shadows, watching.

Markus Kettle was flanked by two other men—senior village leaders, Thorsten presumed. Everyone else had left the clearing. The man on the left handed Kettle something; Thorsten caught the flash of metal and saw it was a key. The mayor bent down and inserted it into the lamppost, opening a tall, narrow panel. Thorsten crept closer, trying to move silently through the undergrowth.

Peering through the bushes, he could just make out something like a thick rope running down the inside of the lamppost. It looked black and charred. Markus Kettle removed his hat, and Thorsten noticed with surprise that his hair was long, fashioned into a braid that was coiled atop his head. When he let it down, the braid fell halfway down his back.

Suddenly, the man on the mayor's right lifted a knife. Instinctively, Thorsten darted forward, but the blade fell not on Markus Kettle's neck but on his head. The man grasped the mayor's braid and cut it close to the scalp, then handed the rope of hair to its owner. The mayor reached inside the lamppost, doing something with the hair that Thorsten couldn't see. He cried out in pain, as if the action burned him, and when he withdrew his hands they were red and blistered. The lamp flared brighter for a moment, then settled down into a strong, steady glow. The men rose and walked back towards the village.

Thorsten sat back on his heels and nodded to himself. Since he'd arrived, he'd been wondering how the curse was sustained, and now he knew. There were many different types, but in this case a sacrificial curse made sense. Most people associated sacrificial curses with blood magic, but in Thorsten's professional opinion, blood magic was for amateurs. It was messy, difficult, and tended to lead to people asking awkward questions. A sacrificial curse like this one, though, was a different matter. Thorsten was impressed with its subtlety, especially as it had apparently remained active for over a hundred years. From what he could tell, it was quite simple: the curse required renewal every year with a bodily sacrifice—in this case, hair—from someone in the bloodline of the curse-maker. In return, Markus Kettle remained powerful—power consolidated, it seemed, by declaring his enemies Shadowless through simple light magic—and Finster remained dark. But the law of curses dictated that nothing came for free. Over time, sacrificial curses exacted terrible tolls on their makers or the makers' descendants, and the only way to be free was to pass the curse on to a younger, fitter heir. But Markus Kettle had no children. It was no wonder the curse was unstable. Thorsten stood and stretched his aching legs, then turned his back on the lamp and followed the path down to the village.

WHEN HE SLIPPED IN among the crowd in the square, he suddenly found himself the centre of attention. Delicately, he began probing about the Festival and the Shadowless, but he quickly discovered that everyone he talked to believed the mayor's words wholeheartedly: the Shadowless were cursed by the Divine and must be banished. He marvelled to himself that it was one of the most effective ways of dealing with dissent that he'd seen. But none of the people seemed to have an inkling of how much trouble the village was in, or that Finster's curse could have come from anything other than a deity.

"It's always been this way," an older woman said, sitting with a young man whom Thorsten presumed was her grandson. "The village is thriving—why would we want it to be any other way?"

"But surely it's difficult without light?" Thorsten said. "How do you grow your food?"

"The Divine has blessed us with wondrous means," the young man said, his face prim and pious. "In the years after the Coming of the Dark there was famine and pain as those of lesser faith fought the wondrous dark. Then the Divine sent a stranger with a gift: a miniature Light of the Divine. He showed us how to balance light and dark to provide for ourselves, and now we have greenhouses and farms the like of which an Outsider could not imagine. But only the most faithful may enter them, lest the constant exposure to so much light uproot their souls."

"The lit world is the work of the Enemy," another man chipped in. "In the darkness is softness and grace; in the light is harshness and heresy. Even the plants and trees have bowed to the will of the Divine and adapted themselves to deep shade."

All those he talked to said the same; they seemed scared of a brightly lit world and opposed to any change.

THE FESTIVAL CELEBRATIONS continued all night, but Thorsten retired early. He lay on his bed, listening to the sounds of revelry drifting up from the taproom and the square below. For the first time in a long time, he was conflicted. Curse-breaking was no easy life, to be sure, but on most of his jobs he brought a welcome end to suffering. When he'd heard about Finster, he'd assumed it would be the same—grateful villagers languishing under a powerful curse, who couldn't be rid of it fast enough. He hadn't expected such resistance, and he wondered what to do. His code of honour bade him to first do no harm—and lifting the curse on a people who didn't wish to be free of it could indeed cause considerable harm. But to leave things as they were would ensure the village's destruction, and with it those who longed for a better life.

He slept little, partly because of the noise, but more due to the uneasiness in his own mind. After dozing briefly in the small hours, he woke to the chiming of the midsummer clock outside his window. A quick glance at his pocket watch showed it was already after nine. He pulled on his clothes and boots, and made his way downstairs.

The inn was quiet, with all the patrons finally gone to their beds. He suspected that most people would spend the day sleeping and recovering from the excesses of the previous night, and he wanted to take the opportunity to look around the village.

He unbolted the door, but jumped when a voice spoke from the shadows.

"Where are you going?" Eleanor asked. She was seated at one of the tables, eating something from a bowl, and looked well-rested. He'd been too caught up in his own thoughts when he came down to notice her.

"Nowhere. Just a walk."

She gave him a shrewd look. "Are you leaving?"

"No." *Not yet,* he thought.

"Are you going to break the curse?" She clearly wasn't one to mince words.

"From what I can tell, nobody wants it to be broken."

"That's not true."

"It certainly appears true, from what I could gather last night."

Eleanor rolled her eyes. "Well, of course they're going to *say* that, aren't they? You were just talking to the wrong people."

"And where can I find the right people?"

She pushed her bowl away and stood up. "Give me half an hour and I can take you to them. Stay here." Then she slipped through the door and was gone.

THORSTEN WAS UNACCUSTOMED to taking orders from anyone, let alone a child, but he did as Eleanor said. And sure enough, as the clock in the square chimed the half-hour, she returned.

"Come on," she said, taking a small hand lamp and leading him out of the inn. Thorsten followed her across the square and down a small alleyway. They twisted and turned behind the buildings until he was thoroughly disoriented, then stopped at the door of what looked like a warehouse. Eleanor rapped a sequence on the door and it slowly opened to admit them. Thorsten approached warily, unable to see beyond the darkened doorway, but Eleanor bounded through with apparent unconcern. Following her, he stepped through and was immediately blinded by the light of a lantern thrust into his face.

"Step back!" he commanded, drawing his knife automatically from long years of practice. The person holding the lantern gasped, apparently not anticipating such a reaction.

"So this is your curse-breaker," someone said sardonically. "How very...dramatic."

"He's our only hope." That was Eleanor's voice.

Thorsten blinked away spots as his vision began to clear. In the dim light he could see around twenty people sitting on boxes and crates, or lounging against the wall. Many of them had a slightly rumpled look that indicated they'd been rudely hauled from their beds. Eleanor was standing before them defiantly, her arms crossed over her chest. She was the only child there.

"Is this your doing?" Thorsten asked her, taking in the faces.

"This is the Light Brigade," she said. "We oppose Markus Kettle and the casting out of the Shadowless." Thorsten looked around the room. They were a motley mix—young and old, male and female, a few couples, but many on their own as well. He wondered what they had in common, but it wasn't hard to guess.

"You've all had loved ones cast out?" he asked.

One by one they nodded. An old woman with a rope of grey hair hanging down her back pulled a worn photograph from the pocket of her apron and thrust it at him. "My daughter, Lilith," she said, her eyes rheumy with tears. Other murmurings began, the names of their loved ones whispered like prayers. Involuntarily, Thorsten patted his breast pocket.

"We just want to be free," a voice said above the susurrus. Thorsten recognised its sardonic tone and traced it to a young man of about twenty leaning languidly against the wall. His face was hidden by a flat cap pulled down low over his eyes.

"Free from what?" Thorsten asked.

"Kettle's tyranny—what else? This eternal darkness. But if we so much as murmur a word of dissent we'll be cast out too."

"So you know about the curse?"

"We're not idiots. *Of course* we know. Anyone who can put two and two together knows. But they never last long."

"Who did you lose?"

"My mother. She got on the wrong side of Kettle."

"How?"

All the others were silent.

"Tell him, William," Eleanor said at last. "You can trust him."

William scowled. "My grandfather is Kettle's right-hand man. My mother had me out of wedlock, and he couldn't stand the shame she brought on the family, so he had Kettle cast her out. He raised me as his son, for all the good it did either of us, and he kept the truth from me for as long as he could. I never knew her, and I'll never forgive him, or Markus Kettle."

Thorsten was momentarily taken aback; he'd heard another story just like it not so long ago. He shook his head to clear it.

"And how have you all avoided being condemned as Shadowless?"

William raised an eyebrow. "We know all about Kettle's little trick with the magic light." He reached into his pocket and pulled out two small mirrors, each just big enough to fit into a palm. "We all carry these. Redirect his light, keep your shadow." He shrugged.

"You forgot to bring yours yesterday?" Thorsten asked Eleanor as the pieces clicked into place in his mind. She nodded, and he turned back to William. "Doesn't Kettle notice?"

"Apparently not. He sees what he wants to see. Anyway, that's not important. What's important is we want to see the sunlight return to Finster."

"I'm not sure I can do that."

The young man snorted. "Then what sort of curse-breaker are you, anyway?"

Thorsten sighed. "A troubled one. If I leave things as they are, the village will be destroyed. But if I lift the curse, it will face a different kind of destruction. Every choice has a consequence."

"So what do you suggest we do?"

"To be frank, I suggest you leave."

"*What?*"

"It's really the only solution. Those of you who wish to live in the light should leave Finster, and those who support Markus Kettle can take their chances with the Divine."

"But this is our home! We have as much right to be here as anyone!" There was an angry muttering of agreement.

Thorsten shrugged. "There is an alternative."

"And what is that?"

"I need to see the mayor. I may have a way to convince him." He thought again of his mother's letter, and briefly wondered if Finster was worth the cost.

"He won't see the likes of you."

"I'm sure I can persuade him."

William laughed mirthlessly. "Good luck. You'll need it."

Thorsten sighed and glanced around the room, meeting each person's eyes in turn. "How badly do you want to save Finster? Because helping me get an audience with the mayor is your best chance." He strode to the door. "When I walk out of here, I'll be heading straight to the road out of town—unless you can show me where to find Markus Kettle."

William appeared to have been struck dumb, and the others shifted uncomfortably.

"Come on!" Eleanor said. "It's the only hope we've got. Do you want little Isadora Keening to grow up without her mother? Another broken person with a loss to mourn, just like us? Because I don't!"

Her words had a stirring effect, and one by one the others also piped up.

"She's right, you know."

"What have we got to lose?"

"My Lilith wouldn't want anyone else cast out."

"Please," Thorsten said.

William sighed, then squared his shoulders and stood up straighter. "Very well," he said. "I'll take him. For Finster. The rest of you stay here." He threw open the door. "Are you coming?"

WILLIAM SET A CRACKING pace down the alleyway and through the village, leaving Thorsten with little time to collect his thoughts. He hoped he'd made the right choice in asking to see the mayor. He didn't need permission to break the curse, and in many cases he'd gone ahead without it when he'd judged it best to do so. But if ever there was a situation that required a compromise, this was it.

He never used to second-guess himself so much, he reflected as they walked. Once upon a time, his ideas of right and wrong had been clearer. Perhaps it was time to retire, to hand over the reins to someone younger. He must take on an apprentice soon.

Markus Kettle's house was at the back of the village, on the edge of the forest. It was the only two-storey house in Finster, with a wide balcony running around the upper level. A single lamp burned in the window and, despite the early hour, a curtain twitched: someone had noticed them there.

William marched up to the door with a swagger that Thorsten recognised as bravado masking a deep fear. He felt a rush of compassion for the lad and mentally kicked himself for asking this of him. He was just about to reach out and tell him to call the whole thing off when the door creaked open, revealing one of Kettle's henchmen.

"What do you want?" he asked, eyeing William up and down. "You've got a nerve showing your face here, boy. Didn't your grandfather make it clear after last time that he wants nothing more to do with you?"

"I'm not here to see Grandfather," William said. He jerked his head at Thorsten. "The curse-breaker has something to say to the mayor. He'll want to hear it."

The man grunted sceptically, but stepped aside. "Fine," he said, waving Thorsten in. Then he resumed his position, blocking William. "You wait outside."

A second man ushered Thorsten upstairs to another closed door off a hallway. The man knocked, then left him. He waited for what seemed like hours, but was probably only a matter of minutes, before the door opened. The room beyond was dark, and Thorsten peered forward, only just able to discern a darker patch of shadow in the blackness.

"What do you want?" Markus Kettle said from the gloom.

"I just want to talk," Thorsten said.

"I have nothing to say to you," Markus Kettle said. "The fact that you choose to keep company with heretics speaks for itself." Thorsten didn't ask how he knew.

"It's important," he said. "I know about the curse, and I know about the Shadowless. And I know that, without a child, it's all collapsing around you. I can help you save the village."

This time the silence had a sharpness to it. Thorsten sensed the danger and let his hand fall to the hilt of his knife.

"No," the mayor said softly. Then he lunged, his fingers twisting like claws. Thorsten was expecting it, but even so, the onslaught of Kettle's rage forced him to take a step back. The mayor lashed out maniacally with his fists—Thorsten was relieved to see he carried no weapons—and caught him a glancing blow on the side of the face, his signet ring opening up a cut on the curse-breaker's cheek. Thorsten rolled his eyes in frustration, and in a few short moments he had Kettle flat on his back in the hallway, without even drawing his knife. He glanced over his shoulder, hoping the mayor's henchmen hadn't heard the scuffle.

"Very well," he said. "If you change your mind, you can find me at the inn. I'll see myself out."

When he emerged from the house, he found that Eleanor and the Light Brigade had followed him and were congregated in the street beneath the single dim lamp, scuffing their boots aimlessly in the dirt. They looked up as he joined them, expressions turning to concern as they saw the blood on his face.

"What happened?" the old woman who'd lost her daughter asked, pulling him close and dabbing at the cut with a corner of her apron.

Thorsten shrugged. "He didn't want to talk," he said.

"He beat you up?" one of the other men said, sounding incredulous.

Thorsten remembered how he'd left the mayor lying whimpering on the floor. "He came off worse than I did."

The old woman rounded on the curse-breaker.

"Oh, what a brilliant idea!" she snapped. "Who do you think he'll come after now? Us, that's who! Why not just break the curse and be done with it? Grow some spine instead of leaving others to sort out your mess!"

Thorsten's head was beginning to throb, and he could feel his self-control slipping away. He usually prided himself on his even temper, but it was so much harder on this job. Everything was that much more personal.

"Well, that's rich!" he said with a withering glance round the group. "You could all just leave, you know. You could walk out tomorrow and find your loved ones instead of just hanging round here whining and waiting for someone like me to come along just so you can blame them for your misery." Even as he said it, he knew he'd gone too far, and one look at their faces had him instantly regretting his words.

"I'm sorry..." he began, but William strode forward and spat at his feet.

"You should go," he said.

"Come on," Eleanor said, tugging at his arm, and Thorsten followed her, feeling numb.

Eleanor said nothing as they walked, but once they were out of sight of the others, she turned to him. "Is diplomacy something they teach you in curse-breaking school?"

"I'm sorry. I shouldn't have said those things. But it was a bit much of them to turn it all back on me, as if I'm to blame for all their problems."

Eleanor sighed. "You really don't understand, do you?"

"Understand what?" It was a point of professional pride that he felt that he could walk into a new place and have a good grip on all its politics and dramas within a few days, if not a few hours. So to be contradicted—by a girl who was little more than a child, no less—stung more than he cared to admit.

"*Why don't you just leave?*" she said, mimicking his tone. "Don't you think each one of us asks ourselves that question every single day? *Of course* they'd leave if they could. I'm going to, as soon as I'm old enough. But it's easy for me—I'm young enough to get a trade, and Aunt Ada said she's put a bit of money aside to give me a start. But the rest of them—what would they do? Even the younger ones have spent their whole lives in Finster. I know you probably can't see it, but from here the outside world looks big and scary, not least because we've all been taught since childhood that we should be afraid of it. And our families could be any-where—we wouldn't even know where to start." She glared at him. "Not everything is as black-and-white as you think, and you've got some nerve, Mister Fancy Curse-Breaker, coming in here and telling us that it is."

Thorsten hung his head, properly chastened for the first time in many years. But Eleanor wasn't finished.

"Plus," she continued, "many people don't want to leave. They love this place, despite its flaws, and they want to stay and make it better, not go running away. Do you know what it's like to grow up without your parents? I wouldn't wish that on any child. But I suppose it's easy to judge when your job is just to waltz in, swan around and then leave whenever it gets too hard."

Thorsten's skin prickled; many years ago, another woman had levelled exactly the same accusation at him. And she'd been right, although he hadn't thought so at the time.

"I'm sorry," he said again, and he meant it. "You're right, I don't always understand. What can I do to make it up to you?"

She looked at him steadily. "Do better," she said. Then she chewed her lip, thinking. "And you can keep your promise. You said that if I told you about the Festival, you'd tell me about the Outside. Well, I did, and you haven't." She frowned. "Don't make me add lying to your list of offences."

"What do you want to know about the Outside?" he asked.

Eleanor's eyes lit up. "Everything."

Thorsten bit back a smile. "I'm afraid you'll have to be a bit more specific."

"Well...what's it like? What are the people like?"

Thorsten thought for a moment. "Let me see. I guess, well, people are...people. Some of them, like me—and like you, I suspect—have an aptitude for magic. The ambitious, social-climbing ones even study to become magicians, but I wouldn't recommend that as a career path—they're wily bastards, the lot of them. They even started a war a few years ago, although you probably don't remember that. But it's a good rule of thumb to never trust a magician." He shrugged. "Basically, people Outside aren't that different to people here. We're all just doing the best we can."

Eleanor scowled, clearly dissatisfied. Then she shrugged. "I guess I'll just have to see for myself," she said.

"One of these days, I'll show you," Thorsten said. "I promise."

"I'll hold you to that, you know."

"I don't doubt it."

THEY RETURNED TO THE square, and Eleanor went to the inn to help her aunt, but Thorsten couldn't face going back to his tiny, stuffy room. A few dedicated revellers were inside propping up Ada's bar; the sound of raucous laughter and drunken singing drifted out the door, but the square itself was empty. He sat on the edge of the fountain, staring up at the midsummer clock. The incident with the mayor had shaken him, because he knew the old woman was right; he'd put the Light Brigade in danger and made things that much worse. When had he started losing his touch? Once upon a time—not so very long ago, even—he would have waltzed into Finster, lifted the curse without a second thought, and waltzed out again, leaving the village to its fate. He wouldn't have dithered about whether it was the right thing to do, or what the people really wanted. A group like the Light Brigade would have been able to persuade him with hardly any effort at all. And yet now here he was, trying to find a complex solution to what was really a very simple problem, as long as you didn't mind ripping the heart out of a place. 'Collateral damage' was what curse-breakers called it when you had to sacrifice a few to save the many, and sometimes it was unavoidable. But if it *could* be avoided, then *shouldn't* it?

He dropped his head into his hands and rubbed his eyes. He never wanted to get too attached to the places where he worked; better to let them sort out their own problems as much as possible, and remain at arm's length. But sometimes a degree of involvement was inevitable, and here he'd misjudged yet again. He'd been emotionally attached right from the start, well before he'd even set foot in the village, from the moment he'd found his mother's letter. And now he had no idea how to make it right, save confronting the mayor again and hoping against hope that this time he'd listen, or at the very least spare the Light Brigade any repercussions. He didn't want to think about the only other solution, even though he'd known it was a possibility when he decided to come here, because he wasn't sure he was prepared to risk his own life for this place. No, he wasn't sure at all.

Suddenly, behind him, he heard a groan. He looked up with a start and turned to see a man staggering across the square, apparently in some pain. Instinctively, Thorsten rose and went to help him, but as he approached he realised it was Markus Kettle. The mayor looked up at him with glowing black eyes. His face seemed more gaunt and sunken that it had even just a few hours before. His skin was ghostly pale and clammy, beaded with an unnatural sheen, and his prominent cheekbones gave him a skull-like look. Thorsten couldn't help staring—it was the worst case of curse-strike he'd ever seen. And it was very advanced: first there would have been the violent mania, which explained the mayor's reaction at the house, and now came the weakness and palsy. Kettle didn't have long left.

"Mr Mayor?" he asked tentatively, reaching out for Kettle's elbow. "Won't you sit down? Let me help you." The mayor shook him off and snarled at him wordlessly, more animal than human. In the back of his mind, Thorsten felt the pulse at the heart of the world quicken like that of someone with a fever.

"I know about you!" Kettle snarled. "You're here to take everything away from me!"

Thorsten shook his head and spoke softly, as if to a frightened child. "Indeed I'm not," he said. "I'm here to bring you back to life. Real life, not this crouching in the dark, a slave. You have a choice, you know—you've always had it. You can lift the curse yourself and restore Finster to its former glory. Your family made it, and you can unmake it. It doesn't have to be this way."

"Never!"

Thorsten sighed, because he'd known that would be the answer. A curse-struck person would do everything they could to protect the status quo. Kettle may once have had the power to lift the curse, when he was young and newly ordained, before he'd literally sacrificed years of his life to the Light. But now he was far too weak to break it even if he wanted to.

Thorsten patted the breast pocket of his coat, where his mother's letter was tucked over his heart. It held the key to the whole thing; it was what had brought him here in the first place, against his better judgement. *Would she have wanted this?* he wondered. After the way Finster had treated her, and after everything she'd had to do to rebuild her life, would she have wanted him to risk everything for this place? Maybe he'd been misguided to even consider it. Then he thought of Eleanor, and of the little girl, Isadora Keening. Maybe his mother wouldn't have cared about the village itself, but she would have been distraught at the thought of yet another child being ripped from its mama's arms. Had it been anywhere else—anywhere less personal—he would have taken action to stop it without a second thought, no matter what the cost. Let them call him arrogant—and many had, over the years—but no-one had ever called him a coward.

Unbidden, the words of the old woman from the Light Brigade rang in Thorsten's mind: *Grow some spine instead of leaving others to sort out your mess.* He'd been hoping to avoid this moment, but now there was really nothing for it. "Come on," he said, hoisting Markus Kettle's arm around his shoulders. "You're coming with me." Kettle struggled ineffectually, but he was too weak to put up much of a fight, and he soon gave up.

"Where are we going?" he mumbled, leaning heavily on Thorsten's shoulder.

"To put an end to this once and for all."

THE PATH UP TO THE Light seemed longer than Thorsten remembered, now that he was dragging the mayor with him. Markus Kettle alternated between babbling and staring vacantly into space, but every now and again he seemed to come back to himself. Thorsten could only hope it wasn't already too late.

When they reached the clearing, Thorsten set his charge down gently, resting him with his back against the lamppost. Kettle's gaze drifted in and out; he seemed to be having trouble holding his focus. Thorsten crouched down in front of him and placed a hand on either side of the man's head, forcing Kettle to look him in the eye.

"There's something you need to know," Thorsten began. He gave him a shake. "Markus! This is important!"

"Nothing matters now," Kettle muttered in a moment of lucidity. His eyelids drooped, and the ground trembled. Thorsten couldn't say for sure what would happen to Finster if the curse took Kettle, but he suspected it wouldn't be pretty. And if he didn't hurry, they would all find out.

"It does matter," he said. "More than anything. I'm your brother."

The words seemed to have a galvanising effect on the mayor; his eyes snapped back into focus, and he appeared to be paying attention.

"Impossible!"

"On the contrary. My mother was a maid in your father's house. She was cast out as Shadowless when it was discovered she was pregnant with me. I have a letter from her detailing everything."

"I have a brother?" Kettle murmured.

"A half-brother, yes. It should be close enough for our purposes."

"What do you mean?"

"I need you to pass the curse on to me—just like you would have to your child. I'm in the Kettle bloodline, so it should work. I'm a curse-breaker—if you transfer it to me I can lift it, before it destroys you and all of Finster. This is what I've been trying to tell you ever since I arrived."

Kettle shook his head. "No," he muttered.

"This isn't a time for power games, Markus!"

Kettle looked Thorsten straight in the eye, the slightest twitch of madness in his gaze. "You think that's what this is about? Maybe it was once. But now...I can't inflict this on another person. Why do you think we never had a child? It's unbearable."

"But I can help you!"

"Do you know that for sure? Or will it kill you too?"

Thorsten paused, then shook his head. "I don't know." He thought of his mother. "But I'm willing to risk it."

"No." Markus Kettle struggled to his feet, propping himself up against the lamppost. "There's another way." He pulled a key from his pocket and unlocked the door. Thorsten tried to grab his arm, but the mayor fought him off, surprisingly strong even in his weakened state.

"Don't do it, Markus!" Thorsten implored, but he was too late. The mayor reached into the lamp with both hands and grabbed the thick rope of hair at its core. Smoke began to rise up, and there was the acrid smell of burning flesh. Markus Kettle screamed. Thorsten attempted to pull him free, but his hands seemed welded to the lamppost. The lamp flared brighter and brighter, until Thorsten had to shield his eyes, but the light burned into them even through his closed eyelids. Markus's keening grew louder until it drowned out all other sounds. Suddenly, with a violent burst of light, the lamp exploded, and Thorsten slumped, unconscious, to the ground.

"MR MACKINDER, SIR? Thorsten? Wake up!" Thorsten drifted thickly back into consciousness, dimly aware of someone shaking his shoulder. He forced his eyes open. It was still dark, but not the pitch black he'd expected, more like a soft grey twilight.

"Oh, Mr Mackinder, you're awake. Thank heavens!" Eleanor was kneeling beside him, concern etched on her face.

"I'm not dead?"

She laughed. "Not even a little bit." Then her smile faded. "Mayor Kettle is, though."

Thorsten propped himself on his elbows and inched slowly into a sitting position, waiting for his head to stop spinning. He appeared to have rolled some way down the hill, perhaps thrown by the shockwave, but sure enough, through the dimness he could see the still-smoking body of the mayor slumped at the foot of the lamp.

"What happened?" he asked, trying to recall.

"I don't really know," Eleanor said. "I was coming to find you, and for some reason I thought you might be here. I was halfway up the path when the Light flared out, and then it all went dark. But now...everything is different. Can't you feel it?"

Now that she mentioned it, Thorsten realised he could. The painful throbbing at the heart of the world was gone, leaving only a sense of release. He hadn't quite realised how oppressive the weight of it had been in his mind.

"Is the village all right?"

Eleanor nodded. "They're fine. They don't even seem to have noticed."

"They will soon enough." Involuntarily he grinned, filled with joy that none of his worst fears had come to pass. It was the sacrifice, he realised. The mayor's—his brother's—final act of selflessness was what had saved them. Even after all these years of curse-breaking, he was still capable of being surprised.

"What do you mean?"

Thorsten glanced towards the eastern sky. "Help me up. I want to show you something—something you've never seen before."

His legs trembled as he stood but, leaning on Eleanor's shoulder, he managed to make his way back up the hill. Towards the east the trees thinned out, exposing a large patch of sky. Eleanor gasped, and together they stood in reverent silence, as the sun rose over the village of Finster.

The Time Flies

Eleanor Darke stood at the edge of the town square, concealed in the shadow of a nearby building. Her eyes were fixed on the row of neat terrace houses across the street. It was early evening; the twilight had deepened, but the lamps hadn't yet been lit. This was the moment she'd dreamed of every night for six years, but now that it was finally here, her hands were shaking.

She pulled a slip of paper from her pocket and checked the address again. If her information was correct, this was it—the house with the blue front door. And yet still she stood rooted to the spot, unwilling—or perhaps unable—to take the step that would change everything. Thorsten often talked about courage, and she'd thought herself brave, but now she wasn't so sure.

As she watched, a lone woman came around the corner at the end of the block and walked up the street. Aged about forty, she wore a nurse's white apron over her full skirts, and a white cap on her head. Her dark hair, streaked with grey, was pulled back in a bun that had probably been neat when she started out, but was now wispy and flyaway. Eleanor's breath caught in her throat and she stifled a sob.

The woman took out a key and let herself in through the blue door. For a moment the world seemed to pause, as if the entire street was holding its breath, then a single candle flared in the front window. Suddenly, Eleanor's legs seemed to be moving of their own accord, propelling her across the street and up to the blue front door. Without a second thought she grabbed the brass knocker and rapped brightly, three times.

Mary Darke stood at the window as she did every evening, watching the light change from gold to purple to darkest blue. It had been a long day and she was weary, but even though it had been six years since she'd left her home village of Finster and its curse of eternal night, sunrises and sunsets were still something she couldn't take for granted. As the stars began to wink out above the rooftops of the town, she lit the single candle that stood in the window—her evening ritual. As always, she remembered lighting a similar candle on her little girl's naming day: the beautiful daughter she'd been forced to leave behind. A single tear trickled down her cheek.

A knock at the door startled her from her reverie, and she quickly wiped her eyes. She went to answer it in some confusion, for people in town didn't generally call on each other after dark without an invitation. It was just one of the many strange customs she'd had to get used to.

She opened the door in some trepidation, wondering if it would be a travelling salesman, or a vagrant begging for food. Her response was already on her lips when she looked down and saw a girl—or young woman, really—clad like a boy in breeches and a shirt, with thick dark hair and piercing blue eyes, just like her father's.

"Hello, Mama," the girl said.

For a moment, Mary thought she was going to faint. She felt herself begin to sway, and the girl reached out a hand to steady her.

"Ellie?" she gasped. "Is it really you?"

Eleanor smiled. "It's really me, Mama. I've come home."

Mary took her daughter's face in her hands and looked at her as a thirsty man looks at a desert oasis. She touched her hair and cheeks, as if trying to convince herself by the evidence of her hands that what her eyes showed her was real. There had been so many times where she'd thought she'd glimpsed Eleanor in a crowd, only for the girl in question to turn out to be nothing like her. But in this young woman there were still echoes of the child she'd been: the little eight-year-old girl that Mary had left screaming underneath the Light at Finster, as men with whips had chased her and Theodore deep into the forest. Out of nowhere, six years of sorrow welled up, and Mary collapsed, sobbing, onto her daughter's shoulder.

ELEANOR COULD BARELY recall her parents' old house in Finster, but as Mary drew her into the cosy sitting room, memories came flooding back. It wasn't exactly the same, of course, for her parents had been forced to flee with nothing but the clothes they were wearing, but they'd recreated the room in much the same style. There was a colourful woven rug on the floor before the fireplace and embroidered cushions on the settee, and her father's intricate replica of the Finster midsummer clock on the mantelpiece. That clock had been made well before she was born, as a prototype for the real thing, and Eleanor had always loved it. She had no idea how her parents had managed to smuggle it out of Finster; she suspected Aunt Ada and Uncle Frank had had a hand in it somehow. *They could take the clock but not me?* The thought felt treasonous, and she damped it down hurriedly, concentrating the ticking of the clock to calm herself. Her father used to say that clockwork was like music: each cog had its own role and specific way of moving in relation to all the others, and the slightest alteration would throw the whole thing out. But when everything worked as planned, it was a symphony in miniature.

Eleanor frowned to herself. Now that she looked closely, she struggled to find signs of her father in the room. Normally there would have been a set of delicate tools on a side table, or a collection of cogs and springs scattered across the mantelpiece for 'safekeeping'. But the room was spotlessly clean and tidy; it seemed somehow unnatural, and the hairs on the back of her neck prickled.

"Mama," she asked, as Mary brought tea and biscuits, "where's Papa?"

"Oh," Mary said, glancing around distractedly, "he's out."

"When will he be back?"

"I...I'm not sure, love. I've been at work since dawn. Between his work and mine, we don't see that much of each other these days."

"You're a nurse?"

"A *doctor*, thank you very much." She smiled proudly.

Eleanor stared, unsure of what to say. She remembered her mother doing the odd bit of work with Finster's healer, but no one would have ever called her a doctor.

"I know it probably seems strange," Mary said. "But when we got here I needed something to...take my mind off things. I started volunteering at the cottage hospital, but they were so shorthanded that I soon had a nurse's apprenticeship, and then a visiting doctor suggested I try for entry to the Academy. And it all just went from there. I graduated last spring and now I'm starting to study magical healing—it turns out I've got an aptitude for it."

"I think you'd make a wonderful doctor," Eleanor said. "I'm so proud of you."

"Thank you, sweetheart. That means a lot. Here, have a biscuit." She passed Eleanor the plate, then took one for herself. "Now," she continued, "tell me how you got away from Finster. You weren't...Shadowless, were you?"

Eleanor smiled and shook her head. "It's all different there now, Mama. The darkness has gone. A curse-breaker came, and now Finster is free." She told her mother all about Thorsten Mackinder and the spectacular demolition of the Light, watching Mary's eyes widen.

"I'm his apprentice now," she added. "I'm going to be a curse-breaker myself someday." In the aftermath of Finster's reclamation, Thorsten had asked her if she'd like to travel with him and learn the trade, and she'd jumped at the chance. Aunt Ada and Uncle Frank had given their blessing, and within two days she was on the road. They'd travelled from town to town, wherever there was work, but all the time Eleanor had been searching for some sign of her parents, and Thorsten knew it. Eventually their investigations had led them here, and Thorsten had told her to stay while he went off to another job. He expected to be gone at least a month, and he would collect her on the way back through.

"A curse-breaker," Mary said in awe. "My little girl. My goodness. And here I was thinking you were bound to be an horologist like your father." Her eyes shone, and she glanced wistfully towards the window.

"Mama, has something happened to Papa?"

Mary started. "Why do you say that?"

"It's just...you would tell me, wouldn't you? He's not...dead?"

Mary put her hand to her mouth. "Oh, my darling, of course not! He's alive and well. There's just been a...problem." She swallowed. "We've had an outbreak of time flies."

Eleanor wracked her brain; the term sounded familiar, but she couldn't quite put her finger on it. "Time flies?"

"You probably don't remember—we didn't really get them much in Finster, and they were easy to contain. They're little flies that live in clocks, especially old ones. They lay their eggs in there and then, when the clock is opened up to be wound, they get out and go and find other clocks to breed in. They don't hurt the clocks, but if they bite you they'll cause you to lose time. We all get bitten by them occasionally—it's why you sometimes end up sleeping through your alarm, or you can't seem to leave the house on time no matter how hard you try. Small children are particularly susceptible to them in that regard. By themselves they're relatively harmless. But if they swarm..." She trailed off.

"And Papa has been attacked by a swarm?"

Mary nodded. "A customer brought in an old clock that he wanted fixed. It was beautiful; a real collector's item. Your father was so excited about getting to work on it. He took it down to the workshop—he works in the cellar—and started looking over it. I was taking him a cup of tea just as he started opening it up. When he took the door off, inside was the biggest time fly nest I've ever seen. He yelled at me to run, and I got out the door just as they started to swarm. I heard him cry out, and then...nothing." Mary rubbed her hand over her face. "Now your father is so chronically late, he's effectively caught in his own time pocket. He probably doesn't even know how much time has passed since it happened. To him it's the same day, but our time moves on while he just gets later and later."

Eleanor reached out and squeezed her hand. "When was this?"

"Two weeks ago."

"*Two weeks*? Is there nothing that can be done?"

Mary's gaze hardened. "Do you think I haven't tried? Every waking hour when I'm not at work I'm down there. I can't open the door or they'll get out and infect the whole town. But I've researched time-fly food and tried to entice them out." She gestured to the midsummer clock. "I took that downstairs in the hope of luring them into it, but I only got one or two, and I very nearly let them all out by accident. I've looked up methods for destroying them, but there's hardly any information, and I can't think of any that would work without hurting your father too. I don't know what more I can do."

A horrible thought occurred to Eleanor. "He won't starve, will he?"

Mary shook her head. "He has plenty of food down there. He's such a scatterbrain about meals—you know what he's like when he's working—that I insisted he stock a larder so that he could eat whenever he remembered to, so he wouldn't have to worry about cooking when I'm at work. And there's a sink with water plumbed in, and a chamber pot. But I don't know how long the food will last. If we can't free him soon, I hate to think what will happen."

"Hmm." Eleanor's first instinct was to call on Thorsten for help. He'd seen many odd things in his time, and surely he'd know what to do. But Thorsten was miles away by now, busy breaking someone else's curse. If anything was to be done, it was up to her to do it.

"Let me think on it," she said. "There must be a way. Now, why don't you let me make supper while you go and rest? You look worn out."

"I'm fine," Mary said. "It's just been a long day. You don't need to mother me, you know."

"Sorry. I'm just trying to help."

Mary sighed. "I know, darling," she said, walking over and kissing the top of her head. "I'm sorry. You don't know how much it means to have you back."

"Everything will be all right," Eleanor said. "You'll see." But her mother just smiled sadly as she went upstairs.

THEODORE DARKE HAD one of the best horology libraries around, with bookshelves lining the walls of what used to be the formal parlour, and it was here that Eleanor went for advice. There were books on every imaginable aspect of clock-making and restoration; it stood to reason that there must be *something* on the subject of time flies. But her search came up fruitless—as her mother had said, there was very little information available. Where she did find a mention of them, it was only ever a line or two, and there was never anything practical about dealing with an outbreak. It seemed like such swarms were sufficiently rare that they failed to warrant expert consideration.

After an hour of getting nowhere, she gave up in frustration and went to the kitchen to prepare supper. Her mother hadn't come down, so she took a tray up to her bedroom, where she found Mary fast asleep. She left the tray on a side table and tiptoed back downstairs. Her poor mama had been through so much—being exiled from Finster, losing her, and now this. She deserved so much better.

The thought fortified Eleanor, and she returned to the library, where she sat in a worn leather armchair and drank tea, turning the problem over and over in her mind. It was like curse-breaking, she reflected: Thorsten had told her that you could encounter the same curse five times and every time it would be different. The method you'd used successfully last time wouldn't necessarily work this time, so every problem had to be approached from scratch. But there was always a key. It was just about finding the weak point in the problem and pressing it until the solution revealed itself.

Perhaps she'd been approaching this all wrong, she thought. Maybe it wasn't about clocks at all, but about the flies themselves. They were natural creatures—albeit rather odd ones—and as such there must be a way to be rid of them. She could feel the germ of an idea itching at the back of her mind, but even as she reached for it and tried to pull it into the light, it slipped away. She sighed and sank back into the chair. It had been a long and emotional day and, without even meaning to, she fell asleep.

When she woke it was deep night, and the lamp on the table beside her chair had burned low. There was no sound save for the odd creak as the house settled. Eleanor blinked blearily, wondering for a moment where she was, then she remembered everything that had happened. A muffled thumping from downstairs startled her, and she jumped. She stood up, grabbing the lamp, and roamed the house until she found the stairs to the cellar. With some trepidation she inched down them, unsure of what she'd find.

The door at the bottom of the stairs was closed, and when she tried it she discovered it to be locked, although the key was hanging on a nail beside it. Her mother must have locked it as an extra precaution. She bent down and peered through the keyhole into the room beyond.

The cellar space—what little she could see of it—was open in the middle, with workbenches lining the walls. Mechanical detritus littered the room, for her father was a notoriously messy worker. The oddest thing was that even though on her side of the door it was the middle of the night, the room on the other side was bathed in noonday sunlight. She realised that she was witnessing her father's time pocket: he was still caught in the day of the swarm. He seemed to have progressed a couple of hours over the preceding weeks—from midmorning to lunchtime—but no more than that. There was a buzzing sound, like the whirring of a very small, very fast clock, which must be the time flies.

Suddenly her father strode into view, picking up a piece from the workbench.

"Papa!" she cried, but there was no indication that he'd heard her. She tried a couple more times, then realised she was literally trying to call into the past. Disheartened, she stood up and made her way back up the stairs. As her mother had said, there was nothing to be done down there right now.

She returned to her chair in the library, sure that the answer must be there somewhere. On the shelves, her father's small clockwork creations glinted in the lamplight. When he wasn't building or fixing clocks, he had a passion for creating small clockwork animals and figurines; he'd given her one for every birthday. Most of them were still in her Aunt Ada's house in Finster, but she'd brought one with her: a little bird called Bertie, which was her most precious possession in the world.

A thought occurred to her, and she raced upstairs to her neat white bedroom. Her haversack was on the floor at the foot of the bed, and she fell to her knees and began to rifle through it. She eventually found Bertie wrapped up in a pair of her socks; she discarded the socks and carried the small clockwork bird back down to the library.

Sitting down in her armchair, she held the little bird up to the lamp and studied him closely. She remembered the day her father had given him to her—her eighth birthday, the day before her parents had been declared Shadowless.

"It's a cuckoo," Papa had said. "He'll keep you on time." As long as he was kept wound, the bird would chirp every hour without fail.

She wound the key in Bertie's side and set him on the floor, where he hopped and pecked his way around the room, just like a real bird. She'd never seen him fly, but when she looked at the mechanics more closely she saw no reason why he couldn't.

"I wonder..." Eleanor murmured to herself. She picked up the clockwork bird and set him on the mantelpiece next to the midsummer clock. She turned the clock to face the bird, then opened the winding cabinet. Sure enough, inside she spotted a cluster of tiny golden pinpricks—the time flies her mother had caught when she'd tried to open the workshop door.

"Shoo," Eleanor whispered, jiggling the clock. "Come on, out you come."

At first she thought they weren't going to leave the clock, but then she caught the familiar high-pitched ticking sound. She hoped her plan would work.

As the flies darted out of the clock, Bertie danced around, snapping at them just like a real bird. She could see the time flies glowing through his intricate brass latticework, then one by one their lights winked out.

Eleanor laughed out loud, then pressed her hand to her mouth, afraid the sound would wake her mother. She couldn't believe it had actually worked. But by itself it wouldn't help her father—Bertie couldn't take on a whole swarm of time flies. She would need many more birds for that to happen.

Exhausted by the day's events, Eleanor picked up the clockwork bird and carried him upstairs to her bedroom, where she set him on the dressing table. Tomorrow, they'd get to work.

ELEANOR SLEPT LATE the next day and was woken by the enticing smell of frying bacon. Downstairs, she found her mother cheerfully cooking breakfast.

"I thought we'd celebrate," Mary said. "It would be a shame if our first breakfast together was merely porridge." Eleanor smiled, for her mother was clearly making an effort, although the lines around her mouth spoke of strain. For the first time, Eleanor wondered what life had really been like for her parents over the past six years. She'd assumed they'd adapted, just as she had, but maybe it hadn't been quite that easy. And now there was this business with her father. In the back of her mind, she also knew she'd have to tell her mother that she'd be leaving soon, but she couldn't bear to hurt her again like that. *Not now*, she thought. *We'll sort out the problem with Papa first.*

"Did you sleep well?" Mary asked.

"Very," Eleanor said, and it was true. The relief of having made some headway into the problem had meant she'd had no trouble dropping off.

"Mama," she asked as Mary set a sizzling plate of eggs and bacon in front of her, "are there any other horologists in town? Or anyone who specialises in clockwork animals, like the ones Papa used to make?"

Mary furrowed her brow in thought. "Well now, I don't really know. Your father's the only one who works on clocks, I believe."

"Oh." Eleanor's shoulders slumped as she felt her plan slipping away.

"At least—he's the only one in town. But he often mentions a colleague in one of the little villages not too far from here. A Maxim something-or-other. I've never met the man, but I believe your father gets him to make the more intricate clockwork parts that he needs. You could try him." She poured tea for both of them. "Is this in relation to the time flies?"

Eleanor nodded, her mouth full of bacon. She swallowed. "I don't want to say any more just yet, in case it doesn't work," she said. "But I have an idea. Can you tell me how to get to Maxim's?"

Eleanor had grown fit and strong in the time she'd been travelling with Thorsten, for they journeyed mostly on foot, occasionally hitching a ride with passing wagons or farm carts. The surrounding countryside was mostly flat, and the weather was perfect for walking—sunny but not too hot, with a refreshing breeze. Her mother had drawn her a rough map showing the way to Maxim's village, and Eleanor had promised to be back by sundown. In truth, she was glad to get out into the countryside again; the town wasn't overly large, as towns went, but she still found it stifling.

Initially she took the main road out of town, walking along the verge while the morning bustle of carts and carriages clattered along beside her. She suspected it was market day, because most of the traffic appeared to be farmers coming into town to sell their produce. There were very few vehicles going in her direction, and none stopped to offer her a lift. In any case, she preferred to walk.

About two miles outside the town, she consulted her mother's map again, then turned off down a cart track through the fields. Rows of corn grew on either side of the lane, taller than she was, giving her the impression of walking down a golden-green tunnel. Eventually the cornfields gave way to spinach, and a small whitewashed farmhouse appeared, popping up unexpectedly among the swathes of green. But the lane ended just beyond the farmhouse, which wasn't marked on her map. Eleanor stopped and peered more closely at it, trying to decipher her mother's directions. She wondered if she'd taken a wrong turn back at the main road, and she didn't relish the thought of having to retrace her steps.

Thankfully, at that moment the farmhouse door opened and a woman appeared, carrying a basket of washing.

"You right, love?" she called. Her tone was friendly enough, but Eleanor could sense the hostility behind her gaze. She supposed they didn't get strangers down here very often.

"I'm afraid I'm lost," she said, walking over to the neat picket fence that separated the farmhouse garden from the lane and the surrounding fields. "I'm looking for the village of Wurt, but I seem to have gone wrong somewhere." She held out her crude map.

The woman's face relaxed, and she set down her basket.

"You've come the back way," she said. "You can cut through the paddock here, and that'll take you right up to the forest, see?" She pointed and, following her arm, Eleanor could just make out a rough track through the fields, leading to a dark smudge of trees about a mile away.

"Then if you follow the path through them woods, you'll end up in Wurt. But next time, better to stick to the main road and then turn off about a mile-and-a-half further on from our lane."

"Thank you very much," Eleanor said. "That's a great help."

"Mind you be careful in them woods," the farmer's wife added. "Wurt's a bit of an odd place."

The path through the fields was little more than a rabbit-track, really, and more than once Eleanor had to stop and make sure she was still going the right way. The woods had looked closer than they actually were, and the sun was getting hot. She pulled out her kerchief and wiped the sweat from her eyes. Gradually, though, the dark wall of trees began to loom taller, and eventually she left the fields and found herself under the eaves of the forest. She stopped to rest on a tree stump, sitting down and unpacking the bread and cheese she'd brought. The shade was a blissful relief.

As she ate, she looked around the forest. It was mostly pine trees; the forest floor was blanketed in a tangy-smelling carpet of last year's needles. A thin track wound its way between the trees, and she assumed it led to Wurt—there was nothing to indicate it did, but there were no other options either. When she was sufficiently refreshed, she stood and followed the track, checking every few steps to make sure she hadn't missed her way.

The forest grew thicker and darker as she progressed, broken only by thin shafts of sunlight that slanted down between the trees. She could hear birds calling, and mysterious scufflings in the undergrowth. Suddenly, ahead of her there was a loud creak and a crash; she jumped, her heart pounding, but it was only a breaking branch. She wondered if spooks haunted woods like this, then berated herself for being so silly. If she was going to be a curse-breaker she'd have to face far worse things than a forest in broad daylight.

She had no indication that the path she was on was leading her to Wurt, but she continued nonetheless. Just as she was beginning to think that she'd misunderstood the farmer's wife's directions, the forest began to thin out, and she glimpsed what appeared to be houses through the trees. She crept closer, afraid of being seen before she knew what she was walking into. On closer inspection it was clear that it was indeed a village, albeit a tiny one. She could see around ten thatched-roof cottages clustered around some sort of village square. Her track led to the back of the square, while a larger road ran away from it, out of the forest. That was probably the way she should have come. All the houses seemed to be shut up tight, and there was nobody around. She wondered how she'd go about finding Maxim, short of knocking on every single door.

There was a communal well in the centre of the village square, and she walked over and lowered the bucket, for she was thirsty from her long walk in the hot sun. As she pulled it up and drank, she heard a noise behind her, like the creaking of a door. She turned but saw no one, although the door of the house directly behind her seemed to be slightly ajar. A twitching curtain in the cottage across the square caught her eye, but when she glanced over all was still.

"Hello?" she called, unsure whom she was speaking to, or indeed if there was anyone around to hear her. "I'm looking for Mr Maxim. He's a friend of my father's...Theodore Darke?"

She heard a noise behind her and turned to find an old crone leaning on a knobbly stick.

"Maxim lives over there, dearie," she said, pointing across the square to a house with a blood-red door, "but won't you come in for a bite to eat first?"

The hair on the back of Eleanor's neck prickled. "Uh...no, thank you," she said. "I really must be getting on." She hurried over to the house with the red door, resisting the urge to glance back over her shoulder. She shivered.

The door was adorned with a brass knocker in the shape of a lion's head; she lifted it and let it fall three times, then waited apprehensively. Just when she thought there was no one home, the door opened, revealing a dark, cavernous hallway. It seemed far bigger than the outside of the small cottage would allow.

"Hello?" Eleanor said, peering into the gloom. "I'm looking for Mr Maxim. My name is Eleanor Darke."

A great big bear of a man stepped out of the shadows and into the doorway, startling her. He was a good foot-and-a-half taller than her and all muscle. He seemed to be about her father's age, with a thick, wiry black beard that cascaded down his chest. His eyes were black and hard, like stones, and he was frowning.

"I am Maxim," he said in a thick accent that Eleanor didn't recognise. "What do you want?"

"I believe you work with my father, sir? Theodore Darke?"

"What of it? Are people telling lies again? Always they accuse me."

Eleanor's eyebrows rose. "No, not at all. He's in some...trouble...and I need your help."

Maxim reached into an umbrella stand beside the door and withdrew an enormous club. "They make trouble for Theodore, I make trouble for them. He is good man. Show me where they are." His eyes narrowed and he thumped the club menacingly into his left palm.

"Actually, I don't think that will work, sir," Eleanor said, taking a deep breath. "He has a problem with time flies. I think I may have a solution, but I can't do it alone."

This seemed to intrigue Maxim, and he let the club drop. "Hmm. Time flies, you say?"

"Yes, sir."

"You come in."

He ushered Eleanor down the hall and into a sparsely furnished sitting room. She was still trying to work out the proportions of the house—she could have sworn it was bigger on the inside than the outside—but eventually she gave up and decided to just accept it.

The sitting room had the air of a place not often used. The carpet and cushions were threadbare, and a thin layer of dust coated everything. Maxim showed her to an armchair and then folded himself awkwardly into one opposite. The chair was too small for his enormous frame, forcing him to perch on the edge like a parrot. Eleanor wondered why he didn't buy larger furniture.

"Coffee," Maxim said, clapping his hands. It wasn't a question, and Eleanor frowned in confusion, for there was no-one else in the room. Then a tea-tray came floating through the door from what she assumed was the kitchen, set with a large coffee pot and two cups. It placed itself neatly on the low table and the pot began to pour, lifted by unseen hands.

"Now, tell me of Theodore," Maxim said, not bothering with further pleasantries. Tearing her eyes away from the coffee cups, Eleanor related the whole story, then reached into her rucksack and withdrew Bertie.

"My father made me this bird some years ago," she said, passing him to Maxim. "I discovered last night that he eats time flies."

Maxim turned the little clockwork bird over in his hands, careful not to crush it. "Remarkable," he said. "Such beautiful work." The gruffness had gone from his voice, and there was a softness to his eyes as he admired the craftsmanship. Eleanor found herself warming to him.

He studied the bird for so long that Eleanor began to wonder if he'd forgotten she was there. But eventually he stirred and looked up at her.

"So you want a flock of these birdies, to eat your father's time flies?"

Eleanor's heart leaped. "Yes, exactly! Do you think you'll be able to do it?"

Maxim didn't bat an eyelid. "Of course. Give me one week."

"You can make an entire flock in a week?"

"I am fast worker. Plus I have assistant." Eleanor jumped as Maxim passed Bertie seemingly into thin air, but rather than falling to the floor, the little brass cuckoo floated and turned as if someone was examining his workings. Maxim laughed. "Just because you not see him, doesn't mean he not there."

Eleanor swallowed. "And...how much will it cost?"

Maxim snorted. "Pfft. No cost to old friends. If I have time flies, he help me too."

"Thank you, sir."

Maxim stood abruptly. "You go now. I must work." He turned on his heel and left the room, leaving Eleanor to show herself out. But when she got to the front door it opened of its own accord, then closed behind her.

"Thank you," she said, to no-one in particular.

THE WAY BACK TO THE main road was much easier than the way she'd come. As she walked, Eleanor hardly noticed her surroundings, so preoccupied was she with the time flies. Finding Maxim had been a stroke of luck, but the clockwork birds only solved half the problem. She still had to figure out how to get them into her father's workshop without letting the time flies out or being overcome by them herself. If the swarm got her too, she'd be in the same precarious situation as her father—so late for everything that she was effectively in her own separate time pocket. There must be a way, but how?

She thought back to the books she'd read in her father's library. One of them had said something about predictability—how time flies thrived on schedules. Organised people with set deadlines and appointments were far more likely to be overcome by time flies than those whose lives followed no set pattern. The problem was that most people by nature craved routine: they rose, ate their meals, went to work, came home, and went to bed at around the same time every day. Her father was messy and a trifle scatterbrained, to be sure, but when it came to his work he always met his deadlines. It was probably only his forgetfulness around meals that had stopped him being wiped out completely.

Eleanor mulled the conundrum over as the miles passed beneath her boots. Perhaps the secret was to make herself unpredictable. Maybe, just maybe, she'd be able to safely enter the workroom if the time flies couldn't sense what was coming.

By the time she got home, she had the beginnings of a plan. It was risky, but she really couldn't think of anything better. But she knew her mother wasn't going to like it.

The sun was almost set as she came down the street, and she could see her mother's candle glowing in the window. Mary had told her how she'd lit a candle for her every night of the six years they'd been apart; now, Eleanor assumed, she was lighting it for Theodore.

Eleanor waited until after supper, when they were enjoying a cup of tea in the sitting room, before she broached the subject of her plan. She'd mentioned the flock of clockwork birds and her encounter with Maxim earlier, and Mary had seemed positive. But the next part was going to be more difficult.

"I've been thinking, Mama," Eleanor began. "We need to sneak the birds into the workshop somehow. We can't keep the door or window open long enough to let them in, because the time flies will get out before we can. What do you think...about me going in there?"

Mary frowned. "No. Absolutely not. I can't lose you again."

"But you wouldn't. I have an idea—I think I can trick them."

"*Trick* time flies? Impossible."

"No, really. I think it will work."

"But you don't know for certain?"

"No, of course not. But it's our only chance to help Papa. I can't see any other way. You do want him back, don't you?"

"Of course," Mary said, but she hesitated just a trifle too long.

"Mama?" Eleanor said, frowning. "What's going on? Is everything all right between you and Papa?"

Mary sighed. "Things...haven't been easy over the past few years," she said. "We both threw ourselves into our work to cope with losing everything—especially with losing you. It was the only way either of us could regain a sense of purpose and some sort of hope. But, well, we've drifted apart lately. To be honest, I don't know if your father even wants to come back."

"But you still love him, don't you?"

"Oh, my darling, I wouldn't expect you to understand. You're still so young, even though you're almost a woman now. Love is...more complicated than that. Of course I love him, not least because he gave me you. But there are days where we don't *like* each other very much, I'm afraid."

Eleanor scowled in exasperation. "Do you even want to try to save him? To save what you had?"

Mary nodded. "Of course."

"Well then, he has to be back here for you to do that, doesn't he?"

"I know." She sighed again. "Go on then—tell me your plan."

Eleanor started her preparations the very next day, by sleeping until nearly lunchtime. She didn't dress or eat immediately, instead waiting until she felt like it. Following her guidance, her mother was careful not to ask her to carry out any tasks or do anything that might be construed as having an appointment or deadline. Eleanor varied her activities according to her whims, alternately reading, napping, and tinkering with the various clockwork parts lying around the house. She ate, slept, and washed only when she felt like it.

She anticipated that it would take a week of such practices before she'd be ready to face the time flies, and she was careful never to do any activity at the same time each day. Life became rather chaotic, but strangely she found she adapted to it better than she'd expected. A curse-breaker's life was seldom ordered, and she'd already had a taste of it on the road with Thorsten, flitting from village to village and town to town, changing their plans at a moment's notice as the work required. For Eleanor, the unpredictability of the job was actually part of the attraction.

A week to the day after her visit to Maxim, there was a knock at the door, and she opened it to find him towering in the doorway with an enormous sack over his shoulder. He lumbered inside and dumped it unceremoniously in the hallway, then nodded to Eleanor and left without another word.

"What a strange man," Mary said, perplexed, as they stood on the step, watching him stride away down the street. "Shall we see what he's brought us?"

Neither of them could lift the sack alone, but between them they managed to get it into the library. Eleanor undid the string around the neck and tipped it over. A cascade of little brass birds tumbled out onto the rug. She picked one up, turning it over so it caught the light. She'd thought her father's work beautiful, but this was something else altogether. It was difficult to comprehend how a man such as Maxim, with his hands the size of dinner plates and fingers as thick as sausages, could produce something so delicate. The brass was worked into an intricate filigree resembling feathers, with just enough of the clockwork showing through to catch the eye. Each bird was slightly different in the tilt of its head, the length of its wings, or the cast of its eyes. It was the finest handiwork she'd ever seen, and she understood now why her father was keen to work with the odd, reclusive man.

Mary wound up the bird she was holding and placed it on the rug. At first it just hopped and pecked around, like Bertie did, but then it suddenly launched itself into the air, swooping around the room like a real bird. Eleanor laughed in sheer delight. If all of them were as wonderful as this, then her plan might just work.

They spent the evening winding the birds and transferring them into smaller sacks, which Eleanor would be able to hang about her person. Winding the birds was a risk, for they were liable to peck at each other in the bags, but she needed to be able to release them as quickly as possible, just in case her protection against the time flies failed her. She wasn't sure if she was ready, but she'd have to act soon, because her father's food must have almost run out.

"When will you do it?" Mary asked as they tied up the last of the sacks.

"Tomorrow," Eleanor said. "I want to make sure I'm properly rested and everything's prepared. Might as well give it my best shot."

Mary nodded, but as they said goodnight, Eleanor noticed she held her longer and more tightly than usual.

SHE SLEPT POORLY, WAKING several times in the night fretting about what she might have forgotten. She woke properly not long after dawn and, unable to go back to sleep, decided to get up. There was no sense in delaying the inevitable.

She'd thought her mother was still in bed, but when she went downstairs she found her in the kitchen, making enormous bowls of porridge.

"Here," Mary said, placing a bowl in front of her. "You'll need your strength." Eleanor smiled and ate dutifully, although her mouth was dry and she could barely taste it.

After breakfast she went back upstairs and dressed in her curse-breaker's clothes: sturdy boots, breeches, a plain shirt, and a waistcoat full of useful pockets. She tied a red-and-white kerchief around her neck and pulled her hair back into a bun. On her belt she hung her knife in its scabbard, and she tucked her pocket-watch into her waistcoat. She slung her rucksack on her shoulders; she'd packed it full of food and water the night before. She glanced at herself in the mirror and straightened her shirt. She certainly looked the part, even if she didn't exactly feel it. She wondered briefly what Thorsten would think of her plan, but really it was no madder than the way he'd saved Finster.

"My, look at you," Mary said with a smile as Eleanor came downstairs. "You're quite the adventurer." There was a wistfulness in her gaze, as if she were wondering when her little girl had turned into such a dashing young woman. Eleanor blushed and busied herself collecting the sacks. Mary helped her haul them down to the cellar, then draped them over her daughter's shoulders.

"Are you sure about this?" she asked.

Eleanor shook her head. "Not really, no," she said. "But we have to try to help Papa." She took a deep breath. "If I'm not back in two days you must fetch Maxim. He may know what to do."

Mary's eyes were bright, but she simply nodded.

"Good luck, my darling," she whispered, drawing her daughter into an embrace. "Your father will be so proud. And I am too."

Eleanor took a deep breath and turned the key in the lock. "Now, remember," she said, "we'll open it just long enough for me to get in. Make sure you close it before too many escape. Use Bertie to catch them if you can."

Mary nodded. "I love you."

"I love you too, Mama."

WHEN THE DOOR OPENED, Eleanor was blinded by a flash of light. At first, she struggled to find its source, but as she blinked away the spots dancing in front of her eyes, she realised it was sunlight from the upper window glinting off the iridescent, brass-coloured bodies of the time flies. There were hundreds, if not thousands of them—they must have bred in the two weeks her father had been trapped, for there was no way they'd have all fitted into a single household clock. One or two flitted out the door behind her, but she managed to slam it shut before too many got out.

The light streaming in through the workshop's high basement window had the golden colour of late afternoon; she wondered if it was still the day of the swarm. She pulled her kerchief up over her nose and mouth, brushing away the mass of flies. So far, they seemed to be leaving her alone, perhaps confounded by her lack of a coherent schedule. With nowhere to be, she had no time to waste and nothing for them to feed on.

The room was lined with workbenches, on which stood clocks in various stages of disassembly, as well as scatterings of tools and parts. A camp bed was set up next to one of the benches—for when her father worked late, she supposed—and on it sat her Papa, looking dazed and confused. Eleanor hurried over to him.

"Papa?" she exclaimed, shaking his shoulders. "Are you all right?" His hair was greyer than she remembered, and his walrus moustache was in need of a trim. There were shadows under his eyes, and he also looked rather thin; a result, she guessed, of having to ration his food.

He peered at her, as if unsure of what he was seeing. "Ellie? No, it can't be."

"It's me, Papa. I'm here to help you."

"But you can't be here...the time flies...they'll get you too..."

"No, they won't, Papa. But we have to act quickly." She offloaded the sacks, in which Maxim's clockwork birds were still fidgeting and chirping. "Help me undo these."

She untied the rope on the nearest sack and reached in to grab one of the birds. It pecked at her fingers, but she was able to catch it with relative ease. Once she had it out of the sack, she double-checked its winding, then flung it high into the air.

For a moment she was terrified it was going to come crashing down onto the flagstone floor, but then the little brass cuckoo stretched its wings and began to soar around the room, snapping at every time fly within its reach. Theodore stared at the bird in amazement.

"I don't understand..."

"You don't have to understand right now, Papa. I'll explain everything, but first help me with these."

Together they began releasing the birds from the sacks, until the room was filled with the clattery beating of clockwork wings. The light in the workshop dimmed as the time flies were snapped up one by one. As each fly disappeared, Theodore began to look more and more like himself.

Eleanor sat down beside him on the camp bed and took his hand. "Now we just have to wait," she said. She was thrilled with how well her plan was working, although she did wonder how they were going to recapture the birds after it was all over. But that was a problem for later.

It took the clockwork cuckoos only an hour to make short work of the time flies. As they did, the world seemed to speed up; the light outside the window changed from late afternoon to evening to morning in the space of a few minutes, over and over, until Eleanor was confident they were back in the time where they were meant to be. Her father still looked dazed, but some colour was returning to his cheeks.

As the birds ate their fill, they gradually came into land, perching on the workbenches, the half-built clocks, the windowsill, and even the edge of the camp bed to roost. Soon there were only two or three still flying, and when there were no more flies to be caught they too settled down, tucked their heads under their wings and went to sleep. Eleanor stood up and stretched.

"I think we should be all right now," she said. "There's someone who wants to see you very much." She hoped it was true.

She helped her father stand, and together they walked over to the door. Eleanor opened it and found Mary was standing just outside, her brow creased with concern. When she saw them both, she gasped, tears springing to her eyes.

"Mary, my love," Theodore said, holding out his hands to her, "I'm so sorry."

Mary pressed a hand to her mouth. "Oh, Teddy," was all she said. Their eyes locked, and for a long moment they just stared at each other.

"Oh, come on," Eleanor said, rolling her eyes and pulling them both into a hug. For a moment her parents held each other stiffly, as if they were no longer accustomed to it, but suddenly Mary began to sob. The three of them clung together, embracing for the first time in six years, and Eleanor, quite unexpectedly, found herself crying too.

THEODORE DIDN'T REMEMBER a lot about the two weeks he was caught with the time flies—a not-unexpected side effect. When Eleanor questioned him, he said he'd known there were things he should have been doing, and he'd had a sense of running terribly late, but he'd been unable to do anything about it. Now, he was full of excitement at his daughter's discovery.

"This is extraordinary, you know," he said as they sat down to an early lunch. "Absolutely extraordinary. You have to write a paper for the *Journal of Horology*. As far as I know, you're the first to discover how to control and defeat the effects of time flies in this way. You'll be famous! You couldn't ask for a better start to your career!"

Eleanor smiled fondly. She'd forgotten just how infectious her father's enthusiasm could be, and for a brief moment she even considered that maybe she *could* be a clockmaker. Certainly there would be satisfaction in eventually being able to produce work like Maxim's—although if she was honest with herself, she wasn't sure she had the talent.

Then she remembered the days on the road with Thorsten, the thrill of new places, and the work of curse-breaking—dangerous sometimes, to be sure, but literally life-changing. She wanted to do for others what Thorsten had done for Finster. Repairing clocks in a small town for the rest of her days would never scratch that itch.

"Leave the girl alone, Teddy," Mary said. "She's already got a career all lined up."

Theodore raised his eyebrows. "Really?"

"I'm sorry, Papa," Eleanor said, "but I'm already an apprentice curse-breaker." Then she had to explain all about Thorsten and Finster, and that she wouldn't be staying with them much beyond the next full moon.

Theodore's face dropped, but he wasn't one to stay down for long. "Ah well," he said, "considering that until a few hours ago I never expected to see you again, let alone have you follow in my footsteps, I suppose I can live with that." He chuckled. "It might even be time for me to take on an apprentice of my own."

A WEEK AFTER HER FATHER'S rescue, Eleanor and Theodore visited Maxim with the intention of returning the clockwork birds, but the reclusive watchmaker wouldn't hear of it, insisting that they were a gift. When they returned home, she helped her father build an enormous aviary for the birds in the yard, and they took to it right away, flapping and swooping happily around the enclosure. From then on, whenever Theodore got a new clock, he always made sure to open it in the aviary first, and more than once the brass cuckoos saved him from errant time flies. He also began to build a thriving side business, hiring out the birds to other horologists.

Eleanor hadn't heard from Thorsten, but at the full moon she received a note, with directions to a village a few miles away where someone had cursed the wells. For a brief moment, she considered tearing it up and staying with her parents, but the lure of the unknown was too strong. The next morning, as she raised her hand to her mother and father, who were standing together on the front step, she knew this would be just one of many farewells, and of homecomings too. After all, they now had all the time in the world.

The Memory Bank

Theodore Darke scratched his head as he sat down to breakfast, his brow furrowing in frustration. Even though life had returned to normal, the lack of recall from the two weeks he'd been pulled out of the world by the time flies still bothered him.

"Everything all right?" Mary asked, passing the toast. Theodore shrugged.

"I suppose so. I just hate feeling like I've forgotten something."

"It's a function of age, I'm afraid."

"Come now, I'm not *that* old."

"Well, neither of us are getting any younger, that's for sure."

"Perhaps. But I've got a lifetime of work all locked up in here." He tapped the side of his head. "What if I forget it all before I have the chance to pass it on to John?" John was Theodore's new apprentice. He was a quick lad, but it would be several years before he'd be truly up to speed.

Mary patted his hand. "That won't happen," she reassured him. "You've got plenty of time left in you yet."

Theodore sighed. "Maybe. But accidents happen." He frowned to himself for a moment. "I think perhaps it's time I went to see Arthur."

"Arthur Denholm? At the Memory Bank?"

"Yes."

"But you've always hated the idea."

"Well, now I see its usefulness. Can't a man change his mind?"

"Of course."

"Anyway, an appointment can't hurt. I don't have to go through with it if I don't want to."

THE MEMORY BANK WAS an imposing stone edifice down by the river. One of the town's oldest buildings, it towered majestically over the other small, rather shabby shops on the street. Its carved cornices bore fanciful swirls capped by human faces with varying expressions; similar features adorned the window-frames. It was both intriguing and grotesque.

Theodore had passed the Memory Bank many times but had never been inside. In many ways its impressive facade reminded him of the regular bank, but there were odd little unsettling details, like the faces, that set it apart. It was mainly the purview of the wealthy, who felt that their memories were worth preserving and had the means to do so, and occasionally those like him, who had unique knowledge that they didn't want to lose. He'd known the manager, Arthur Denholm, socially for around five years—they belonged to the same chess club—but he'd never called on him professionally before.

Theodore climbed the wide stone staircase to the front door and took a deep breath. He reminded himself that he was just finding out the particulars—he didn't have to commit to anything today. He'd expected the doors to be wide open but, strangely, they were shut. He glanced at the plaque by the door and saw that he was well within the opening hours. He reached for the big brass handle and pushed, expecting to find the door locked, but with a bit of effort it gave way, opening into the bank's cavernous interior. Against his better judgement, Theodore stepped through.

Much as in a regular bank, the main door opened directly onto a great hall lined with tellers' booths, but all were empty. There were no customers, and no staff that he could see. The hall was cool and dim, and smelled of dust and old paper. Some daylight trickled in through the windows, but many of them were covered with thick velvet drapes. Only one or two of the gas lamps were lit.

"Hello?" Theodore called. His voice echoed off the cavernous ceiling and the polished wooden floor, bouncing back at him like a lonely ghost.

"It's Theodore Darke here...I'm looking for Mr Denholm. I'm hoping to do business with him...?" He trailed off, aware of how ridiculous he sounded, talking to an empty room as if it could hear him. Then a voice spoke.

"Mr Denholm will see you in his office." It was a female voice, but its owner was nowhere to be seen. Theodore looked around, unnerved.

"And, uh, which way is that?" He was beginning to wonder if this was such a good idea. Perhaps he should just go home and forget all about it. But the incident with the time flies still nagged at him. Memories were so ephemeral, and he couldn't afford to lose everything he'd learned over the years.

"Down the hallway, to the left," the voice said.

"Well...thank you..."

"You're welcome."

Theodore dutifully followed the voice's instructions, and soon found himself standing before an ornate wooden door on which the words 'Arthur Denholm, Manager,' were inscribed in swirling gold letters. He raised his hand and knocked, trying to ignore the churning in his stomach. For a moment there was no response, then he heard a gruff "Enter," and obeyed.

Like everything in the building, the office was overly large. A beautiful wooden desk, which Theodore immediately valued as Very Expensive, was the centrepiece of the room, but even it seemed dwarfed by the expansive floor space. There were bookshelves along each wall, crammed with leather-bound tomes that glowed like jewels, and Theodore thought wryly that Arthur must get his required daily exercise just by walking between them.

The man himself was seated behind the desk, looking smaller and greyer than Theodore remembered. It had been some time since they'd seen each other, for the last time Theodore had attended the chess club was before the time flies incident. He wondered if Arthur even knew about it, although they had enough mutual acquaintances that the news had probably got back to him.

"How are you, Arthur?" Theodore asked companionably. "Long time no see."

Arthur Denholm raised his head, and Theodore was shocked at how gaunt he'd become. His eyes were shadowed, and his mop of silver hair was wispy and uncombed. Theodore remembered him as always being impeccably dressed in a three-piece suit, with a bowler hat and cane, but today his necktie was loose, his waistcoat unbuttoned and his shirt rumpled, almost as if he'd slept in it. His jacket had been thrown haphazardly across a nearby armchair, and he sat there in his shirtsleeves looking like a completely different man.

"What can I do for you, sir?" he asked in a bored tone, as if Theodore were just another customer. Theodore frowned in confusion.

"You don't remember me, Arthur? It's Theodore Darke. From the chess club."

The bank manager shrugged. "I'm a busy man."

"Surely not too busy to help an old friend?" Without waiting for an invitation, Theodore sat down on a chair in front of the desk. He leaned on the desk and peered forward. Something was clearly wrong. Arthur's eyes were darting around, as if he was having trouble concentrating, or was searching for something.

As he caught his friend's eye, Arthur seemed to snap back into himself. "Theodore?" he said. Theodore grinned.

"That's right. You had me worried there for a minute."

"I'm sorry, sir, if you could just fill in your details here. Wouldn't want to forget these things, now, would we?" Arthur chortled to himself, the familiarity gone.

"Is everything all right, Arthur?"

"Quite all right, I assure you. And I must ask that we maintain propriety and that you address me as Mr Denholm."

Surprised at his own daring, Theodore reached out and patted his old friend's hand. "Are you sure?"

The contact seemed to revive Arthur, and lucidity came back into his eyes. "Oh, Theodore, thank goodness you're here. I've done something terribly stupid."

"What have you done?"

"I've banked my memories."

"Um..." Theodore wasn't quite sure what to say. It made sense, he supposed, that the manager should avail himself of his own services. "Why does that matter?"

Arthur sighed. He clutched at Theodore's hand as if it were a lifeline. "I went too far. I was trying out our new feature—connected memories. You store your memories—*all* your memories—in the bank and then just access them as needed, rather than only banking one or two. It would have been so lucrative for us, charging for storage space. But..."

"It doesn't work?" Theodore ventured.

Arthur shook his head. "I stored all the bank's access codes in there. Now I have no way of retrieving them, and the forgetting is taking over..." He bowed his head, his shoulders shaking with sobs.

"There, there," Theodore said, patting his friend's hand again in what he hoped was a reassuring manner. "I'm sure it can all be sorted out. Where are all the staff?"

Arthur looked up tearfully. "I can't remember. Perhaps I sent them away, or perhaps they left of their own accord. I don't know."

"What about the voice in the foyer that gave me directions?"

"A Simple Memory Processor. She's just a memory of someone uttering a few standard phrases. She doesn't exist. But she's all I've got left now."

Theodore huffed to himself and twirled his moustache absently around one finger, as he always did when he was thinking. "Well now, that's a pretty pickle you've got yourself into. Looks like we're just going to have to figure it out."

"We?"

"Well, you're clearly in no state to do it on your own. I'll give you a hand. Now tell me, where exactly are these memories stored?"

"There's a vault downstairs. It's where we keep all the memories. It's well-protected, but I can't remember how."

Theodore sighed. "Well, I guess there's nothing for it. You and I are going to have to become bank robbers."

Arthur stared at him, his eyes wide. "Oh no, I couldn't possibly."

"Do you want your memories back or not?"

"Well yes, of course...but..."

"And I can't think of a better way, can you?"

"No..."

"Well, then."

"But I wouldn't even know where to start."

"To start, you'll come home with me. You can't stay here, and you need feeding and cleaning up a bit. Then we'll get our things together and come back tomorrow with everything we need. How does that sound?"

Arthur nodded, seemingly relieved that someone else was taking charge. "It sounds good." His eyes clouded. "Who are you again?"

MARY HEARD THEODORE come in and went to meet him in the hallway.

"How did it go?" she asked, then stopped short at the sight of the rather bedraggled little man trailing behind her husband. "Surely that can't be...?" She stared at Theodore, questions in her eyes.

"Arthur, you remember my wife, Mary?" Theodore asked, ushering the bank manager in front of him.

"I'm afraid I don't, ma'am," Arthur said rather apologetically, "but I'm nevertheless very pleased to make your acquaintance."

"What's going on?" Mary whispered to Theodore as they showed Arthur through to the sitting room. The bank manager had been their dinner guest numerous times over the past five years, and he'd never forgotten her before.

"It's a long story," Theodore murmured. "I'll explain later. Can we get him something to eat?"

"Of course."

When Mary brought in a plate of bread, cheese, cold meats and pickles, Arthur fell on it and wolfed it down as if he hadn't eaten in days. Remembering the empty bank and his friend's dishevelled appearance, Theodore suspected that may very well have been the case. After the meal was over,

Arthur slipped into a happy, sleepy trance, until Mary suggested he take a nap and showed him to the guest room.

"Go on, then," she said as she returned to the sitting room. "Explain, because I'm *this close* to taking him to the hospital. He looks awful."

Theodore sighed. "It's complicated. The poor man appears to have become a victim of his own success. He tried out some new feature the bank was working on, and the upshot is that all his memories are now locked in the bank vault and he can barely remember his own name. And of course the codes for opening the vault are in there too."

"He didn't build in any fail-safes?" Mary asked, her eyebrows rising.

Theodore shook his head. "You know Arthur. He always tended a bit to the rash side. Even in our chess games he'd take unnecessary risks. More often than not they paid off, but sometimes..." he trailed off.

"So you've decided to help him?"

"Well, someone has to do something, and I'm really all he's got. The bank staff have all disappeared to goodness knows where, and he hasn't got that many friends anymore. As far as I know, his life is just work and chess club."

Mary sighed. "I know. Poor Arthur. So what are you planning to do?"

"We're going to rob the bank."

"You're going to *what*?"

"It's the only way."

"What a ridiculous notion. What if you get caught?"

"Well, I should think the bank manager would be unlikely to press charges against himself."

"This isn't a joke!"

Theodore put his arm around her consolingly. "I know, love. But it'll be fine, I promise."

Mary shook her head. "And you accuse Arthur of being rash. You need to think things through, Teddy. I've nearly lost you once already this year—I don't want it to happen again. Remember, Ellie isn't around to save you this time."

"I promise I won't do anything stupid. If it seems like it's too dangerous, I'll turn back. But we can't let him go on like this. Sooner or later it'll kill him. Anyway, I thought you of all people would be on board. Didn't you take an oath to help people?"

Mary turned her stony gaze on him. "Don't even *think* about playing that game," she said, then sighed. "But you're right. I suppose it has to be done." She glanced at the clock on the mantelpiece. "I have to go or I'll be late for my shift." She gave Theodore a peck on the cheek and then left without another word.

THEODORE SPENT THE rest of the day preparing all the tools and supplies he could think of, but he couldn't help feeling that he was missing something. Arthur was still in bed, and Theodore left him there, for the manager was no help at all when it came to remembering anything useful about the bank's security systems. As afternoon turned into evening, Theodore couldn't shake the idea that he'd bitten off far more than he could chew. Unbidden, he thought of Ellie and wished she were there—her solution to the time flies had been nothing short of brilliant, and she'd surely know what to do. At what point, he wondered, did parents start relying on their children, rather than the other way around?

He sat up thinking late into the night, until Mary returned from work and ushered him up to bed. But even when he did sleep, it was fitful and punctuated by strange dreams.

It was just after dawn when he woke, but try as he might, he couldn't get back to sleep. He rose quietly, careful not to disturb Mary, and went out to the aviary, where he stood and watched his clockwork birds chirping and swooping, the rising sun glinting off their brass filigree. He held out his hand and one landed on his finger; as always, he was captivated by the intricacy of the work. He'd always felt much more at home with clockwork than people. People were unpredictable and difficult to understand, but with clockwork you always knew that if you got the right components in the right order, marvellous things would happen. He reflected that he'd be utterly useless in a job like Arthur's, dealing as it did in the vagaries of the human condition.

Thinking of Arthur brought him back to the present, and to the task that awaited them. Theodore could pick a lock with the best of them—the legacy of a misspent youth—but a bank vault was a whole other matter. What kind of security could a vault storing people's most precious possessions—their memories—possibly need? He shook his head in frustration and went back inside to see if Arthur was awake.

He found the bank manager in his dressing gown, sitting at the kitchen table with Mary, not only awake but more lucid than Theodore had yet seen him. It seemed that a decent meal and a sleep had worked wonders. He still drifted off periodically, but he seemed to have a much firmer grip on who they were, which could only be a good thing.

"How are you feeling, Arthur?" Theodore asked as he sat down to his breakfast.

Arthur smiled. "Much better, thank you. Less...vague."

"I'm glad to hear it. Are you all set for our adventure?"

Arthur's gaze shifted, and he looked confused. "Remind me what we're doing, again?"

"We're going to break into the Memory Bank and see if we can retrieve what you've lost."

"Ah, yes, that's right! I remember now."

"I don't suppose you remember anything about the vault—specifically its security systems?"

Arthur chewed this over for a minute. "I remember there's a key," he said eventually.

"Good! And where's the key kept?"

"Um...I can't quite recall. You have to access it somehow. By solving a puzzle or something? I don't know; I may be barking up entirely the wrong tree there. Sorry."

Theodore suppressed a sigh. "That's fine, old fellow. I know it's difficult. Looks like we're just going to have to play it by ear. What say you get dressed and ready to go, and then we head off?"

"Smashing idea," Arthur said. "Once more unto the breach and all that!" He stood, nodded to Mary, and headed back upstairs.

"Puzzles?" Mary said. "That sounds...intriguing."

"I know," Theodore said. "It's got me worried too." He grinned boyishly at her. "Want to come?"

In spite of herself, Mary grinned back. "I wish I could," she said, "but I have to be at work in a few hours."

"Take the day off."

Mary sighed. "You know I can't, Teddy."

"Yes," he said. "I know." He finished his breakfast, so distracted he hardly tasted it, then went into the hall to pack their rucksacks.

It was mid-morning when they eventually set off, for Arthur had been slow to get ready, leaving Theodore pacing the hallway in frustration. It was just a short walk to the Memory Bank, and entering thankfully required no breaking of anything, as Arthur had a key.

The interior of the bank was dark, for they'd turned out the gas lamps before they left the previous day, and not much light came in from outside. Theodore groped his way over to one of the large windows and threw open the thick drapes, letting the sunlight pour in. Dust motes danced in the beams.

"So far, so good." Theodore shrugged, glancing over at Arthur. Being back at the bank seemed to be having a poor effect on him—the dazed look was returning to his eyes.

"Which way is the vault?" Theodore asked, concerned that Arthur would forget before he was able to give directions. But thankfully the bank manager's gaze sharpened, and he pointed towards a vast marble staircase that dominated the end of the banking hall.

"Downstairs," he said.

"Right," Theodore said, with businesslike cheerfulness. "Off we go, then."

He took Arthur's arm, marching him past the empty tellers' desks with their polished wood and brass fittings, to the staircase. They descended to the next level, but Arthur shook his head.

"It's right at the bottom," he said. "As far as you can go."

The staircase seemed interminable, and Theodore began to wonder just how many basements and sub-basements the Memory Bank held, and what exactly went on in them. Certainly the building was far bigger than it appeared from the street, being mostly underground. As the staircase opened out onto each new landing, he peered through the doorways, trying to get glimpses of its inner workings, but he could never see very much. As soon as they descended past the first bend, they lost all light from the main hall, and Theodore stopped to untie a lantern from his pack and light it. Its warm glow was comforting, but it made the shadows around them seem darker, and the further they went, the less comfortable he became. He'd never really been underground before, and he fancied he could feel the weight of the building pressing in on them from every side. Arthur, on the other hand, seemed totally unperturbed. Theodore supposed he must have made this journey hundreds of times.

Eventually, just when he thought they were doomed to go on descending until they went right through the centre of the earth and out the other side, the staircase ended. Ahead of them was a large brass door adorned with a massive combination lock.

Theodore went up to it and held the lantern high. "Well, Arthur," he said, "what's the combination?"

The manager had been marching along stoically, and in apparently good spirits, during their descent, but now he stared around him as if he'd never been there before.

"I'm not sure I should tell you that, Mr...what was it again? Security and all that."

Theodore closed his eyes briefly and took a deep breath. "You remember, Arthur. I'm your friend, and we're going to retrieve your memories."

Arthur frowned for a minute. "Oh, yes. Sorry, Theodore. It all just slipped my mind for a moment."

"That's perfectly all right. Now, the combination?"

A series of pained expressions crossed Arthur's face, as if he were thinking hard. "Nope...gone completely."

"Of course it is." Theodore sighed.

He set his pack and the lantern on the ground and stood staring at the door, thinking. Finally he reached into his bag and dug out a listening device on a long cord. He placed the smaller end in his ear, and the larger he held against the door. It had been many years since he'd used this skill—something he'd developed as a young man, along with the lock-picking—and he hoped he hadn't forgotten how. Slowly and carefully he turned the combination lock, listening for the telltale clicking. It was so faint that at first he thought he'd imagined it, but after several painstaking minutes he stood up, stretched, and tried the handle. It turned easily beneath his fingers, and when he pulled on it the door swung open on well-oiled hinges.

Theodore had fully expected a vault on the other side, although he'd wondered about the level of security—if an amateur like him could crack it so easily, it didn't inspire much confidence. But to his amazement, when he stepped through the door it wasn't into a strongroom, but rather an enormous underground cavern. The bank—and indeed, the rest of the town—must have been built on top of a natural cave network. He'd had no idea.

Running just in front of the door was a line of narrow-gauge railway tracks, the kind used for mining trucks.

"Oh, goody!" Arthur exclaimed, bouncing through the door behind him. "I've always liked this part."

"What's this?" Theodore asked, astonished.

"This is how we get down to the vault," Arthur said. "I remember now." He punched a series of brass numbers that were set into the stone wall, then hit a button. There was a rattling further up the line, and Theodore glanced along the rails just as a small cart came bumping into view. It diverted off a branch line and stopped right in front of them.

"Is it...safe?"

"Oh, perfectly. There was only that one time...but we don't really talk about that."

The cart was narrow but was fitted out with two seats, one behind the other. Theodore pointed to the front one.

"I suppose you should drive, since you know what you're doing."

"Why, thank you. Happy to." Arthur clambered into the front seat, while Theodore climbed in behind him, praying that the manager's memory wouldn't desert him again before they reached the end of this crazy ride.

"All ready?" Arthur asked. "Good. Here we go." He threw forward a lever on the cart, and they began to move, slowly at first, then faster and faster, until Theodore felt his moustache being whipped back by the wind.

"I say, old fellow," he yelled in Arthur's ear, "is it really necessary to go *quite* so fast?"

"Only one speed!" Arthur yelled back. "Hold on!" His words were swept away as the cart careered round a bend. Theodore looked down at the drop to their left, and instantly regretted it. He squeezed his eyes shut, but that was worse. His stomach began to churn from the motion.

Down they went, further and further into the depths of the earth. Theodore briefly wondered how they were going to get back out again, but he supposed the bank vault's architects had thought that through—at least, he hoped they had. The air on his face was getting cooler as they descended, and he caught the smell of damp. There had to be water around somewhere.

Finally, just when he thought he couldn't take much more of the bumping and rattling, the cart began to level out and slow down. In a few minutes they came to a stop outside another locked door. Theodore clambered out, breathing deeply and trying not to lose his breakfast. The smell of damp was stronger now, and he fancied he could also hear the rush of running water. He turned back to the truck to find Arthur still in it, giggling like a child.

"I could do that all day!" he exclaimed, flinging his arms above his head. "Whee!"

Theodore rolled his eyes surreptitiously. "Well, thankfully we don't have to. Come on, out you get." He took

Arthur's elbow and helped him out of the cart, but he was unable to stop a smile. He'd always thought of his friend as rather stuffy and a little pompous at times, but the loss of his memories seemed to have freed something in him. Theodore guessed he'd forgotten how a man in his position was supposed to act.

The lock on the second brass door had apparently been designed by the same person who'd made the one above, and Theodore made equally short work of it. Now that the stomach-churning ride was behind them, he was actually starting to enjoy himself. It had been years since he'd had anything that could possibly be described as an adventure—fleeing Finster was probably the closest thing, and that had brought more pain than pleasure, at least in the short term. He loved his work, but he'd always harboured a hankering for exploration, fostered, he suspected, by a strict childhood reading diet of penny dreadfuls and boys-own-adventure stories.

As he finished his work on the door, he glanced across at Arthur, who had gone quiet again.

"Would you like to open this one?" he asked. Arthur shrugged unconcernedly, but walked over and turned the handle.

The smell and roar of water rolled over them and, stepping through the door, Theodore immediately understood why. They were standing on the bank of an underground river; not a large one, but fast-flowing by virtue of its narrowness. Theodore held up the lantern and glanced to his right, downstream, but the river quickly disappeared into blackness beyond the circle of light, and he couldn't tell how far it ran or where it led. The rock shelf they were standing on petered out to either side; there was no way to walk alongside the water.

"What do we do now?" Theodore asked. Arthur frowned.

"Just give me a minute…"

Theodore took off his pack and sat down. He pulled out his water flask and took a long swig, then offered it to Arthur, who shook his head. He was scuffing at the floor with the toe of his boot, clearly deep in thought.

Theodore said nothing, not wanting to distract his companion from the retrieval of such fragile memories. After a time he pulled out some dried fruit, more for something to do than because he was actually hungry. He passed them over and Arthur munched absently on an apricot as he continued to contemplate the floor.

After they'd been sitting there for about half an hour, Theodore began to wonder if Arthur had truly forgotten and, if so, how they were going to get out again. He hadn't seen a way back up the railway track, but then again he hadn't been looking for one. Perhaps it was designed that way to deter thieves—if you couldn't make it past all the security measures, you were doomed to die of hunger down here in the blackness.

It was an uncomfortable thought, and as soon as it bubbled up he wished it hadn't, but the image was impossible to unsee. He took a deep breath to steady his nerves.

"How's it going, Arthur?"

Arthur glanced over at him, and Theodore was relieved to see lucidity in his gaze.

"I think I've almost got it," he said. "It's on the edge of my recollection. Just a few more minutes."

"Arthur?"

"Mm?"

"What's it like—forgetting?"

Arthur looked up at him, his grey eyes sad. "Forgetting?" he said. "That's the easy part. Forgetting is soft and floating, like a featherbed. It's when I remember I've forgotten that it hurts. I know I had a mother and a sister once, but I can't picture their faces." He sighed. "Although sometimes I wonder if it's just because my life really hasn't been that memorable. But then I think there's things I'd want to remember, even so." He shrugged. "Does that make sense?"

Theodore nodded, and Arthur went back to gazing at the floor. Then he looked up again.

"I remember now!" he exclaimed. "There's a hidden boat, and we have to navigate the rapids. It's like a maze, or a lock."

"And you know the way?"

"It's the first thing you're taught when you're taken on as staff here. I've done it hundreds of times. Even if my mind can't quite remember, my hands will."

This explanation wasn't entirely satisfactory, but Theodore reflected that he had no option but to trust his friend.

"So where do we find this boat, then?"

Arthur laughed. "It's been here all along. We just couldn't see it." He gestured at the rock ledge beneath their feet, and Theodore realised that it was edged with cracks outlining a canoe. Arthur reached around to a seemingly innocuous knob of rock on the wall and twisted it, and the ledge in front of them split away until the canoe itself was visible.

"Hop in," Arthur said. "I'll need to be in the back, to steer." He pulled two paddles out of the canoe and handed one to Theodore. They quickly stowed their gear, then lowered the canoe into the water, where a convenient eddy brushed up against the ledge. Theodore felt the familiar churning in his stomach start up again—he'd had enough wild rides for one day. But before he could even say anything, Arthur had pushed them off and they were being swept downstream by the current.

"You paddle on the right, and I'll take the left!" Arthur yelled. "Don't stop paddling unless I tell you to!"

For the first few minutes the river was relatively calm, albeit fast-flowing, but then they hit their first set of rapids. Theodore gripped his paddle so tightly his knuckles turned white, but Arthur got them through it with nonchalant ease.

It continued in this way for what felt like miles, although Theodore knew that realistically it couldn't be. Just as they left a rapid and he started to relax, they'd hit another one. His nerves felt frayed to ribbons.

By the time the rapids receded and they pulled into another rock ledge, he was a quivering wreck. Hoisting himself from the canoe, he felt his knees wobbling under him, and he sat down as gracefully as possible, pretending he'd intended to do so all along. He dug in his rucksack for the sandwiches he'd packed. The bag was wet, but the sandwiches thankfully were none the worse for wear.

"I think this is an excellent place to stop for lunch," he said. "It'll do us good to have a breather." Arthur acquiesced and took a sandwich, but he didn't look anywhere near as wrung out as Theodore felt; in fact, he was positively sprightly. If anything, the wild career down the rapids appeared to have done him good.

By the time they'd finished their lunch, Theodore had recovered his spirits. "Right!" he said with renewed enthusiasm. "What's next?"

The next thing was yet another brass door, but this one was different from those they'd encountered previously. There was no lock, for one thing, just a panel with a series of small squares set into it. Theodore touched the doorknob and the squares began to light up randomly, one after the other, in a complicated sequence.

"What do we do with this?" Theodore asked, but Arthur merely shrugged. His former exhilaration had disappeared, and he now looked very tired.

Theodore stared at the sequence, which lit up differently every time he touched the door handle. It was like a puzzle, he reflected, but how was he supposed to solve it?

Unbidden, a memory surfaced of a game he used to play with Eleanor when she was small. It had involved a series of cards, each painted with a brightly-coloured picture—a horse, a ball, a tree. The cards were laid out in a sequence, turned over briefly, and then replaced face-down, and the players had to remember what order the pictures were in. Ellie had triumphed without fail—even as a child she'd had a phenomenal memory.

Perhaps this was something similar, Theodore thought. Maybe it was as simple—and as complicated—as remembering a sequence. He gripped the handle again and the squares flashed white. This time, he tried to count where each one appeared: three across, two down; six across, ten down; one across, four down. When the last square stopped flashing, he reached out and pressed the square he remembered as flashing first. It lit up green beneath his thumb, and he grinned to himself. He got the next four without a problem, but on the sixth one he stumbled. The square flashed red, then the whole grid flared and went dark. He wondered how many attempts he had left, but there was nothing to indicate.

"What are you doing?" Arthur asked, peering interestedly at the wall. Theodore explained, and he nodded. "Why don't we break it up?" he suggested. "You take the first five and I'll take the last five. Easier for both of us that way."

Theodore thought about this strategy briefly, then agreed. He wasn't sure he'd be able to remember all ten squares alone, and Arthur's short-term memory did seem to be improving.

"All right, then," he said. "Here we go again." He gripped the door handle and the squares flashed up. This time he got all five of his correct, and Arthur managed three, slipping up on the second-last one.

"Do you know how many tries we get?" Theodore asked.

"Three, I think," Arthur said. "I can't remember for sure, but with things like this it's usually three."

"Well then, it's our last chance. No pressure."

Theodore had got the hang of it now, and he breezed through his set confidently. Arthur got four correct without hesitation, but on the fifth he paused, his thumb hovering between two squares.

"Everything all right?" Theodore asked anxiously.

"I just can't...quite...remember," Arthur said. "I think it's this one, but I'm not completely sure."

Theodore tried to bring up the pattern in his mind. "No, I think it's the one next to it."

"Are you sure?"

"Um..."

"Oh well," Arthur said with a shrug, planting his thumb on his original choice. Theodore held his breath, and then the square flashed green and there was a click. He turned the doorknob and the door swung open. Beyond lay a long hallway cut into the rock. There were no obvious puzzles or traps, but by this stage Theodore was getting suspicious.

"Any idea what comes next?" he asked, but Arthur shook his head. Theodore hoisted his lantern and they set off down the hall.

At first it was easy going, for the way was straight and even, with no roughness underfoot to trip them up. Theodore had initially thought it was a single corridor, but as they got further in he began to wonder. Sure enough, they soon came to an intersection where three tunnels branched off in different directions.

"A maze?" he said. "Really? How...quaint." He hoped there were no monsters lurking in the depths. Arthur said nothing.

"So, which way do we go, then?" Theodore asked. Arthur stood for a moment, his eyes closed, as if he was trying to smell or feel something. Then he pointed to the right.

"That way."

Theodore didn't even bother asking if he was certain this time; he knew he wasn't.

"Just a second," he said, as Arthur made to walk down the tunnel. He undid a pocket of his rucksack and pulled out a large piece of chalk, which he'd packed just in case. As they set off, he trailed it along the right-hand side of the tunnel wall. At least this way they could find their way back if they needed to.

As they went deeper into the maze, Arthur's confidence seemed to grow. At each intersection he picked a tunnel with hardly a pause. Theodore followed without a word, hoping his faith wasn't misplaced. He lost track of how long they'd been walking; it could have been minutes or days.

Finally, they rounded a bend and came upon what was unmistakably a vault door. It was firmly locked, however, and Theodore could tell just by looking at it that it was way beyond his safe-cracking skills. He sighed and shrugged off his pack.

"Let's take a break," he said. "I'm beat." He pulled out his canteen, wondering what on earth the vault builders had been thinking. Surely there were easier ways to ensure security?

Arthur, sitting with his back against the vault door, was off in his own little world, humming happily to himself. Theodore closed his eyes and leaned his head back against the wall. All he could hear was Arthur's humming. It was rather tuneless at first, but then it gradually resolved itself into some sort of melody. Arthur hummed it again, and then he was singing it, growing more and more full-voiced.

Theodore opened his eyes and looked at his friend, who was gazing blankly into space, singing.

Suddenly there was a *thunk*, and the great handle on the vault door began to turn of its own accord. Theodore jumped up and pulled Arthur to his feet.

"You did it!" he exclaimed. "That song must have been the key!"

"I did?" Arthur said, looking puzzled. "I didn't even re-alise. This tune just came into my head, and I felt like singing."

"Well, anyway, we're in. Look!"

The vault door had swung open, revealing row upon row of shelves, each stacked with large glass bottles. Theodore peered at one nearby; it appeared to be filled with some sort of swirling, multicoloured liquid—or was it gas?

"Are these what memories look like?" he asked.

Arthur shrugged. "I guess so."

Each bottle was neatly labelled with its owner's name and a brief description of the contents: 'Childhood years,' 'Recollections of ACME Corporation,' and one Theodore couldn't decipher, which was simply 'MTSUSSS'.

"What's MTSUSSS?"

Arthur chewed his lip. "Most Top-Secret Ultra-Sensitive State Secrets, I think. It really should be locked away, not left on a shelf like that. I'll file a complaint with the manager." He guffawed at his own joke, and Theodore smiled wanly.

The Memory Bank had clearly been doing well, for there seemed to be thousands of bottles. At first, Theodore assumed they were in alphabetical order by surname, but he quickly realised that wasn't the case and, when questioned,

Arthur had no clue about the cataloguing system. How on earth were they going to find one little bottle of a bank manager's memories among all this?

He thought long and hard, but he could come up with no better solution than to start at the far row and work their way along. It would probably take them hours and hours with just their single lantern—for although the vault surely possessed some means of illumination, neither of them could find how to activate it—but there was really no other way without having access to the catalogue. With a sigh, Theodore led Arthur over to the top of the far row, and together they started along it, reading off the names one by one.

They had no joy in that row, nor the next, nor the two after that. Theodore called a halt for sustenance and they both sat on the floor, leaning against the shelves, while they ate more of the dried fruit.

"We're never going to find it, are we?" Arthur said despondently. "It will all just slip away until there's nothing left." He turned to Theodore and grasped his hands urgently. "Will you look after me when it does—you and Mary? I know it's a lot to ask, but...well, I don't have anyone else. And of all the things I planned for, I never thought it would be this that took me. My life has been built on memories. I don't know who I'll be without them."

"Of course we will," Theodore said. "You don't need to worry about that. And anyway," he added, more enthusiastically than he felt, "it must be here somewhere. Are you sure you can't remember anything about where it was filed?"

Arthur scratched his head. "There's just some vague images," he said. "I think there was a glass box."

"A box? Like a small one that the bottle was kept in?"

"No, like a room. That was where they did the extraction. And I think there were some bottles on shelves along the walls."

"And it was down here?"

"I'm pretty sure, yes."

"Well, then, let's change our approach."

It seemed to make sense that the mysterious glass room would be somewhere towards the back of the vault, away from the doors. Theodore walked down the miles of shelving until he reached the back wall, then walked along the second side of the square. He was beginning to think that Arthur had imagined it, or even if he hadn't, that the glass box had been somewhere else entirely, when he caught his reflection staring back at him. He'd come upon it almost without realising.

As Arthur had described it, the room was a simple box, with glass walls on three sides and the fourth set into the back wall of the vault. An inscription on the door read 'Memory Extraction Chamber'. Theodore tried the door, but of course it was locked, and the lock appeared too complex to pick.

"I don't suppose you have a key, do you?" he asked Arthur, half-joking.

"Actually," Arthur said, digging in his pocket, "I do, although I'm not sure if it's *the* key. I can't remember."

"Worth a try," Theodore said, gesturing to the door. Arthur slipped the big brass key into the lock and turned it.

For a second nothing happened, then the lock rotated with a click and the door swung open.

Theodore lifted his lantern high as he entered, looking around the room. The light bounced off the glass walls, and more than once he jumped at his own reflection. In the centre of the room was an elongated chair, surrounded by a mess of wires and cogs. The odd machine culminated in what looked like a kind of headgear made of copper wire. Theodore assumed that this was where people sat to get their memories extracted, although how the process actually worked, he couldn't tell. To the right of the extraction chair was a desk, upon which rested a large, very thick ledger. Theodore flicked through it and realised it was the catalogue, listing every person's name and the location of the bottle containing their memories as defined on a grid system. He hurriedly turned the pages, looking for Arthur's name, but as he'd thought, there were several thousand entries dating back years. The Memory Bank must have attracted clients from all over, for there was no way they could get that many just from their small town. He supposed it *was* quite a specialised service, after all.

Arthur, meanwhile, had been perusing the shelves of bottles that lined the back wall of the room, and now he cried out in triumph. "It's here! I've found it!"

Theodore hurried over and, sure enough, saw 'Arthur Denholm' written on the bottle's label in neat letters, along with a date some two weeks earlier and the words 'For Memory Cloud'. The memories inside were various colours and swirling like gaseous streamers.

"How do you get them back?"

Arthur unstoppered the bottle and held it up, taking a long sniff. The memory-gas surged up the neck of the bottle. Arthur's eyes widened, and the vague look that had been haunting him suddenly vanished. He hurriedly put the cork back in the bottle.

"What are you doing?" Theodore asked, perplexed.

"I remember how it works now!" Arthur exclaimed jubilantly. "Just that little bit gave me a jolt. Here—" he hurried over to another contraption, which looked like a large, slightly misshapen glass ball with two holes cut in it. The larger one on top was lined with leather padding. Arthur handed Theodore the bottle, then sat in a chair in front of the sphere.

"I'm going to put my face in there," he said, gesturing to the larger opening on top of the sphere. "When I do, you need to uncork the bottle and plug it into the small hole underneath. The memories will escape upwards and dissipate, and I'll be able to breathe them in. Ready?"

Theodore did as instructed, and once Arthur was settled with his face pointing into the sphere, he opened the bottle. The memories seemed keen to escape; they rushed up the neck of the bottle and poured into the sphere. Arthur breathed deeply, his eyes closed, and slowly each memory returned to its rightful owner. When there were no strands of coloured gas left, Theodore tapped on the glass, and Arthur opened his eyes. He sat up, looked around him, and laughed—the kind of laugh one gives upon waking up from a nightmare and realising everything in it wasn't real.

"Theodore, old fellow!" he cried, springing up and clapping his friend on the back.

Theodore couldn't help grinning. "It's good to have you back," he said. He noticed Arthur looking around rather confusedly. "Do you remember how we got here?"

"Sort of...not really. Just bits and pieces."

"Well, what can I say? You were magnificent. And now everything can go back to normal."

Arthur inclined his head and gave a small smile. "Perhaps."

"Now," Theodore continued, "I don't suppose you know how to get out of here?" He thought about paddling back up the river—if such a thing were even possible against the rapids and the current—and sighed inwardly. He suddenly felt very tired.

"Oh yes," Arthur said. "That's easy." He walked to the wall at the back of the room and pressed a button. Theodore heard a grinding of gears, and a section of the wall slid open, revealing a small room.

"What's this?" he asked.

"Our very own invention," Arthur said proudly. "The only one of its kind anywhere—that I know of, at least. We call it a lift, because you get in and...well, it lifts you."

Theodore's mouth fell open. "That's extraordinary," he said. "How does it work?"

"This little room is actually a box attached to a long rope, which runs on a pulley and is guided by rails," Arthur said. "And in that little room there—" he gestured to a small door that Theodore hadn't noticed—"we have a clockwork automaton who hauls on the rope. Then when it gets to the top he lets it down again."

"You've got to be joking," Theodore said. "All that mess with the railway and the river and the maze and we could have just taken the lift?"

"Well, not exactly," Arthur said. "It only goes up, not down—the door at the top is concealed and you can't activate the automaton from up there. It goes back down again as soon as everyone has got out. Security, you know."

"I suppose that's something," Theodore muttered, not entirely mollified. They entered the lift and it carried them upwards, more smoothly and faster than Theodore had anticipated. But nevertheless, he found the clanking of the gears disconcerting, and he couldn't help thinking of the enormous chasm below them, into which they'd drop if the ropes snapped or if the clockwork automaton hauling them failed. He was profoundly glad when at last the machine ground to a halt and Arthur pushed the doors open.

At first he wasn't sure where in the Memory Bank they were, but looking around he realised they'd emerged in a corridor just around the corner from Arthur's office. When the lift doors slid shut they merged smoothly into the wall, the outline fitting in perfectly with the panelling. He realised Arthur was right—there was no way to tell it was there if you didn't know, and certainly no way to call it to travel down to the vault. They'd gone the only possible way. The thought made him feel better.

The light slanting in through the windows was now the golden colour of late afternoon, although Theodore felt like they'd been travelling for days. They returned to Arthur's office, where the bank manager went through his desk, packing things into a box. A bowler hat and cane from the hatstand in the corner went on top.

"What are you doing, old fellow?" Theodore asked, perplexed. "Surely you'll be back here tomorrow?"

Arthur shook his head. "I think it's time I retired," he said, smiling serenely. "You know, so many of the memories in that bottle were about work. That was the only reason I went ahead with the trial—corporate knowledge. But when they disappeared, I realised there was hardly anything left. All I've done for my entire life is work. But not anymore."

"So what will you do?"

"I think I'm going to buy myself a little cottage in the country and do some gardening, at least to start with," Arthur said. "Somewhere where the people are friendly and the sky is blue."

"Won't you miss it here?" Theodore asked as they walked back through the great hall.

Arthur considered this. "You know, I don't think I will," he said. "I'll miss you and Mary, of course, but you're the only real friends I've got here. And as for this place—" he waved his arm at the vaulted ceilings—"I can't wait to see the back of it. It's taken the best years of my life. And it would have taken a lot more if it hadn't been for you."

They stepped out into the early evening light, and Arthur closed the big wooden door behind them, with a thud that sounded to Theodore particularly final. He shook Arthur's hand.

"Go well, old chap," he said. "Don't forget to write."

"Goodbye, Theodore. And thank you. Oh, and one more thing."

"Yes?"

"My mother's name was Janice. She had beautiful dark curls and blue eyes, and a smile that was like coming home. And my sister was Ophelia. We were twins, but we were nothing alike."

Theodore grinned. "I wish I could have met them. Farewell, my friend."

Arthur tucked his box under his arm, placed his bowler hat on his head and picked up his cane. Theodore watched him as he headed off down the road towards the setting sun, whistling. Halfway down the road a great rush of joy seemed to overtake him, and he leaped into the air, box and all, clicking his heels together in merriment. Theodore smiled and turned away.

Walking home through the twilight, he saw Mary coming down the street on her way back from the hospital. When she caught sight of him, he hurried towards her and lifted her off her feet in an embrace.

"What's this for?" she exclaimed, laughing as he spun her round.

"Nothing special," he said, kissing her. "I've just remembered something important."

The Weathermen

Wetterdale was, Arthur Denholm reflected, quite the perfect village. He sipped his morning tea and looked out across his garden, where the early roses were blooming. It was a perfect spring day, neither too hot nor too cold, with small white puffy clouds dotting the azure sky. In the six months Arthur had lived there, in fact, he couldn't recall a day where the weather hadn't been perfect. He'd moved in in the autumn, when the foliage had been a riot of colour, the nights cool and the days pleasantly clear. Then had come the winter, with its dusting of picture-perfect snow—just enough for atmosphere, but not enough for inconvenience. And a few weeks ago the thaw had arrived, and with it the first flowers had begun pushing their way up through the loam. There'd been just enough rain to nourish the growing things, but it always fell during the night or at generally convenient times.

Arthur finished his tea and readied himself for his morning walk. Since his retirement, he'd developed an unchanging daily routine—get up at a respectable hour, enjoy a nice cup of tea looking out onto the garden, walk into the village and greet the shopkeepers, perhaps catch up on the latest gossip with other locals, return home in time for lunch, and then spend the afternoon working on his memoirs. In the evening, he sometimes repaired to the local pub for a meal and a chat, or simply spent the time in contemplation by his fireside with a pipe. It was a quiet, uneventful existence, and he liked it that way; he'd had adventure enough to last a lifetime, and he was thoroughly sick of the frenetic pace of town life.

"Morning, Arthur," his neighbour, Maisie Andrews, called as he passed. She was working in her garden as she did every morning, and Arthur tipped his hat to her, as was his wont.

"Morning, Maisie. How goes it?"

"Smashing. A few more days like this will do my tomatoes the world of good."

"Glad to hear it." Maisie Andrews' tomatoes were legendary in Wetterdale and won all the prizes at the district fair. Arthur was very much looking forward to sampling them when the time came, and he didn't doubt that she'd have a bumper crop as always. If there was one thing you could count on in Wetterdale, it was the weather.

Leaving Maisie to her gardening, he continued on his perambulation. He always took the same route—down along the river, then looping back behind the pub and ending up at the village green. Then he'd pop into the general store for the morning paper, and the tea shop for a bun.

In fact, it had been on one such morning walk three months ago, not long after he'd arrived, that he'd first learned the truth about Wetterdale's highly clement weather. He'd been in the general store buying the paper, when the proprietor, James Mason, had noticed him flipping to the weather forecast. "Wouldn't bother with that," he said with a shrug. "It don't apply to us."

Arthur looked up, interested. "Why not?" he asked. "The forecast is for town, but it's close enough that it shouldn't make a difference."

"Aye," James said. "It shouldn't, but it does."

"How can that be?"

"You're new here, so you probably haven't met the twins yet, have you?"

"The twins? No." Arthur had no idea what he was talking about. He thought he'd met just about everyone in the village.

"Sol and Sturm. They're what gives Wetterdale its lovely weather."

"I'm not sure I follow."

"Aye. But you'll see soon enough." He gave Arthur an enormous wink and handed him his change.

Arthur left the shop feeling rather dazed. He wasn't sure what James meant, or who the mysterious twins were, or how on earth any of that could possibly affect the weather. Shaking his head, he put the whole odd conversation from his mind.

He'd almost forgotten about it when, two days later, he'd encountered the strangest personages he'd ever seen, right in the middle of the village green. They were two young men, aged perhaps in their early thirties, as like as two peas in a pod. But it wasn't just their identical faces that made Arthur do a double-take. They both wore impeccably cut three-piece suits and bowler hats, and each carried a closed umbrella. Their outfits were something special—from the tops of their hats to the tips of their brightly polished shoes, they were patterned with an azure autumn sky, pockmarked with fluffy white clouds. They turned together as Arthur passed by, lifting their hats to him as one.

"Good morning," they said in unison.

"Good morning," Arthur said, somewhat bemused. It was the first out-of-the-ordinary thing he'd encountered since moving to Wetterdale. "Lovely day for it."

"Thank you."

Arthur frowned to himself in confusion and continued into the tea shop, where June Linwood had his usual currant bun all ready and waiting for him.

"Are you all right, Arthur?" she asked, peering at him. "You look like you've seen a ghost."

"I think perhaps I have. Two, in fact."

June grinned. "Ah," she said, "I see you've met the twins."

Arthur glanced over his shoulder, out the bakery door towards the green. "*They're* the twins?"

"What, couldn't you tell?"

"No, I...well...it's just..." He realised he was babbling and closed his mouth.

"It's all right," June said with a laugh. "Everyone who's not from round here reacts like that the first time. They *are* a bit odd-looking, I suppose."

"Why do they dress like that?"

"Because that's who they are. They're the Weathermen."

"You mean they forecast the weather?"

"No, not forecast it. Cause it."

"I'm sorry, *what*?" He coughed. "I mean, I beg your pardon, but I'm afraid I don't quite understand."

June came out from behind the counter and ushered him to the small table by the window.

"Here," she said. "Have a seat. It's a bit of a story."

Arthur sat, and June took the other chair across from him. "No one knows where they came from, or how old they really are," she said. "But they've always been here. Sol and Sturm are their names, although I can never quite tell which one's which. No last name that I know of. Anyway, they control the weather for Wetterdale. It changes with their moods, and when they're in agreement their suits change too, and we get the result. Lucky for us they're pretty even-tempered!" She laughed as she said this. "It's why we don't get many storms. They know what they're doing."

Arthur shook his head in amazement. "Well, I never."

"You won't see them round here all that often," she said. "They mostly keep themselves to themselves. But we're all of us grateful for them."

In the months that followed, Arthur encountered the Weathermen only twice more. The first time was on a frosty but clear winter's day, and the second was just after the thaw, in the middle of a warm spring shower. Both times, Sol's and Sturm's hats, suits, shoes and umbrellas had matched the weather around them so neatly that they were almost camouflaged—they were in perfect agreement with each other and their surroundings. Arthur had nodded 'good day' to them and thought nothing further of it, and life in Wetterdale had continued on apace.

Today, he could have sworn he glimpsed them as he walked along beside the green. Out of the corner of his eye he'd definitely seen the flash of a bright blue suit ducking down one of the alleys between the cottages, but only one. He wondered idly whether it was Sol or Sturm, and where the other twin had got to. He'd never seen them alone before. But he shrugged and put the mystery, such as it was, from his mind.

The rest of the day passed uneventfully in his usual pursuits. In the afternoon he did a couple of hours' work on his memoirs, sitting out in the garden in the lovely spring sunshine, only stopping when it became too dim to see. Before he went in, he glanced at the sky, which was unusually overcast—purple tinged with a sickly yellow, the colour of an old bruise. For some reason he found the tint in the air unsettling, and he hurried inside to light the lamps.

It was just as he was eating his dinner that the rain started, thudding down on the roof in great gushing drops. Soon the droplets became a torrent, and Arthur couldn't help glancing at the ceiling, for he'd never heard it rain so heavily in Wetterdale before. He wondered what was going on.

It was agreed, afterwards, that even the oldest resident of Wetterdale had never seen anything like it. No gentle spring shower, this: around eight o'clock the wind came up, battering at the windows and howling around the eaves. Trees began crashing down as hail pounded the village, in some cases even shattering windowpanes. The villagers cowered in their homes, wondering if the apocalypse had been foisted upon them. Arthur, unable to sleep, ended up spending the night in his armchair with an oil lamp burning on the table beside him. He tried valiantly to keep the fire going, but the rain spattered down the chimney to drop, hissing, onto the coals, and the gusts of wind down the flue and through the cracks in the doors and windows guttered the fire until it was all but out. Eventually he drifted into a doze, half-waking every time the fire sputtered.

When the day dawned, wan and grey, it showed a scene of utter devastation outside his window. His beautiful flowers had been pummelled into the ground by the violent rain, the beds intersected by gushing rivulets. He dressed hurriedly and went outside to examine the destruction. He didn't have to go far: Wetterdale was a mess, and it seemed like every resident was outside surveying the damage. Fallen branches had blocked roads and staved in roofs, and everyone agreed it was a mercy nobody had been killed. Standing in the street, looking at what had become of their trim little cottages and neat, colourful gardens, the residents were all rather perplexed. Wetterdale was one of the most climatically stable places in the realm, if not the world. Storms like this just didn't happen there. Sol and Sturm wouldn't let them. Except, apparently, they had.

As Arthur followed his usual route around the village, dodging fallen trees and stepping over puddles, he heard the same thing being muttered over and over again. What had happened to the twins? The Weathermen would never normally let such a fierce storm land on their village. Something was terribly wrong.

This sentiment was only confirmed as the day wore on. The morning had been cool and fresh, one of the few happy side-effects of the storm, but as the hours ticked by, the temperature rose and rose, with no sign of stopping. By mid-afternoon, Wetterdale was baking in a heatwave. Village summers were always pleasant—warm enough for summer amusements, like eating ices and paddling in the stream, but never hot enough to be truly uncomfortable, and always cool at night. None of the villagers had ever experienced anything like it. Work on clearing up the debris from the storm ground to a halt as everyone retreated indoors, away from the blazing heat of the sun. Arthur couldn't believe that just the night before he'd had the fire going and had been wrapped up cosily in his dressing-gown; now the very thought made him break out in a sweat.

Another sleepless night ensued as the village sweltered in the unseasonable heat. Arthur again spent the night in his chair—for it was cooler downstairs—fanning himself with some pages from his manuscript. It was too hot for the oil lamp, let alone the fire, so he sat there in the dark, a tall glass of cold water beside him.

Around dawn the heatwave seemed to break, and when Arthur woke from his fitful sleep it was, ironically, because he was cold. After bathing, he went and stood outside, revelling in the cool, refreshing air. He walked out into the street and found Maisie Andrews clearing up her garden as best she could. The prize-winning tomatoes, Arthur saw sadly, were now nothing but withered stalks.

"Morning, Maisie! Odd weather we're having, isn't it?" He couldn't help feeling that he was understating it a little, and Maisie apparently agreed.

"Odd! I'll say! Heaven knows what it'll be next!"

"Has anyone spoken to the twins about it?"

"Not that I know of." She shrugged. "It's probably just a hiccup. We've been spoiled here in Wetterdale—we forget how volatile the weather is elsewhere. I daresay things will be back to normal soon." She poked sadly at the shrivelled tomato plants with the toe of her boot. "Too late for these, though."

Arthur left her sighing over her vegetables and continued his walk around the village. Everyone he spoke to agreed with Maisie—Wetterdale had had a bad run lately, but that was probably to be expected every now and then. Things would be fine again soon, in every sense. Arthur nodded and smiled, but inside, he wondered.

That night, the snow came.

It wasn't just a fine dusting like the village usually got in the winter; this was a proper blizzard, and when Arthur rose the next morning he found his back door jammed shut by drifted snow. Luckily he had a snow-shovel left over from his time in town, and even more luckily it was stored in the utility cupboard in the house—he'd been meaning to move it to the shed for weeks but had kept forgetting. Pulling on an assortment of winter clothes, he opened the large casement window onto the porch, dropped the shovel through and clambered after it. He shovelled the snow away from the door, then went around to the front and did the same there. He'd often had to shovel snow in town, but they hadn't had a fall like this all winter in the village. After eating breakfast, he picked up his shovel and went to check on his neighbours.

Three people in his street alone, all of them elderly, were trapped in their houses by the wind-blown snow, and Arthur spent the morning digging them out and shovelling paths through their gardens. By the time he was halfway through, he was already hankering for a nice cup of tea. His back ached and the tip of his nose was numb. Finally, the last path was cleared and he was able to put his shovel over his shoulder and stagger wearily home. He'd never really thought of himself as old, but the aches in his body reminded him that he was certainly no longer young.

When he got home, he changed his wet clothes, lit the fire and slumped gratefully into his chair. Storms, heat, snow—and all in the space of a few days. Surely that was the worst of it over, but he couldn't help wondering what the next day would bring.

Those in Wetterdale who had been expecting the weather to go back to normal were disappointed. Over the next week the violent changes continued, alternating rain, hail, snow and blazing sun. Some people got sick from the heat or the cold, and many more began to be worried. Whatever was going on, it certainly wasn't normal.

At the end of the second week, a town meeting was called. As a relative outsider, Arthur was unaware of it until the last minute, when he opened his door one evening to find Maisie Andrews standing on his step in the pouring rain.

"Everything all right?" he asked, frowning in concern.

"Oh yes," she said. "I was just wondering if you're coming to the town meeting. I thought we could go together."

"First I've heard of it, but of course we can," he said. "Let me get my things." He pulled on his galoshes and raincoat, and grabbed his large striped umbrella from the stand beside the door. Maisie took his arm, and together they walked down to the village hall.

It seemed to Arthur that just about everyone in the village was there, crowded into the hall. He added his umbrella to the collection in the entryway, then followed Maisie inside. There were chairs laid out in neat rows facing a table where the parish council were seated, but whoever had arranged the chairs had grossly underestimated the number of attendees, and the back was standing room only. Arthur slipped through a gap, grateful for once that he wasn't tall, and took up a position against one wall, where he had a good view of the proceedings.

When it was clear that nobody else was coming—or, more to the point, could fit into the space—the chairman, whose name Arthur couldn't remember, called the meeting to order.

"Thank you for coming, everyone," he said. "As you know, we're here tonight to discuss the village's response to the current spate of wild weather." A murmur broke out among the crowd, but he held up his hand for silence.

"Our first order of business will be to form volunteer committees to oversee the recovery from the weather damage, and to attend to those who are unable to look after themselves. Now, do I have someone to lead the clean-up operation?"

A few hands rose, and the chairman began allocating roles. Arthur tuned out a little as the meeting dragged on, sorting out the various bureaucratic responses. He wondered when they'd get to the nub of the problem.

It was when the chairman called for any final business that he realised they weren't intending to. Without even being sure of what he was doing, he raised his hand.

The chairman gestured to him. "Yes, Mr Denholm?"

"Thank you. I was just wondering if the council has consulted the Weathermen about the unseasonable weather we've been having, and what their response was?"

The chairman looked flustered. "The Weathermen, you say? We haven't seen the need to consult the twins yet, err...no. This is simply seasonal variability—no need to drag them into it."

"But surely, since we have such experts on hand, their opinion would be worth knowing?" Others in the crowd began to murmur in assent, and the council members looked, if possible, even more uncomfortable. Suddenly Arthur had a realisation: They were *scared* of Sol and Sturm. These small-minded villagers, who'd never lived anywhere else or encountered any lives different from theirs, were terrified of the twins. They'd never openly admit it, of course—because the Weathermen were undoubtedly an asset to the village—and it was much easier to just keep themselves separate, under the guise of living and letting live. But the thought of having to bring the twins into anything to do with the village's day-to-day life, much less ask their advice, was anathema to the council.

"Arthur has a point," a man in the crowd called out. "What if it *is* their fault? What if they're trying to hurt the village?"

"No," Arthur said, "that's not what I..."

"Aye," a woman interjected. "They've always been a bit odd. What if they've been plotting against us this whole time?"

"Maybe we should *all* pay them a visit!"

Arthur shook his head as the muttering increased and the chairman shifted awkwardly in his seat. He raised his hand again and the chairman shot him a look that, once upon a time, would have quailed his heart. He wasn't used to being a troublemaker—all his life he'd done exactly what everyone had expected. His sister Ophelia had accused him of being a doormat who always took the path of least resistance, and it was only now, some eight years after her death, that he could concede she'd had a point. Standing idly by was infinitely easier than standing up, but in this case he just couldn't see what there was to be afraid of. He'd dealt with all sorts of people at the Memory Bank, and a little eccentricity had never bothered him. And he didn't like the way the mood in the room had suddenly turned— he worried what might happen to the twins if he didn't do something.

"Let's all just take a deep breath," he said. "I volunteer to lead a deputation to consult Sol and Sturm—to *consult* them, mind, not accuse them. We should be drawing on all available resources during this time of difficulty."

"I...uh...well, that is to say, thank you," the chairman blustered. Arthur knew he couldn't very well refuse the offer without appearing weak to the rest of the village, but he looked relieved that it wouldn't be him having to deal with the twins. The crowd murmured their agreement and glanced across at Arthur with approving nods, but when it came to selecting the members of the delegation, it seemed that no one else was particularly keen either, despite their earlier threats. In the end, the only volunteer was Maisie Andrews. She turned to Arthur as the meeting broke up.

"Well, this is a fine business," she said. "I'm glad you at least had the gumption to point out the obvious to old Harrow there."

Arthur chuckled.

"What's so funny?"

"Oh, nothing." He shrugged. "I just think that's the first time anyone's ever accused me of having gumption."

"Tosh," Maisie said. "You may think yourself just a stodgy old bank manager, but I'll wager there's more to you than meets the eye, Arthur Denholm."

Arthur opened his mouth to speak, then closed it again, unsure of what to say.

"Might I suggest we convene over a nice cup of tea to make our plans?" Maisie said. "My parlour is so much cosier than this draughty hall."

Arthur finally found his words. "That sounds like a fine idea."

In fifteen minutes they were ensconced in Maisie's parlour, with cups of tea on their laps and the lamps lit against the blustery night outside.

"Well," Arthur said as Maisie plied him with tea-cake, "in the first instance, I think the only thing to be done is to talk to the twins directly. Weather is their business and their life—they must have some idea of what's causing it."

"What if they won't speak to us?" she asked.

"Then we come up with another plan," Arthur said. "But they must be involved somehow. It's too much of a coincidence for it to be anything else."

"You're right," Maisie said. "We'll go first thing tomorrow. The sooner this gets resolved, the better." She went to the sideboard and drew out a bottle of scotch. "Fancy a nip?"

"I...I probably shouldn't." The wind howled, and Arthur fancied he heard Ophelia laughing at him. "Oh, go on then," he said. "Let's live a little."

"You know, I don't think I ever asked you why you moved to Wetterdale," Maisie said as the bottle made its fourth round. "Beyond retirement, I mean."

Arthur shrugged. "I wanted somewhere peaceful to write my memoirs. Memories are...precious to me, and I need to get them down. And there wasn't anything keeping me in town."

"No family?"

"Just my mother and my sister, and they've both passed. I never married. Never met the right lady." He blinked; his head was growing pleasantly fuzzy. "Ophelia and I were twins, you know."

"Like the Weathermen?"

Arthur giggled, imagining him and Ophelia in suits the colour of the sky. "Nooo...not like the Weathermen." He gestured with his glass, almost sloshing the liquid over the side. "My sister—now there was someone with real gumption. I was such a disappointment to her."

"I'm sure that's not true."

"You know how she died? She was a *bounty hunter.* She tracked down rogue magicians for the King in the aftermath of the Five-Month War, to bring them in for trial. One of them got her." He took another gulp of scotch. "And look at me. What have I done?"

Maisie smiled. "Sometimes us small folk change the world too, even if we're not remembered for it." She held out her glass. "I'll have a top-up, if you don't mind."

THE NEXT MORNING, ARTHUR woke with a headache that reminded him why he rarely he drank spirits. Parts of the previous evening were fuzzy, but he distinctly remembered getting morose somewhere around his fourth glass. He hoped he hadn't embarrassed himself in front of Maisie.

Thankfully the rain had stopped, although the air was cool and the sky overcast. As he walked over to Maisie's, Arthur glanced up at the leaden clouds with some apprehension. These days, there was no telling what was in store for them next.

Maisie met him at the door, carrying a large round tin. She opened it to reveal one of her most toothsome concoctions, a carrot cake with fluffy white icing, made to her secret recipe. Arthur had been lucky enough to receive one as a housewarming gift back in the autumn, and the smell of this new-baked specimen made his mouth water. If this didn't win the twins over, nothing would.

"You're a genius, Maisie," he said.

"I figure it never hurts to be neighbourly," Maisie replied, smiling and taking his proffered arm.

"I...I'm sorry about last night," Arthur said, feeling that he should clear the air. "I think I got a bit carried away."

"Nonsense," Maisie said, giving his arm a squeeze. "It was good to see you're as human as the rest of us."

They were out earlier than usual, and the village was still under a haze of sleepiness; they saw very few people as they made their way past the green and along the outbound road. Arthur was familiar with the way into town, but he'd never explored beyond Wetterdale in the other direction. He'd heard that the village was the last one for some miles, and down the outbound road lay only woods and farmland.

He'd never thought much about where Sol and Sturm lived, although he knew it was on the village outskirts, but Maisie seemed to know the way. A short while after leaving the last of the cottages behind them, she turned off the main road and down a rather rutted track that wove its way between two fields. A copse of trees rose up to meet them, and as they got closer, Arthur could spy a trim little cottage nestled under the eaves of the wood.

"That's odd," Maisie said, frowning slightly as they got closer.

"What is?"

"That cloud there." She pointed, and Arthur realised that a solitary dark cloud was hanging over the roof of the little house, suspended in an otherwise clear blue sky.

"What do you think it means?"

Maisie shook her head.

"I've got no idea. But I've been here a couple of times before and I've never seen anything like it. I'll wager it can't be good."

Arthur was inclined to agree, and he felt a flutter of trepidation in his stomach as they approached the cottage. There was no sound—even the birds seemed to have stopped singing—and it seemed as if the little house was deserted.

Perhaps, Arthur thought, this was the reason for their troubles—the Weathermen had gone away and now Wetterdale was catching up on years of unstable weather. But then he saw the faintest twitch of a curtain in the front window. Someone was there—but whether they'd welcome him and Maisie was a whole other question.

Beside him, Maisie seemed undaunted; she marched up to the cottage and rapped smartly at the blue-painted door. As the echoing of the knock died away, the silence enveloped them, lasting so long that Arthur began to wonder if he'd imagined the face at the window. But just as he was about to suggest they give it up as a bad job and head home for a nice cup of tea, there was the sound of footsteps in the hall and the door was opened gingerly.

Standing before them was one of the Weathermen—Arthur couldn't tell which one—looking thoroughly miserable. His suit, which was usually so neat and trim, was rumpled, and it looked as if he'd slept in it several times over.

"I...uh, excuse me, Mr...Sturm, is it?"

"Sol," the Weatherman said, his mouth turning down at the corners. His expression reminded Arthur of a basset hound.

"Sol, I beg your pardon. I'm Arthur Denholm and this is Maisie Andrews, from the village. We just wanted to check that, uh, everything is all right?"

Sol stared at them, his eyes big and liquid. "You...came to check on me...?" he murmured.

"And your brother, dear," Maisie piped up. "Where is Sturm?"

"He's...he's not here." Sol hiccupped, then quite unexpectedly burst into floods of tears. The sky darkened and rumbled in response, and fat raindrops began to fall.

"Oh, you poor dear," Maisie said. "Why don't we come in and put the kettle on, and you can tell us all about it? I've brought cake." She put her arm around the sobbing Weatherman and led him into the cottage, nodding to Arthur over his shoulder.

The little house had clearly been much neglected over the past two weeks. Dust was beginning to pool on surfaces, and the sink was full of dirty dishes. A broken plate lay in the hearth, which hadn't been swept for some time. Sol was clearly going to pieces without his brother.

Maisie, all business, lit the stove and retrieved the kettle from under a pile of dishes, while Arthur guided the still-distraught Weatherman to the settee. Somehow, Maisie managed to find some clean cups and plates, and busied herself making tea. She sniffed the milk in the bottle and pulled a face.

"It'll have to be black, I'm afraid," she said, slicing up the carrot cake. Arthur cleared a space for the tea things on the cluttered coffee table, then settled into an armchair. Maisie brought the tray over and perched next to Sol.

"Now then, love," she said, handing him a cup and a generous slice of cake, "tell us all about it. Where's Sturm? Did you two have an argument?"

Sol nodded, sniffing. "He wanted an adventure," he said. "He was sick of being stuck here all the time, doing the same old things, so he said."

"But you didn't want to go?"

Sol shook his head. "I like it here," he said. "It's all so...predictable. I like to know what to expect."

Arthur nodded in agreement. "I know what you mean," he said. He remembered having several similar conversations—well, fights, if he was completely honest—with Ophelia, back when they were young.

"So you argued, and then Sturm left?" Maisie asked gently.

Sol nodded. "He said...he was going to visit Mother."

"Your mother?" Arthur asked, glancing at Maisie. For some reason it had never occurred to him that the twins had a mother. "Where does she live?"

Sol stared at the carpet, rubbing the toe of his shoe against a patterned rose. "In the Witherwood."

The name meant nothing to Arthur, but Maisie started. "Not...the Witherwood Witch?"

Sol nodded again. "We swore we'd never go back. And now Sturm has abandoned me..." He broke into sobs again, the tears rolling down his nose.

"There, there," Maisie said distractedly, patting his hand. "Why don't you go and have a little lie down? Arthur and I will clean up here."

"You...you won't go, will you?" he said in a small voice.

"Of course not, dear."

"All right, then." Sol rose and went down the little hallway, which Arthur assumed led to bedrooms at the back of the cottage.

"Well," Maisie said, picking up the cups and plates, "here's a to-do, and no mistake." She cleared a space in the sink, added the remaining hot water, and set the kettle to boil again.

"What's the Witherwood?" Arthur asked, picking up a dishcloth.

"It's an enormous forest a few miles from here. It has a fearsome reputation. When I was growing up, children would sometimes go missing. We were warned to stay away lest the Witherwood Witch get us."

She shook her head, banging a dish into the draining board. "I always thought it was just a ridiculous superstition," she said. "But maybe not."

"So the Witherwood Witch had twin boys, and they eventually left and vowed never to go back," Arthur said. "And now, out of the blue, Sturm has suddenly decided he wants to visit his dear old mum, and the resulting fight has sent Wetterdale's weather crazy."

"I'd say that's an accurate summary. The question is what we're going to do about it."

They worked for some time in silence, mulling over the problem. Eventually, Arthur sighed.

"I'm not sure there's anything else to be done—we'll have to take Sol and go in search of his brother. The only way this is going to be resolved is if the two of them sort it out."

"I was thinking the same thing," Maisie said. "And I suppose there's no time like the present."

"You don't think we should go back and fetch supplies or something?"

Maisie bit her lip. "I think if we give Sol too much time to think about it, he'll back out," she said. "He's clearly at the end of his tether as it is. We'll just have to try it and hope it all works out. The good thing is it's not all that far to the Witherwood."

By the time the Weatherman emerged, looking much rested and refreshed, Arthur and Maisie had scrubbed the kitchen and tidied the small sitting room, and the cottage was back in something resembling its usual pristine state. Sol started when he saw it, and seemed rather touched by their kindness.

"I'm sorry for my terrible hospitality," he said, glancing around the room. "I haven't been myself lately."

"We understand," Maisie said with a smile. "And we've been thinking—how would you like us to come with you to find Sturm? The two of you need to work this out."

Sol's smile faded. "I...I'm not sure that's a good idea. I can get by without him. I'm fine."

"You know," Arthur said, "I'm a twin too."

"You are?"

He nodded. "And for a long time—years—I thought I could get by without my sister. We were so different, so we went our separate ways."

"Well, you did get by," Sol said. "Look at you—your life has been a success."

Arthur smiled sadly. "By some measure, I suppose it has," he said. "But I didn't realise until much too late that without Ophelia I'm missing half of myself. We needed each other's differences, just like light needs shade, or sun needs storm. We thought they made us weaker, but we were wrong. We could have been so much more together. I don't want you to make the same mistake I did."

Sol shrugged. "Our situations aren't alike. I'll be fine alone."

"Sol," Arthur said, feeling that the time had come to speak frankly, "if the weather goes on the way it has been, someone in Wetterdale is going to die. Do you really want that on your conscience?"

The Weatherman stared at the floor for a few seconds, then shook his head. "Has it really been that bad?"

"In the last two weeks we've had snow, blistering heat, and flash flooding," Arthur said. "People are terrified of what's going to happen next."

"I'm sorry."

"It's all right, dear," Maisie said, glancing at Arthur. "But I think we'll all be a lot happier if you and Sturm can resolve this little misunderstanding. What do you think?"

Sol sighed. "Very well," he said. "I suppose I should try, at least."

"Good lad," Maisie said. "Now, what's the best way to the Witherwood?"

They locked the cottage and set off down the lane in the opposite direction to Wetterdale. Arthur noticed that the day became more overcast as they went along—it was as if Sol's gloominess was literally following them around like a little black cloud. None of them spoke much; Sol seemed preoccupied with his own thoughts, and Arthur was busy worrying about what the Witherwood Witch was like and whether they were walking to their doom. Maisie was the only one who seemed relatively unconcerned. Arthur knew that she generally took things in her stride, and he admired her for it. It was something he'd never really been able to do himself.

After they'd gone a couple of miles, Arthur noticed the dark smudge of an enormous forest on the horizon, and it grew rapidly closer, as if the trees themselves were advancing to swallow them. As the road approached the wood it turned sharply away, clearly happy to take the longer way around rather than risk going through. Sol stopped at the bend, glanced around, then led them off the main road along a rutted, overgrown track that ran directly into the forest. Arthur took a deep breath, glancing up at the dark pines rising above him, then plunged into the wood.

He hadn't been in many forests in his time, but he vaguely recalled that usually the light receded gradually as one walked further in. In the Witherwood, however, it was like someone had blown out a candle; as soon as they stepped over the threshold, the wan grey daylight was replaced by a deep greenish gloom. Arthur felt all his senses heighten, and he glanced at Maisie beside him. Even she seemed to have lost a little of her composure—she was breathing shallowly, and her eyes darted around nervously. Their hands brushed, then clasped. He squeezed her fingers reassuringly, and she gave him a watery smile. Ahead of them, Sol strode on, apparently unconcerned; if he was feeling any trepidation now about visiting his mother and brother, he showed no sign of it.

Time did strange things in the Witherwood, and Arthur quickly lost track of how long they'd been walking. He began to feel like they'd been treading this path for ever, and that he would never again see the sun or feel the wind on his face.

Maisie, too, was slowing down; there was something about the stuffy atmosphere of the forest that lay heavily on the soul.

Just when he thought he couldn't take much more of it, the trees began to thin out and gave way to a clearing. Sol stopped at the edge of the clearing, so suddenly that Arthur and Maisie almost ran into him. A thin ray of sunlight slanted down, illuminating the thatched roof of a picture-perfect little cottage. Its walls were of dark wood, standing out against the glowing gold of the thatch. A neatly pebbled path ran from the red front door to the edge of the clearing, with clusters of pansies blooming along its borders. A well stood on the other side of the clearing.

"Is this where you grew up?" Maisie asked Sol quietly. The Weatherman nodded.

"Why did you leave?"

Sol shrugged. "We wanted to see the world. Then we did, and we realised the world wasn't as nice as it looked. We were chased from town to town, called freaks, sometimes even pelted with rotten fruit." He shuddered. "Then we found Wetterdale, and it seemed like we'd finally found a place we could call home, almost right back where we started."

"But Sturm got restless?" Arthur asked.

"He said he was sick of wasting his life. He thinks that we should go back out into the world and really show them what we can do. If they're mean to us, we can just bring a storm down on their heads. But I don't see the point. Why go chasing trouble? We'll never fit in anywhere else. And even the Wetterdale people are scared of us. We can tell by the way they look at us."

Arthur wanted to reassure him, but he found he couldn't. He remembered the town meeting, and how quickly the parish council's reluctance to approach the twins had flared into something more sinister. If the extreme weather continued, how long before that fear ignited into anger, and then exploded into violence? It would only take a weather-related death or serious injury to make even the peace-loving folk of Wetterdale reach for their torches and pitchforks. It was a sobering thought.

"So why did Sturm come back here?" Maisie asked.

"When we left, our mother warned us," Sol said. "She told us that the world would be unkind to the likes of us. She offered to give us a spell that would help us, but we refused. I think he's come for that."

Arthur wanted to ask what the spell did, but just then the cottage's front door opened, and Sturm came out carrying a bucket. He walked over to the well, attached the bucket to the rope, and began to turn the windlass. Sol started forward as if drawn by an invisible thread, and his twin, catching the movement from the corner of his eye, looked up. There was a splash as he let go of the windlass and the bucket, forgotten, plunged into the water below.

Arthur had half-expected the twins to embrace and all to be forgiven, but it was clear from the way they stood some distance apart, eyeing each other warily, that this wasn't to be. He couldn't hear their words, but Sol gestured back to where he and Maisie were standing, evidently explaining how and why they'd come. Sturm shrugged and inclined his head towards the cottage, then turned and walked back inside. Sol waved at Arthur and Maisie.

"Come in," he said as they joined him. He shrugged. "At least he didn't tell me to go away."

The two of them followed Sol into the little cottage, which turned out to be much bigger on the inside than it looked from outside. The door opened directly onto an enormous kitchen, where a great iron oven roared away in the hearth. There was an enticing smell of baking, and Arthur's mouth began to water.

An old woman was pulling a loaf of bread from the oven on a long wooden paddle. She deposited it on the bench in the middle of the room, then transferred an uncooked loaf to the paddle and slid it into the oven. As she turned, Arthur saw that her face and arms were horribly scarred. Sturm was leaning against the bench, arms folded defensively.

The old woman looked up as the door closed, and saw Sol. The paddle clattered to the floor. She covered the space between them in two paces and wrapped him in an embrace, kissing him fondly on both cheeks.

"You came back!" she said. "I never thought you would."

"Hello, Mother," Sol said, smiling in spite of himself. "It's good to see you."

His mother glanced over his shoulder and spied Arthur and Maisie. "And who are these?"

"This is Arthur Denholm and Maisie Andrews," Sol said. "They're friends of mine from Wetterdale."

Sturm snorted.

"What?" Sol demanded.

"We don't have *friends* in Wetterdale."

"*You* don't."

The sunshine that had been pouring in through the kitchen window faded, and Arthur caught the rumble of thunder outside.

"Stop that this instant!" the twins' mother exclaimed, and both of them looked chastened. The light in the room returned to its former golden colour.

"Forgive me," she said, holding out her hand to Arthur and Maisie. "I'm Bertha—although you've probably heard me called the Witch of the Witherwood." She raised a twisted eyebrow sardonically.

"Pleased to meet you," Arthur said, and he meant it. Bertha wasn't at all what he'd expected.

"I understand my lads have been causing trouble," she said, glancing at the twins, who were still staring at their shoes like reprimanded puppies.

"Well..." Arthur wasn't quite sure how to respond. 'Trouble' seemed to be overstating it, but there was also no question that Wetterdale couldn't continue to suffer from the vagaries of the Weathermen's moods.

Bertha sighed. "So now that I've got you all here," she said, "what am I to do with you?"

"You know I only came for the spell, Mother," Sturm said, with a stubborn set to his mouth. "Why won't you give it to me?"

Bertha smiled and shook her head. "Put the kettle on, Sol," she said. Sol dutifully did as he was asked, and Bertha led Arthur and Maisie into a small sitting room. They could hear the twins bickering over the tea things, but although Arthur braced himself for the smashing of crockery, all the cups and saucers arrived intact. The twins sat on opposite ends of the settee, and Bertha poured the tea, exchanging pleasantries with Maisie.

"So you only came for the spell, did you?" Bertha asked finally, addressing Sturm. "Not to see your dear old mother?"

Sturm had the good grace to blush. "That's not what I meant..."

"In any case, you're out of luck," she said. "There is no spell."

"What do you mean?" Sturm asked, frowning.

"I don't understand, Mother," Sol said. "Before we left all those years ago, you said you could tell us a spell that would change the way the world saw us."

Sturm nodded in agreement. Both twins were sitting forward in anticipation, and Arthur noticed that, without even thinking about it, they'd moved closer together.

Bertha smiled wistfully. "I'm afraid your memories are playing you a trick, my dears. I didn't say I had a spell that would change the way the world saw you; I said I had a *secret* that would change how *you* saw the *world*. It's really not the same thing at all."

"But why didn't you tell us?" Sturm asked.

His mother shrugged. "You didn't want to hear it. Some things you have to learn for yourselves."

"I want to hear it now."

"Very well. Do you know why they call me the Witch of the Witherwood?"

The twins glanced at each other, as if they each thought they should know the answer but couldn't quite put their fingers on it.

"Because you're magical...?" Sol ventured eventually, but Bertha shook her head.

"Forgive me," Maisie said, "but I heard some of the stories, long ago. They said you brought plagues and misfortunes upon the villages and stole children from their beds. They also said you could heal all ills, and make people fall in love."

Bertha laughed mirthlessly. "If only," she said. "The truth is, I haven't got a magical bone in my body." She glanced at the twins. "Your father is the magical one."

"I know," Sturm said, frowning in confusion, "but..."

"They called me a witch because I was always an outsider," Bertha said. "My family died one by one of the fever when I was small, and as the only survivor it was assumed that I'd somehow killed them. From there the stories multiplied. I managed to apprentice myself to a healer outside the village for a few years, but when I returned nobody would let me ply my trade. My shop was burned to the ground three times in two years. Once I nearly burned with it. Funnily enough, it was your father who rescued me. He was passing through the village and heard my screams. He took me to my old mistress, who was able to save my life, and he stayed with me all the long months that followed. Those people gave me this face, but he saw beyond that." She paused and wiped her eyes.

"After I recovered, he persuaded me to leave the village and built us this house—even though I knew he wouldn't be able to stay forever. And then you two came along. You were so much like him, right from the start, that I knew that all my hopes for a normal life for you would be in vain." She sipped her tea, and when she replaced the cup, it rattled in the saucer.

"When you said you wanted to see the world, I was so afraid for you," she said. "I wanted to tell you this story—my great secret—to persuade you to stay with me, to avoid the danger of the world. Because I knew it wasn't as open-minded and friendly as you thought, and I didn't want you to suffer like I did."

"Is that why you're telling us now?" Sol interjected. "To get us to come home?"

Bertha shook her head. "After you left, I realised how wrong I'd been," she said. "You can't hide from the world. You'll encounter pain, and perhaps even persecution, but you'll also find people like Arthur and Maisie here—people like your father—who will take your side. Don't ever take that for granted. I used to think that the only way to live was to fight, but there are other ways to move through life, rather than throwing yourself up against it all the time."

"I understand what you're saying, Mother," Sturm said, "but that doesn't change the fact that we want different things. Sol wants to stay in Wetterdale for the rest of his life, and I want to go and see what else is out there."

"So why don't you?" Bertha said. "There's no reason why you always have to do everything together. Live your lives, and when the time is right I have no doubt you'll find your way back to each other."

The twins stared at her, mouths open, looking so alike that Arthur had to stifle a smile. They'd clearly spent so long together that the thought of doing things apart was utterly foreign to them. And for the first time, he wondered if his regrets over Ophelia had been misplaced. She'd never really left him, he saw now, despite all the years they'd spent apart. Even now, she was still the voice in his head that urged him to be more than he thought he could. And was it possible that he had been the same for her? He hoped so.

"Mother's right, you know…" Sol said in amazement. He glanced at Arthur and Maisie. "If I stay, could I perhaps come and visit you? I've never really had friends before—I don't quite know how it works."

"Of course, dear boy!" Maisie exclaimed. "And we'll come and see you too. Perhaps we can even call on your mother from time to time."

"I'd like that," Bertha said. "I do miss my lads."

"I won't be away forever," Sturm said. "And it would mean a lot knowing I had a home to come back to."

"Well then," Bertha said, "that's settled. Honestly, talk about a storm in a teacup. Now, have some more cake."

They stayed at the cottage until the shadows grew long and it was almost too dark to find their way back through the wood. But even in the dark, Arthur felt that the sense of threat he'd experienced before had disappeared. Bertha came with them to the edge of the forest but would go no farther, despite the twins' urging that she come and spend the night with them.

"Perhaps one day," she said, embracing them in turn. "For now, my place is here."

Arthur and Maisie left the twins at their cottage and walked home in the gathering dusk. The stars were glittering above them in a perfectly clear sky, and the air was mild. Maisie took Arthur's arm as they walked.

"That was very well done," she said at last. "Ophelia would have been proud."

"Yes," Arthur said with a smile, "I think she would have."

They walked on in silence for some time.

"Do you think they'll be all right?" Maisie asked, referring to the twins.

"You know what?" Arthur said. "I really think they will. Everything is going to be just fine."

The Model Village

Sol stood at his kitchen window, watching the sun rise over the distant Witherwood. It had been a month since his brother had gone adventuring, and he'd taken to watching every night and morning for his return. It wasn't that he was lonely, exactly, but even his new friends in Wetterdale couldn't truly understand what life was like for him. The only person who ever really could was Sturm. He'd promised to come back, but when that would be, Sol didn't know. In the last few days, he'd even begun to wonder whether he should have gone forth on an adventure too. Staying behind wasn't as much fun as he'd thought it would be.

As the light strengthened, he went about his usual routine for the time of year, with spring turning into summer. After tidying the cottage, he went out into the garden to check on the flowers and the bees and ensure all was as it should be. The other day they'd been showing signs of heat stress, so he'd brought rain to the region during the night, and they were all much happier now. The last of the daffodils and bluebells were dancing merrily in the light breeze, and the bees were buzzing in the blossoming fruit trees; there'd be a grand crop come autumn.

He'd left his own garden and was inspecting the crops in the fields across the lane when he heard the whistling of the postman. There weren't many houses down this way, so his visit was out of the ordinary. Sol climbed over the stile and stood in the road, waiting for him. The postman stopped and tipped his hat.

"Grand morning we're having," he said. "Got a letter for you."

"For me?" Sol couldn't recall the last time he'd received a letter.

The postman handed it to him. "That's what it says here. Cheerio." He adjusted his satchel on his shoulder, turned on his heel and headed back the way he'd come, whistling like a blackbird.

Sol turned the envelope over in his hands, wondering what it could be. It was unremarkable in appearance, but he immediately recognised the handwriting—Sturm. He hurried indoors and sliced open the envelope with a paring knife, then sat down at the table to read it.

My dear brother, the letter said, *I hope you're well. This last month has been a whirlwind of adventure for me, and I'm looking forward to telling you all about my travels. I'd planned to be home soon, but I'm writing to you because of an unexpected development and to request your assistance.*

I recently arrived in a quaint little village called Guildthorpe. It's not all that far from home in the scheme of things, but I'd never heard of it before passing through. But I've met the most extraordinary person—the village toymaker, who is a master craftswoman of prodigious talent. We've become friends, but I'm growing increasingly concerned. It's really impossible to explain why in this medium, so I'm writing to beg that you'll join me here and help me get to the bottom of the malaise afflicting my friend. I don't feel it's exaggerating to say that the fate of the village and the surrounding country is likely to hang in the balance.

I've booked a room for you at the local inn and have enclosed the address and a map. If you take the train to Relthorpe it's an easy day's walk from there. I hope to see you here soon.

Your loving brother,

Sturm

Sol sat for some time, staring at the paper in his hand. He read it and reread it, trying to make sense of it. It was heartening to know that Sturm was on his way home, and that all trace of their disagreement appeared to have been erased, but he was confused by the reference to the toymaker and her mysterious illness. He was no doctor—what help could he possibly be?

He set the letter aside and unfolded the enclosed map. A train ticket tumbled out with it. It looked like an easy enough journey, and perhaps it would do him good to get away for a while. After all, he'd just been lamenting his lack of adventures, and now here one was, fallen neatly into his lap.

Having made up his mind, Sol spent the rest of the day packing and readying the house for his departure. He hoped that the people of Wetterdale wouldn't mind a few days of unpredictable weather. It hadn't been that easy, managing without Sturm, but he'd somehow kept things relatively calm. Now they'd have to make do with whatever nature chose to throw at them, just like everyone else.

The next morning he rose before dawn and, after a final check of his plants, he was out the door as the sun was peeking over the horizon. He shouldered his pack and walked up the lane to the main road. There wasn't much traffic so early in the morning, but he'd only been walking a short while before he heard the clop of horses' hooves behind him, and turned to see a cart driven by Farmer Joseph, who owned the land opposite the cottage.

The farmer drew his horse to a halt as he recognised Sol. "Hello there!" he said. "Where are you off to?"

Sol lifted his hat politely, fighting back a predictable feeling of shyness. "The railway station. I'm going away for a few days."

Farmer Joseph looked concerned. "But you'll be back soon? We'll have a hard time without you."

"Of course," Sol said. "I'm just going to meet my brother. It won't be for too long."

"Hop in," the farmer said with evident relief. "I'm headed into town myself. I can easily drop you at the station."

"Thank you, that's very kind."

Sol clambered up to sit beside Farmer Joseph, and the old man clicked to the horses. The miles vanished easily under the wheels, and it seemed no time at all before they were pulling into the little branch-line station.

"Thanks again," Sol said as he disembarked. Farmer Joseph passed his pack down after him.

"My pleasure," he said. "Safe travels, and come back soon, eh?"

Sol nodded and walked onto the platform. There were a few others waiting for the train, all bleary-eyed and lost in their own worlds, and no one was talking. He leaned against a post and gazed out at the fields and trees beyond the tracks. He knew that in the other direction, beyond the station, lay the town, but he had no interest in it. Sol had always cared more about the wild places. It was Sturm who craved civilisation.

Eventually the silence was broken by the puff-puff of a small red engine pulling two carriages and a goods van. Sol stepped back from the onslaught of steam and smoke, thinking longingly of the peace of his garden. He clambered aboard the beast and found himself a window seat, then settled back as the train took off again with a crashing and rattling of wheels.

By the time the guard called, "Next station—Relthorpe!" he felt like he'd been travelling for days, although it had really only been a couple of hours. He was prepared to admit that there was something nice about just sitting and watching the world go by, but he wouldn't want to do it too often. He wondered how Sturm could stand it.

Relthorpe was a small town, and the train stopped just long enough for the few alighting passengers to scramble off and gather their luggage. Sol left the tiny, single-platform station and paused in the road, pulling out Sturm's map. Away to his right, a small cluster of shops and houses marked the town, while to the left the road ran up a hill to he knew not where. According to his brother's map, this was the way to Guildthorpe. Sol slung his haversack over his shoulder and went on his way.

The road was well-made, and he found the going quite easy, for he was used to traversing the woods and fields around his home. At the crest of the hill he came across a milestone, which confirmed he was on the right path. He paused for a moment, taking in the surrounding vista. It was beautiful country, neat and well-ordered, a patchwork of green and brown fields, broken here and there by the bright yellow flowers of a canola crop, or a dark expanse of woodland. His gaze followed the pale ribbon of the road down into the lowlands and along to where it branched in two. The main road continued on until it met a patch of haze that Sol assumed indicated another town, while the fork continued on through the fields to what looked like a small cluster of houses. He held the map up at eye level, comparing it to the view. Unless he was mistaken, that would be Guildthorpe.

From the top of the hill he'd estimated the distance to be about three miles, but as he descended he quickly realised that the view had been deceptive, and by the time he reached the fork in the road he knew it was likely to be nearly double his original guess. Still, it was a lovely day for a country stroll, and Sol was in his element. He always felt at his best when he was out alone in the countryside; he rarely craved the company of others, and even though he'd been lonely at times without Sturm, in general he'd borne the solitude well. People confused him; they'd often say one thing but mean another, and he could never quite tell what they were thinking. Nature was much more straightforward.

By the time he approached the outskirts of Guildthorpe the sun was low in the sky, and he felt a flutter of apprehension in his chest. He had no idea where to find his brother, but Sturm had said he'd reserved him a room at the local inn, so he supposed that was the best place to start. He smoothed down his suit, which was now the colours of the setting sun, and tried to walk boldly, as if it was perfectly normal for him to go striding through unfamiliar villages. In truth, he hadn't left Wetterdale for many years.

The Crossed Keys was a charming, warm-looking place, with a wooden sign above its rather crooked door. It looked like a child's model of a building rather than something structurally sound, but Sol thought it had character. He pushed open the door and entered the dark-panelled, dimly lit interior.

Although it was still early, there was a respectable number of drinkers at the bar, who all turned at the sound of the door. An older man, whom Sol assumed was the landlord, was pulling a beer behind the bar. He placed it in front of a customer and looked up, and Sol caught the confusion in his eyes. He glanced around the room and quickly figured out why: Sturm was sitting at a table in the corner, apparently deep in thought, his suit and hat, like Sol's own, mirroring the sunset outside. The landlord looked from Sturm to Sol and back again, his brow furrowing, and Sol nearly laughed out loud at the poor man's expression.

"It's all right," he said, approaching the bar with a daring that he would never have expected of himself. "I'm his brother." He held out his hand and the landlord shook it, evidently glad to have it confirmed that he wasn't in fact seeing double. Sol walked over to Sturm's table and dropped his haversack with a thud on the wooden floor. Sturm jumped, his reverie broken, then, seeing Sol, leapt to his feet.

"Brother!" he exclaimed, embracing Sol tightly and thumping him on the back. "It's so good to see you! I wasn't sure if you'd come."

Sol shrugged, trying to hide his happiness at this warm reception. "You know I'll always come if you need me. But I *have* been wondering what this is all about..." he trailed off, suddenly becoming acutely aware that every eye in the place was fixed on them.

"First things first," Sturm said, picking up Sol's haversack. "I'll show you to your room, and then we can have some dinner and I'll tell you all about it." He spoke to the landlord, who took a key off a hook behind the bar and joined them. Sol followed them to the back of the pub and up a set of small, rather crooked wooden stairs, to a corridor with several doors opening along it. Sturm turned the key in the door marked '7', and it opened onto a neat little room, with a bed and fireplace, and a small diamond-paned window overlooking the street.

"Is there anything else you need, sir?" the landlord asked.

"Just a meal for two," Sturm said. "We'll be down shortly."

"Very good, sir." He nodded to Sol and headed back towards the stairs, leaving the twins alone together.

Sturm went in and dumped Sol's haversack at the foot of the bed. "I suppose you want to know what I've been up to," he said.

Sol nodded.

"To be honest, it's all been pretty uneventful," Sturm said. "I've just been travelling around, seeing the sights. I was on my way home when I took a wrong turn and ended up here. That was a couple of weeks ago. But this is no talk for an empty stomach. Come back downstairs—they do a fabulous stew here."

When they were seated at a table with steaming plates in front of them, and the buzz of the pub had returned to normal, Sturm continued.

"It was such a charming little place that I decided to stay for a few days," he said. "But...well, you probably haven't noticed it yet, but there's something a bit odd going on."

Sol sighed with relief. He'd been feeling a niggle at the back of his mind, like an itch he couldn't quite scratch, since he'd arrived in Guildthorpe. He'd assumed was just his unease at being away from home—but perhaps not.

"I started poking around a bit," Sturm said, "but nobody seemed to think anything was really wrong. I couldn't work out if it was just because they hadn't noticed, or if they were covering something up. Anyway, I eventually found my way to a little place on the outskirts of town, and that was where I met Marley."

"This is your friend? The toymaker?"

"That's right. She's a lovely woman but...well, that's where the strangeness is coming from." He shook his head in frustration. "I'm sorry, I'm doing a terrible job of explaining it. It'll be much easier if I just show you."

"Now?"

"No. You won't be able to see much in the dark. First thing tomorrow would be best." He pushed his bowl back and stretched. "I should probably get going. I'm staying with Marley, and I didn't quite get round to telling her you were coming. Best if I do that tonight so it's not a shock tomorrow."

To his own surprise, Sol wasn't sorry to part company. It had been a long day and the travel was catching up with him.

"How do I find this place tomorrow?"

"Keep walking through the village until you get out the other side," Sturm said. "Her house is on the main road, right up against the wood. You can't miss it. See you then." He clasped Sol's hand in farewell then left, the bell on the door tinkling behind him. Sol glanced briefly at the other patrons, who were staring again, then climbed the stairs to his room. He was asleep almost as soon as his head hit the pillow.

THE NEXT MORNING, SOL woke just as the sun was beginning to stream in at the window. For a moment he lay still as the events of the previous day trickled back to him. It had been good to see Sturm again—and particularly to reunite without any trace of the old disagreement—but he couldn't help wondering what his brother had got them both into. His mind, which had always had a tendency to churn through all the worst possibilities, started turning out all sorts of grisly scenarios. He sat up in frustration, shaking his head to clear it, then dressed and went downstairs.

Unsurprisingly, the taproom was empty, with even the landlord apparently still in bed. Sol unbolted the front door and let himself out, closing it gently behind him. Outside, the air was cool and crisp, with a slight fog burning off in the rapidly increasing sunlight. It looked like it was shaping up to be a beautiful day. There weren't many people around, but the enticing smell of newly baked bread led him across the market square. He bought a sweet roll at a shop that looked as if it could have been lifted from the pages of a storybook and perched on the edge of the fountain to eat it.

He hadn't really had the chance to look around the village properly the previous night—he'd been too focused on finding Sturm, and then it had been too dark. Now, as he sat and savoured his breakfast, he glanced around the market square, and the niggle at the back of his mind returned, stronger than before. He frowned to himself, trying to figure out what it was that unsettled him so. Finally he decided that it was the buildings themselves. He'd been to many villages and towns, big and small, over the years before he'd settled in Wetterdale, and although they'd varied widely, there had always been a sense of coherence to them. It had been possible to trace their heritage in the buildings: the way the old had gradually adapted into the new—or conversely, how the entire village seemed to have been built in a single rush and then not modified since. But Guildthorpe was different. The more Sol looked at it, the more he got the feeling that it had been fashioned by some sort of moody, changeable architect with no concerted sense of style. The oldest buildings, like the pub and the bakery, had an almost childlike quality about them—they were squat and square, with uniform windows and doors and peaked roofs—while others reflected a madcap style, like they'd been put together by a rebellious adolescent who was discovering new concepts for the first time. The overall effect was strange and disjointed: a kind of charming unease.

Sol finished his roll and stood up, brushing the crumbs from his knees. The village was slowly coming to life around him, and he decided it was time to meet Sturm, before he had to answer any awkward questions. He left the square in the opposite direction from the way he'd come the previous night, following his brother's directions. Before long, the main village gave way to cottages in the same strange mishmash of styles, and then these gradually thinned out as the road was reclaimed by the countryside. Ahead, the horizon was hidden by a dark-green mass of trees.

The road began to slope upwards towards the wood, and Sol started to wonder if he'd somehow missed the toymaker's house. Just as he was on the verge of turning back and retracing his steps, he saw a sign up ahead. On it was painted a jack-in-the-box with a slightly manic expression, and the words 'Marley Cotton, Master Toymaker' underneath. The house itself was screened by trees, with only the top of its thatched roof visible from the road. Sol pushed open the wrought-iron gate, which squeaked in protest, and walked down a rather overgrown path of white stones.

The cottage itself was what he thought of as 'chocolate box'—white walls, small square windows, a green-painted wooden front door, and of course the thatched roof. Flowering creepers clambered up the walls and crept along the eaves, but they were wild rather than cultivated and, coupled with the unkempt front garden, gave the impression that nature was gradually reclaiming its own. Sol lifted the round brass knocker on the door and let it fall. The plants seemed to absorb the dull thudding sound, and he shifted his weight nervously from foot to foot.

He was just beginning to wonder if anyone was home, when the door opened to reveal Sturm. Like Sol, his suit reflected the sunny blue sky outside, but his expression was troubled.

"Come in," he murmured. "I'm glad you came."

"Why are you whispering?" Sol asked in his normal voice, only for Sturm to hiss "Shh!" Sol raised his eyebrows but said nothing, following his brother into the house.

The interior was dim and cool, for the sun had not yet managed to penetrate the small windows. The front door opened onto a short hallway, which led into a sitting room slung with low, dark beams. A stone fireplace dominated the far end of the room, but it clearly hadn't been used for some time. The furniture was cosy but threadbare and, like the rest of the house and garden, had an air of neglect about it.

Sturm led the way through the sitting room to a kitchen that opened onto the back garden. It was lighter and brighter than the rest of the house, with whitewashed walls. Glancing out the window, Sol could see that the garden itself provided a magnificent view down the hill into the village.

"Where's Marley?" Sol asked in a low voice.

"In the workshop," Sturm said. "She's *creating*." He opened a door off the kitchen into what was clearly an addition to the original building. Sol had expected a small outhouse, but instead he found himself in an expansive workshop. Inside was organised chaos—a long workbench ran the length of the room and was covered with tools, wood shavings, and half-finished creations that Sol couldn't identify, but which he assumed to be toys of some sort. Wide windows looked out onto the back garden and the view of

Guildthorpe. At the far end of the room, a dark-skinned, middle-aged woman with tightly curled salt-and-pepper hair was bent over the workbench, tapping away at a chisel. She didn't look up as the door opened and, after a quick glance around, Sturm ushered his brother out and closed it again behind them.

"I'm afraid I still don't understand what's going on," Sol said, more confused than ever. Sturm put a finger to his lips and led him back through the kitchen and out the back door into the garden.

"It's best not to disturb her too much when she's working," Sturm said in his normal voice once they were outside. "She hasn't been quite herself lately."

"What's she making?"

"Come and see."

He led Sol through a tangle of bushes, as wild as the front yard, to a flat area that had been carved out of the hillside. Sol wasn't sure what he'd been expecting, but it hadn't been this. Laid out before them was a model village, the roofs of the houses barely reaching his knee. He could see straight away that it was a perfect recreation of Guildthorpe. He glanced from the model village down to the view of the real thing below—even the colours of the roofs were exactly the same. He squatted down, peering at the little buildings. Without much difficulty he was able to find The Crossed Keys, the market square, and even the little misshapen bakery where he'd bought his breakfast. Every detail was exactly the same as the real thing, only far more intricate. He couldn't begin to imagine how many hours of work had gone into it.

"This is extraordinary," he murmured.

"Isn't it, though?" Sturm said.

"She must have spent years on it—to study every building and recreate it so perfectly. It's amazing."

"Ah, but that's where you're wrong."

"What do you mean?"

"She didn't base it off the buildings down there. The village is a copy of *this* one, not the other way around."

"I don't understand."

At that moment the workshop door opened and Marley emerged, carrying a small wooden house. She seemed completely unfazed to see Sol standing beside his brother; he guessed, wryly, that she was used to working with doubles.

"What do you think?" she said to Sturm, holding up the house for inspection.

"Very nice," he said. "It's very...modern."

"Yes indeed. It'll do very well on Lovers' Lane, I think." She bent down, her hand hovering over the model village before alighting on an old-fashioned thatched cottage. Deftly, she plucked the model out of its place and replaced it with the new house. Sturm nudged Sol, gesturing towards Guildthorpe.

Down below them there was a puff of dust, as if a building had been demolished. Sol peered at it and fancied he could see something growing. Within minutes a new house—an exact, life-sized copy of the one in the model village—had appeared where the old cottage used to be. Sol gaped, open-mouthed, at his brother. Sturm shrugged. He didn't say anything, but Sol could read his thoughts: *Now do you see what I mean?*

Marley dusted off her hands and nodded in satisfaction. "That's much better," she said. Without waiting for a reply, she turned and went back into the workshop, the door banging behind her with what Sol thought was a rather ominous finality.

He sat down on a small boulder at the edge of the clearing, staring down towards Guildthorpe, his thoughts swirling. There seemed to be a hubbub down in the village—people were running around the new house as if in distress, and a horrible thought occurred to him.

"Sturm," he said.

"Mm?"

"What would happen if there were people in a house when she...changed it?"

Sturm closed his eyes briefly and shook his head, telling Sol everything he needed to know. He put his hand to his mouth in horror.

"You can see what the problem is now, can't you?" Sturm said. Sol nodded dumbly.

"Why doesn't she just create new houses instead of replacing the old ones?" he asked. "There's plenty of space."

Sturm was silent for a moment. "I don't think it's the act of creation that interests her," he said at last. "I think it's the act of destruction."

Sol gaped at him.

"It didn't used to be like this, apparently," Sturm continued. "The art runs in Marley's family—her grandfather was the first Architect of Guildthorpe, and then he passed it to her mother and eventually to her. They've always worked with the village leadership to help revitalise it."

"And now?" Sol asked.

Sturm shrugged. "She seems to have gone rogue. The village council hasn't seen hide nor hair of her for a long time, apparently, and when they come calling she refuses to answer the door."

"Why?"

"I don't know. She won't talk about it. She's a lively conversationalist on other matters, but every time I've raised it she's just clammed up. But it's almost like she's punishing them for something."

Sol chewed this over for a moment. "Has the village...lost...many people?" he asked. It was an unpleasant thought, but he had to know.

"Not yet," Sturm said. "Unless there was someone in that cottage just now. But there's been some injuries, and I'm afraid it's only a matter of time before there'll be a death." He shook his head ruefully. "And when there is, I don't doubt they'll come after her. Sometimes I think she wants them to."

"So what do you want me to do?" Sol asked. He still didn't really see how he could help.

Sturm's shoulders slumped, and Sol realised this was taking quite a toll on him.

"I don't know," he said. "But I'm all out of ideas, and I just hoped you might be able to think of something."

"Why do you care so much?"

"She's my friend." But there was something in the way he said it that made Sol look at him sharply. This wasn't simply about friendship, he realised. Somehow, in the few short weeks he'd been in Guildthorpe, Sturm had fallen in love with Marley Cotton.

Sol felt as if a veil had been lifted from his eyes, revealing a truth that, once seen, couldn't be unseen. There was a roiling in his stomach that couldn't be entirely attributed to his meagre breakfast. He and Sturm had always been a pair—as children, their mother had often told them how at their birth Sol had come out literally holding his brother's heel. They'd always done everything together—until recently, at least—and there'd never been even the thought of someone else coming between them. Sol had always assumed that, when Sturm returned from his adventures, things would go back to the way they'd always been. He'd never thought that his brother might have changed or, worse, that he'd be so stupid as to go and fall in love. And with a magical toymaker who was nursing a god complex, no less.

Sol sighed. He just wanted things to be easy again, back to the way they used to be. He glanced down at his suit, which was darkening to the purple-grey of an approaching storm. He took a deep breath and forced himself to think of more pleasant things, like the smell of his garden after rain. He didn't want Sturm to sense what he was feeling. But his brother was looking down towards the town, lost in thought. Sol straightened his shoulders and made a decision. It seemed that the only way to get his twin back, to rescue him from the jaws of this monster called love, was to help Marley recover from whatever it was that was causing her to wreak such havoc on Guildthorpe. It never occurred to him to ask whether she returned Sturm's regard.

Just then, the workshop door opened and the object of his thoughts emerged again. If Sol had had any doubts about Sturm's feelings, they were put to rest as soon as he saw his brother standing up straighter and adjusting his suit self-consciously. Sol took the opportunity to have a proper look at the master toymaker. She was younger than he'd initially thought—probably in her late thirties or early forties, despite her grey hair. Her mop of curls was cropped short and her black eyes blazed like coals. She wore a pair of patched overalls and a plaid shirt. Her skin was as dark as Sol's was fair, and her hands as rough as his were smooth. He felt strangely self-conscious in her presence.

Marley glanced from Sturm to Sol and back again.

"So this is your brother," she said to Sturm. Sol was impressed; most people, even those who'd known them for a while, had trouble telling them apart, but Marley hadn't flinched. He wondered how someone so clearly observant could miss the obvious effect she was having on her own village. But then people often only saw what they wanted to, he reflected. Or maybe she *did* know, and simply didn't care.

"This is Sol," Sturm said, and Sol held out his hand. Marley's grip was strong and self-assured; the term 'force of nature' kept popping into Sol's head. He wondered if Sturm would be able to keep up with her.

"Sturm said you happened to be passing through," Marley said. Sol shot a questioning glance at his brother, then quickly schooled his expression back to neutral.

"That's right," he said. "When I got Sturm's letter saying what a lovely place Guildthorpe is, I thought I'd stop by and see it for myself." It wasn't entirely untrue, he told himself, even if he was omitting one or two major facts.

Marley sighed. "It's not what it was," she said, looking out over the town. She seemed to be focusing on something a long way away.

"How so?" From the corner of his eye, Sol caught Sturm making a 'keep going' gesture.

"Well, I don't know if you noticed, but there are no children in the village anymore. Not one."

Sol hadn't really noticed, but now that she mentioned it, he realised he hadn't seen a single child during his time in Guildthorpe. Whenever he went into Wetterdale there were always a few around, playing on the green or shopping with their parents. A village without children was indeed very odd.

He was about to ask Marley to elaborate, but it was as if a curtain had fallen across her face.

"Tea?" she asked, and Sol let the subject go.

"Please," he said. "Can we help?"

"No, no. Just make yourselves comfortable." She gestured to a wooden table and chairs set on a paved area near the back door.

Sol and Sturm sat down, and when the door closed behind their host, Sturm turned to his brother.

"Well done," he said. "She must like you."

"Has she ever mentioned that before, about there not being any children in the village?"

Sturm shook his head. "Never. It might explain things, though. Imagine being a toymaker in a place with no children. You'd lose all reason for existing."

"Surely that's not reason enough to begin attacking the place, though? That's quite a drastic action."

Sturm shrugged. "Maybe. But the two things are connected, you mark my words."

They fell silent as the door opened and Marley emerged holding a tea tray. Sturm jumped up to help her, and when she smiled at him in thanks, Sol felt a strange lurch in his stomach. He suddenly realised that Sturm's feelings might just be reciprocated. Would that mean his brother would remain in Guildthorpe? But what about their little cottage and the life they'd built together? He fought down a rising panic as Marley sat down and poured the tea. He'd never particularly liked change, and this would be a change of the most profound sort.

"So, Sol," Marley said, passing the sugar bowl, "how do you like Guildthorpe?"

"It's...charming," Sol said, trying to be diplomatic. And it was, in a way, although he found its mishmash of architecture odd and a little unsettling.

"My family built this village," Marley said proudly. "I'm the fourth-generation Architect in the Cotton family. There are buildings down there—" she gestured towards the valley— "that my mother, grandfather and great-grandmother built."

"But you chose to become a toymaker as well?" Sol asked, curious. He figured he might as well take advantage of Marley's expansive mood.

"There wasn't a lot of work for an Architect to do," Marley said. "After four generations, there's only so many buildings you need in a village this size. So instead of making houses, I made toys." Sol noticed that she used the past tense.

"But you don't make toys now?' he asked.

Marley shrugged. "Not much point, is there, with no children?" Her voice took on a sharper edge, and it was clear the subject was closed. For some minutes, the three of them sipped their tea in awkward silence.

"It's lovely weather we're having," Sol said eventually.

"I guess that'd be down to the two of you, wouldn't it?" Marley said.

"Not exactly," Sturm replied, and proceeded to explain as best he could how their magic worked. Sol was only half-listening, lost in thought about the toymaker and the missing children.

After a while it became clear that Marley was itching to get back to work. Sturm was still babbling on obliviously, so Sol rose to his feet.

"Thank you for the tea," he said. "I'm going to take a look around the rest of the village. He glanced pointedly at his brother. "Care to show me the sights?"

"SO?" STURM ASKED AS they made their way back down the hill towards Guildthorpe.

"So what?"

"What do you think?"

"About what?"

Sturm rolled his eyes. "About all this. Marley. The problem."

"It's certainly a thorny one," Sol said, biting his lip. "She seems nice enough. But I really don't understand what you expect me to do."

Sturm shrugged. "I don't know," he said. "But we have to do something."

"Do we, really, though? It's none of our business. Surely it's up to the villagers to sort it out. It's their home she's destroying."

Sturm sighed. "I know," he said. "But she could be so much more. And I can't just stand by and watch her—and by extension, everyone else—suffer. So I asked you to come because, well...I just don't seem to think as clearly on my own."

Sol glanced across at his twin, but Sturm was staring resolutely ahead. It was the closest he'd ever come to sentimentality, but Sol knew what he meant. In his brother's absence he too felt he'd been living in something of a fog; now that they were together again, it was as if the mist had lifted.

They walked the rest of the way into the village in silence. Sturm looked as glum as Sol had ever seen him. One way or another, they had to solve this conundrum.

When they reached the square, Sol gestured towards the pub, thinking of lunch, but Sturm shook his head.

"You go ahead," he said. "I'm going to go for a walk. I'd like to be alone for a while."

"Well...if you're sure..."

"I am."

"All right." Sol shrugged, trying not to let his brother see his concern. He watched Sturm walk across the square towards the woods at the other end of the village, then entered the pub.

The lunchtime rush—such as it was in a place the size of Guildthorpe—hadn't yet started, and he was the only customer, apart from a grizzled old man hunched over a mug in a corner booth. Sol took a seat at the bar and waited. It didn't take long for the landlord to come bustling in.

"Ah, Mr Sturm. What can I do for you?" he asked jovially.

"Actually, I'm Sol," Sol said, twisting his fingers together. It always made him anxious when people mixed them up. To him, he and Sturm were as different as could be; to be told otherwise felt like a kind of erasure.

"Apologies, Mr Sol," the landlord said, a flush creeping up his cheeks.

"It's all right," Sol said. "I confess, I've forgotten your name too."

The landlord chuckled. "George," he said, holding out his hand. "George Bannister." Sol shook it.

"Now," George said, "are you after a meal? A drink? Both?"

"Both, please," Sol said. Usually he abstained from strong drink, but after the morning he'd had, he felt a pint of cider was just the thing to help him get his thoughts in order.

"Been to see the toymaker, have you?" George asked as he placed a frosted glass of cider on the bar. Sol stared at him in surprise but didn't ask how he knew; nothing was secret for long in a small village. Wetterdale was the same. Besides, Sturm hadn't exactly said it needed to be a secret, and there was no better source of information than the proprietor of the local tavern.

"Yes," he said. "You know her?"

George laughed. "Know her?" he said. "Marley and I grew up together. We were best friends until we were in our teens."

"What happened?"

He shrugged. "Young love. On my part, at least. She didn't want a bar of me. I was hurt pretty bad, so I went off to lick my wounds for a while. It was years before we could even stand to be in the same room together, and things have never really been right since."

"But you still love her," Sol said, because it was written all over George's face. He remembered, too late, that Sturm had told him more than once that it was rude to just come out and say things like that, but George didn't seem to mind.

"Aye, I guess I do, after a fashion," he said. "I never married, you know, while she ended up with Andrew Calvert, of all people, and had little Sara."

"She had a child?"

George Bannister suddenly seemed to realise how much he'd let slip, and caught himself. His face closed as if a curtain had been drawn, and he simply nodded.

"I've noticed there aren't many children in the village," Sol said, figuring if he was in for a penny he might as well go in for a pound.

"Aye," George said again, his eyes narrowing. "Why are you so interested in that, anyway?"

Sol shrugged. "I know Marley hasn't been quite herself for a while now," he said. "And I also know it's having quite an impact on the village. And it seems to me that it's all got something to do with her no longer being able to ply her true calling. So in the interest of helping Guildthorpe—and Marley—I wanted to find out what happened to the children." He stopped, surprised at himself; he wasn't usually given to long speeches.

George Bannister leaned on the bar and rubbed his face. He looked suddenly older. "Do you remember the Five-Month War?" he asked.

Sol nodded. "Of course." The Five-Month War was the reason he and Sol had moved to Wetterdale in the first place, eight years ago. They had been quite young then, barely into adulthood, and had been off seeing the world, when some magicians on the Provincial Council had decided to mount a coup. The resulting resistance had quickly turned violent, and the twins had realised that their obvious magic put them at risk. So they'd retreated to their little cottage near the Witherwood—for despite Wetterdale's proximity to Guildthorpe, the provincial boundary ran between them, along the railway line. The day after Sol and Sturm had crossed to safety, the border had been closed, and it had remained that way until the coup attempt was suppressed and the instigators had been dealt with, nearly a year later. But the scars of the short but brutal conflict took much longer to heal.

George sighed. "Many Guildthorpe folk have magical heritage, not just the Cottons," he said. "So when the magicians came through, they rounded up all the children with magical aptitude—which was basically all of them—and took them away to be apprentices or slaves or something. The village leadership did nothing to stop it. Little Sara was only ten, but she was quite clearly her mother's daughter. Marley fought them with everything she had, but it wasn't enough. Afterwards, she made no secret of the fact that she blamed the village council for not fighting back. She stopped making toys, and with that model village of hers she's been remaking the place steadily ever since. It's like she wants to erase all trace of what Guildthorpe was before."

"Why does the council let her?"

George shrugged. "Because," he said, "deep down, they know she's right. They should have fought harder. We never managed to find the children, though we searched far and wide in the days following the war. Not all the magicians were captured, and those that evaded justice went to ground. Now so much time has passed, I doubt we'll ever find out what happened to them. And as the final straw, no one in Guildthorpe has been able to bear a child since. We didn't even know the blighters had cursed us until recently."

Sol could hear the sorrow in his voice, and felt his own heart lurch. He was no parent, but to lose a child was a terrible thing. Despite the years-long falling-out with his own mother, it had been an urgent message from her that had sent him and Sturm dashing back across the provincial line to safety. Poor Marley.

The landlord seemed exhausted by his tale, so Sol thanked him and took his meal and drink to a private booth overlooking the village square. As he ate, he stared out the window, turning over everything he'd learned in his mind. The village children, he concluded, were the key to this whole mess. Find them, and there was some chance of saving Guildthorpe. George had said the townspeople had looked everywhere with no success—but then, they hadn't had him and Sturm on their side.

SOL SPENT THE REMAINDER of the afternoon roaming the woods and fields around Guildthorpe. He always thought more clearly when he was out in nature—towns and buildings and people could be so stifling. It wasn't until the sun was beginning to set that he wended his way back to the village, where he found Sturm sitting alone by the fountain in the square.

"How's Marley?" Sol asked.

His brother shrugged. "Same as usual." He indicated a pile of rubble where the bakery had been. "Or perhaps getting worse. I can't imagine people will be happy about that."

"I found out something interesting today." Sol said, and proceeded to relate what George had told him. Sturm's eyes widened.

"That makes sense," he said. "But I'm not sure it helps us much."

"Actually, I've been thinking," Sol said, lowering his eyes. Sturm was always the one with the ideas; he was usually content to just go along with whatever was proposed.

"Go on."

"We need to find out what happened to those children, and I thought that maybe Father might know."

Sturm was silent for a long moment; so long, in fact, that Sol was sure he thought it was a terrible idea.

"Sol, you're a genius," he said at last, clapping him on the back. "If anyone would know, Father would. He sees everything."

"Do you think he'll mind us getting in touch after all this time?"

Sturm shrugged. "If he does, we're no worse off than we were before, are we?" It was a good point.

"I don't want to get Marley's hopes up," Sol said, "but I think we should tell George."

The landlord, not unexpectedly, raised his eyebrows when they confided their plan. Sturm had told him a little about their magic, especially their effect on the weather, but this was stretching the boundaries of his credulity, and since the war the people of Guildthorpe in general had developed a strong distrust of anything—and anyone—magical.

"We'll let you know how it goes," Sol said. George let out a mirthless laugh.

"Oh no you won't," he replied. "This, I have to see for myself."

THE NEXT MORNING, SOL woke before dawn. He met George outside the pub and together they walked in silence to Marley's house. As they'd agreed, Sturm was waiting for them there, his suit camouflaged against the twilight. There was little any of them really wanted to say, so they simply nodded a greeting and continued up the hill in silence. The air was solemn and expectant, with just the faintest breeze, as if it knew what was to come.

None of them saw a soft grey shadow slip out into the road behind them and pursue them up the hill.

The hill above Marley's culminated in a lookout—little more than a flat area with a small plaque etched into a rock, and magnificent views over Guildthorpe and the surrounding countryside.

"This'll do very well," Sturm said, surveying the scene. He gestured to the flat-topped rock and addressed George.

"You sit there, and don't move, no matter what happens."

George paled.

"It's all right," Sol reassured him. "There's nothing dangerous."

The publican didn't look convinced, but he took his seat and said nothing.

Sol strode to the edge of the lookout and gazed northwards, out over Marley's house and Guildthorpe below. The model village was visible on Marley's block as a series of tiny dots, mirrored by the larger squares of Guildthorpe's houses nestled at the bottom of the hill. A soft pre-dawn breeze ruffled his hair.

There was a stirring at his shoulder as Sturm came up beside him. "Ready?" he asked.

Sol nodded, and Sturm began to hum softly. Sol joined in with the harmony. It was a tune they'd been taught at their mother's knee, although they hadn't had much cause to use it in recent years. The breeze grew stronger, whipping around their ears and tugging at the hems of their jackets. Away to the east the light was growing, until suddenly the first rays of the rising sun came slanting through the trees. The wind gave a final powerful gust and died away to nothing. And, suddenly, he was there.

As always, Sol didn't manage to capture the exact moment of their father's arrival. All he knew was that one minute the place next to Sturm was empty, and the next it was occupied by a man. He was both old and young at the same time; his hair and beard appeared a youthful brown in one moment, peppercorn grey in the next. But his grey-blue eyes were ageless and unchanging.

"Hello, Father," Sturm said, and Sol greeted him likewise. Their father simply inclined his head.

"Long time no see," Sturm said. He was attempting to keep his tone light, but Sol could hear the strain in his voice and knew he was thinking of Marley.

Their father looked vaguely puzzled by this. "Yes," he said at last, "I suppose it is." It had, in fact, been the better part of ten years since the twins had last seen him, but Sol knew that such a period probably seemed like the blink of an eye to him. Immortals viewed time differently to ordinary people, and the Winds especially so. He remembered their mother explaining to them, after one of their father's childhood visits to the cottage in the Witherwood, that there were many types of magic in the world, and his was some of the oldest and most powerful. He wasn't a god—although over the centuries he'd been worshipped as one. He was simply the North Wind, but their mother had always just called him Ned.

Ned glanced around, taking stock of his surroundings. "What have we here?" he asked. "You're a long way from home, lads." Sol glanced at Sturm, waiting for his brother to take the lead, but Sturm seemed suddenly bashful.

"We need your help, Father," Sol said. "We're trying to find some little ones who were taken by magicians during the Five-Month War."

There was a long, expectant silence.

"A lot of children were taken, if I remember rightly," Ned said at last. "The air smelled of ash and sulphur and blood. You're going to have to be more specific."

Sol turned and beckoned to George. The innkeeper came over slowly, almost reluctantly, and Sol saw that his knees were trembling.

"We need to know the children's names and descriptions," Sol said. "Can you remember?"

George nodded and began to list them. Ned looked at him solemnly, his grey eyes taking it all in. When the list was done, the North Wind said nothing, just gazed out over the escarpment in the growing dawn. Sol gradually became aware of a faint humming, less a sound than a feeling, emanating from his father. Every now and then a bird or an insect would come and perch on his shoulder, while leaves drifted and swirled around him, seemingly out of nowhere.

Ned stood like this for so long that Sol began to wonder if his father had somehow dozed off with his eyes still open. Eventually, however, Ned blinked, as if returning to himself from far away.

"There were so many children I saw, and so widely scattered," he said. "Of the ones you seek: three were sold at the market in Hermansville, and the rest were smuggled across the provincial line by a magician with a scarred eye and a drooped lip. After that, I know not where they went."

Sol saw Sturm's shoulders slump, because although it was a starting point, it wasn't the easy answer he knew his brother had hoped for.

"What of the three who were sold?" Sol asked. "Do you know anything more of them?"

"Two boys and a girl," Ned said. "All with strong magical auras, the girl most of all. The boys were sold to some minor lord, but the girl was bought by the chairman of the magicians' Grand High Council."

"What did she look like, this girl?" George asked.

Ned shrugged. "You described her to me before. Around ten years old, dark hair, eyes of fire." He sighed. "I should like to know what happened to her. I suspect she gave her master a run for his money. But contrary to popular belief, even the North Wind cannot be everywhere at once."

George shot the twins an astonished glance. "Sara," he said. He turned to Ned. "Is she alive?" he asked.

"I don't know," Ned said. "But with talent like that, I expect so. Too smart—and too valuable." He glanced around, turning his face to the dawn.

"Is that all?" he asked. "If so, I'll be off. Your Aunt South's on her way and she doesn't much like me interfering. I get on well enough with East and West, but South and I can't really stand being around each other more than we can help."

"Goodbye, Father, and thank you," Sol called. His father raised a hand in farewell, then he was gone, although Sol didn't quite see him leave.

The three of them stood in stunned silence, trying to come to terms with everything they'd learned. Sol hoped it would be enough, scant as it was, to give George and the villagers—and Marley, of course—a starting point for tracking the missing children. He couldn't think of anything more they could have done.

A rustle in the bushes behind them broke them out of their reverie. "Is it true?" a voice said. "Could she really be alive?"

Sol whirled around to see Marley standing at the edge of the lookout, just under the trees.

"You followed us!" he exclaimed.

"You should have told me," she said, rounding on Sturm. He stared at the ground, scuffing the toe of his shoe. Eventually he looked up and met her eyes.

"Yes," he said, "we should have. I wanted to spare you any pain, in case we learned nothing of use, but I was wrong. You had a right to know."

Marley seemed thrown by such an open admission of error, as if she'd been expecting a fight. She stared at Sturm for a few seconds, then turned on her heel and marched back down the road. By the time they'd collected themselves enough to follow, she was a good distance away and moving too quickly to catch.

WHEN THEY ARRIVED AT Marley's gate, Sturm turned to his companions. "You go ahead," he said. "This is something I need to handle on my own."

"Are you sure?" Sol asked, for his brother seemed unusually sombre.

Sturm nodded. "I'll meet you at the pub later."

"Well?" Sol asked hesitantly as he and George walked down the hill. "Did that help at all?"

George nodded. His eyes were slightly unfocused, as if he was trying to take it all in. "It gave us a starting point," he said. "It's going to be a hard road, but at least now we have some idea of where to begin, and for that I'm grateful."

"I'm glad," Sol said, and he was. It hadn't seemed like much help on his part, but they'd given the villagers hope, he and Sturm, and that was something that had clearly been in short supply.

"Will you be staying on?" George asked as they arrived on the outskirts of the village. "We could use your help with the search."

Sol shook his head. He'd been thinking about it since the previous evening, and he'd come to a decision—adventures were undoubtedly exciting, but when it came down to it, they really weren't for him. He missed the peace of his garden, and he even missed Wetterdale, where everyone knew him, and where he didn't have to pretend to be someone or something he wasn't.

"And what about Mr Sturm?"

"I don't know." Sol supposed that all depended on Marley.

When they reached the pub, George busied himself with tidying, but Sol just sat in a booth and stared out the window, drumming his fingers on the table. It seemed an age but eventually, when the morning sun was closer to noon than dawn, he spotted his brother coming through the square. To Sol's great surprise, Marley was with him.

"I came to thank you," she said, when they were all seated and George had finished pouring drinks. "And to say goodbye."

George started at this. "I say," he said, "where are you off to, old girl?"

The toymaker shrugged. "I don't rightly know," she said. "But I'm going to find out what happened to my Sara, so I suppose the first step will be tracking down what's left of the Grand High Council."

"You don't want to stick with us and all search together?"

Marley shook her head, and Sol knew she still harboured animosity towards the village elders. She probably didn't trust them to execute a proper search, and he couldn't really blame her.

The four of them ate lunch together, but the meal was strained, as Marley was clearly keen to be off. When the time came for farewells, she shook Sol's hand, but kissed Sturm on the cheek.

"Thank you," she said. "For everything. I hope we'll meet again one day."

"I hope so too," Sturm said. "You'll always be welcome if you're ever passing through Wetterdale." She nodded, then turned back up the hill towards her house. Just before they lost sight of her round a bend, she turned and raised a hand in farewell. Then she was gone.

"I'M SORRY IT DIDN'T work out," Sol said, as he and Sturm set off for the train station. They'd taken their leave not long after Marley; as Sturm had said, they'd solved the town's problem with the errant Architect, and had given them a way to find the children too, so their work there was done.

Sturm shrugged. "It's all right," he said. "I suppose it's better this way." He sounded like he was trying to convince himself.

"You weren't tempted to go with Marley?" As glad as he was to have his brother returning to Wetterdale with him, Sol couldn't help wondering how long it would be before the wanderlust struck again.

"She didn't want me to," Sturm said. Sol remembered the look between them that he'd intercepted in the garden and was surprised—granted, he wasn't much chop at all this feelings business, but he'd really thought that Marley had reciprocated Sturm's regard.

"Oh," he said.

"She hasn't said 'never,'" Sturm clarified, "but until she finds out what happened to Sara, she can't move on with her life. She said once that happens, she'll come and visit, and we'll see how it goes."

"Do you think she will?"

Sturm shrugged, eyes downcast. "I hope so," was all he said.

The sky clouded over, and little drops of rain spattered their suits as they walked. Sol took his brother's arm and squeezed. He said nothing, but up ahead a ray of sunshine broke through the clouds. Sol smiled, and together they walked on.

The Ventriloquist

Marley Cotton was dreaming. It was the same dream as always: a dark-haired child was standing on a road, staring at her, holding out her arms in a mute entreaty, but as the toymaker ran towards her she got farther and farther away, until she vanished completely over the horizon.

And as always, Marley woke up crying. Three months had passed since she'd left Guildthorpe to seek her daughter, but she was no closer to finding Sara than when she'd first heard that, miraculously, her little girl—a young woman, now—was likely still alive. The only clue she'd had was what she'd heard from the North Wind, that a child matching Sara's description had been sold to the head of the Grand High Council of Magicians, presumably to become either a slave or an apprentice. Marley had been aware of her daughter's burgeoning magical aptitude, but not aware enough. Not enough to protect her.

In the three months since leaving home, she'd scoured the length and breadth of the province, seeking to find out what she could about the Grand High Council, and what had happened in the aftermath of the Five-Month War to those who'd served on it. One particularly fruitful discovery had furnished her with a list of names, but that had been weeks ago, and the only magicians she'd been able to track down since were those who had been tried, found guilty of treason and publicly hanged. Of Hugo Sweeney, the Council chairman, she could find no trace. Her eventual conclusion was that he'd fled the province, and so she found herself in a second-rate inn in a one-horse border town, trying to ferret out information from taciturn locals and dreaming every night of a child who no longer existed.

Marley sighed, wiping her eyes with a corner of the sheet. It was still early, with the grey dawn light just beginning to creep through the shutters, but she couldn't return to sleep. She lay there glumly for some time, then pulled herself together and got up. By the time she'd dressed and splashed some water on her face, she was feeling better.

She'd been in the border town of Hamsby for three days, and she was beginning to feel that she'd exhausted its possibilities. The town sat on the banks of the River Ham, and the ferry manned by the townsfolk was the only border crossing for miles. If Hugo Sweeney had fled the province, he most likely would have come through Hamsby, either on the ferry or on a private boat. She was sure that someone knew something, but for the life of her she couldn't convince anyone to talk. In despair, she'd decided to give herself one more day before taking the ferry and trying her luck in the unknown lands across the river.

She decided to skip breakfast, having discovered through bitter experience that the inn didn't serve porridge so much as grey sludge. The morning air was crisp and pleasant, and Marley felt her spirits lift as she left the inn and strolled along the waterfront. Perhaps today would be her lucky day. It felt different, somehow, like the world was holding its breath in anticipation of some great change. She shook her head, exasperated at her own folly. She'd felt this way several times before, and all it had invariably led to was disappointment.

She'd become quite familiar with the river walk, having taken it every morning she'd been in Hamsby in the hope of meeting someone—a ferryman or fisherman, perhaps—who'd encountered Hugo Sweeney. So far, all her efforts had been in vain, as had the questions she'd posed at the inn and around town—but she'd discovered a nice route.

Hamsby's commercial district, such as it was, was clustered along the riverbank—the docks, fish markets, public houses, and the odd red-doored parlour of ill-repute. The air stank of fish and brine, for the town was built on the Ham estuary, and the water was salt. At this time of the morning the docks were bustling with fishing boats returning and unloading their catch. Marley dodged the crowds, the quay slick beneath her boots. She relished the feeling of anonymity, something she'd never experienced at home.

It didn't take long before the cluster of shops began to give way to cottages—densely packed at first, then spaced gradually further and further apart, until she was walking along a dirt towpath through fields, with only the odd farmhouse breaking the greenery.

Marley enjoyed this part of the walk the most, because it was peaceful enough that, for a short time at least, she was able to still her racing thoughts. Today, however, something was different. A large red-and- yellow tent had sprung up, literally overnight, in a field just beyond the town's outskirts. Marley found herself irresistibly drawn to it, like a bee to a flower. She abandoned her plan and set off across the fields, keen for a closer look.

As she got nearer, it became apparent that the circus had only just arrived. The area around the tent was a hive of activity and organised chaos—people were darting here and there, but they all seemed to know what needed to be done, and no one was standing idle. In among the throng she caught a glimpse of an elephant, and she fancied she heard the roar of a lion over the din, although she wasn't quite sure if she'd imagined it. The last time she'd been to the circus had been many years ago, when Sara was just five years old. Her little girl had been entranced by it all—the music, the lights, the dazzling costumes, the feats of daring. She'd talked of nothing else for days afterwards.

A large wooden sign at the edge of the meadow proclaimed the evening's show: "Fitz Bros. Circus and Funfair—Grand Opening!" There followed a list of attractions: The Human Serpent, the Double-Bodied Man, Jane of the Jungle, the Aristocratic Acrobats, the Strongest Man in the World...and on and on it went. Marley looked at the sign and made a decision. Sara would have loved this, and attending the show felt in some strange way like paying homage to her daughter. In any case, it would be a nice diversion on her last night before she returned to the hardships of the road.

When she got back to town, she found that the circus was all anyone could talk about. Its arrival had engendered an air of palpable excitement among the usually grim folk of Hamsby, and the town had something of a holiday atmosphere about it. Even the sour-faced landlady at the inn seemed to have been affected, flashing Marley a smile as she sat down to lunch—an act so unexpected that the toymaker started in shock.

When evening came, it seemed like most of the town was also making a beeline for the circus, and as Marley made her way to the field in the twilight, she found herself part of a cheerful throng. The air was mild, the sun setting in a purple-golden haze, and the smell of woodsmoke and cooking drifted over from the circus folk's camp. The townspeople wandered cheerfully along the rough track to the camp, laughing and joking; Marley even caught the occasional snatch of song. No one was angry or jostling, although she couldn't help wondering if that would change as the night wore on.

The show wasn't due to start for another hour, but she'd purposely arrived early so as to have time to look around the sideshow. The sideshow and funfair spread across the field like spokes from the main tent, with numerous smaller tents and rides packed closely together and creating small alleys between them. Marley let herself get drawn along with the crowd into the maze of tents. Flaming torches and strings of coloured lamps formed a bulwark against the encroaching dark and gave the place a festive air. Here and there small grills were set up, selling skewers of barbecued meat. Marley bought herself a couple, less because she was hungry than because it was all part of the attraction. The meat was tender, rubbed with a smoky spice that left a tingling sensation on her tongue. After she'd finished, she treated herself to dessert in the form of deep-fried dough balls dripping with honey. Sara would have loved this, she thought again with a flash of melancholy, but it was rushed from her mind as she turned a corner and found herself in the freak show.

Marley had never much liked this aspect of the circus—it was, she believed, a way for someone to make money off the magical or otherwise unusual folk who were desperate enough to have no other options. She thought of Sturm—if he and his brother had been born to less-scrupulous parents, they might very well have ended up in a place like this. Heck, even she could have—Architects were rare enough, and weren't exactly well-understood.

A sign on the first tent proclaimed 'The Human Serpent', and despite her philosophical objections, Marley dropped a coin in the promoter's bucket and went in. The Human Serpent was standing on a platform at the far end of the tent. Squinting a little in the dim light, Marley realised that his entire body, including his face, was painted—no, tattooed—with scales that glinted greenish-black in the lamplight. As the tent filled up with fascinated gawkers, he began an elaborate routine, moving sinuously across the stage and contorting himself into ever more complicated poses. His motion did indeed remind Marley of a snake, and she was both fascinated and repulsed, unable to look away. The Human Serpent ended his act by tying himself in a knot, his face to the crowd, and when he opened his mouth in a wide grin Marley was unable to bite back a gasp at the realisation that his tongue was split in two, forked like a snake's. There was a second of shock, then the crowd burst into applause. Marley left as quickly as she could, unsure quite what to think. Unable to move easily against the tide of people, she was carried by the crowd deeper into the freak show.

She managed to extract herself and catch her breath near a small stage, set up just to the side of the main thoroughfare.

A banner stretching across it proclaimed: 'The Double- Bodied Man'. She was just contemplating the possibilities of what this could be—all of them rather horrifying—when a small man bounded on stage, addressing the crowd through a brass horn almost as big as his head.

"Roll up, roll up, ladies and gents! Come and see the amazing Double-Bodied Man! I guarantee you've never seen the like of this before! Roll up, roll up!"

His announcement had the desired effect, and people were crowding in behind Marley, so that she couldn't have left even if she'd wanted to. She held her breath, wondering what sort of person—people?—would emerge from behind the curtain. She'd just decided it was going to be Siamese twins, when the curtains parted, and the Double-Bodied Man stepped through.

One of his bodies was normal adult-sized, and the other was much smaller. At first, Marley thought he was carrying a child in his arms, but its movements were jerky and unnatural, and she realised it was in fact a dummy.

He's a ventriloquist, she thought to herself with dawning comprehension. Others in the crowd must have realised the same thing, for a chorus of boos and jeers broke out, doubtless led by those who felt that plain old ventriloquism didn't quite meet their expected standards of freakishness. But when the ventriloquist began to speak—or, rather, his dummy did—the jeering stopped.

"Wow," the dummy said in a rather shrill voice, turning its head from side to side to take in the crowd, "look at all these people. Hi there!" He waved, and a few people in the crowd called out greetings.

"Good evening," the ventriloquist said. "My name's Zeb and this is Stanley. He does most of the talking."

"I'm the brains of the outfit," the dummy said, and a few people tittered. "I say," he continued, "Do any of you here own a cat?" There was some nodding, and one or two people raised their hands.

"Why do you want to know that, Stanley?" the ventriloquist asked.

The dummy shrugged. "Well, I borrowed the wagon earlier, and unfortunately I ran over a cat."

The ventriloquist raised his eyebrows. "You ran over a cat? What did it look like?"

"Oh," Stanley said, "like *this*." He pulled a grotesque, squashed-looking face, and the audience laughed.

The man was extraordinary, Marley thought; it really was as if the dummy was alive and talking of its own volition. She peered at it, trying to discern its inner workings. There was something odd about it but, try as she might, she couldn't quite put her finger on it. She was only half-listening to the show, and before she knew it, it was over and the crowd began to disperse. The toymaker frowned; a deep-seated unease writhed in her belly, but if asked, she wouldn't have been able to say why.

She was jerked from her thoughts by a clanging gong announcing the main show. The crowd buzzed with excitement as people began to file into the big top and take their seats. By the time the last person had settled, the tent was full, and it was standing room only at the back.

A trumpet fanfare sounded and a spotlight lit up the centre of the ring. Into it stepped the ringmaster, richly adorned in a red velvet coat, black trousers, white shirt and gold cravat. An immaculate black top hat was perched on his head, and his shoes were so highly polished that they reflected the lamps. He swung a silver-topped ebony cane theatrically.

"Welcome, ladies and gentlemen, boys and girls!" he declared. "Welcome to our wonder of wonders! Tonight you'll see things you've never dreamed of, and may never see again! And now—" he paused for effect— "on with the show!" The crowd roared, not settling down until the lights dimmed and then rose again on the first act.

Marley had always been suspicious of big talkers, but she had to admit that the show lived up to the high expectations the ringmaster had set. Jane of the Jungle turned out to be a petite young woman who rode elephants and had lions literally eating out of her hand. The Aristocratic Acrobats' routine was part tumbling, part comedy, which subtly—and sometimes not so subtly—skewered the upper classes. There was also a rather sad-looking clown; a troupe of trapeze artists and tightrope walkers, whose act elicited horrified gasps from the crowd; a husband-and-wife knife-throwing act; and a conjurer, the Great Majesto. Then the ringmaster returned to announce the next act: the Double-Bodied Man.

Marley sat up straighter as the ventriloquist walked into the ring. Sitting in the second row, she had a good view as he took his place on a tall stool in the spotlight. As it had previously, the sight of the dummy gave her an inexplicable feeling of unease, but this time she also noticed something else. The ventriloquist himself spoke quite woodenly, as if blandly reading off a script, while the dummy itself was animated and engaging. She supposed this could all just be part of the act, but there was something not quite right about it.

The feeling continued to niggle at her during the rest of the show, and she found it difficult to re-immerse herself in what was happening in the ring. The crowd greeted the finale with a standing ovation, and Marley joined in, her eyes seeking out the ventriloquist as the performers took their final bows, but she couldn't spot him.

"Did you enjoy the show?" one of the attendants asked as she waited to file out of the tent.

"Oh yes," Marley said. "Very much. How long are you here for?"

"Not long, I'm afraid," he said. "We leave the day after tomorrow. We're heading across the river. It'll be the first time we've been out of the province in a year. It'll make a nice change."

"Well, best of luck," Marley said distractedly. A mad idea had just occurred to her. *No*, she thought, *it's crazy. It wouldn't be possible—would it?* There was only one way to find out.

Outside, people were milling around in the flame-lit dark, eagerly talking over the show, or slowly starting to make their way back towards Hamsby. Marley, a little surprised at her own daring, glanced quickly around and then darted away behind the big top. It was a bit like going backstage at a theatre—all the glamour of the audience-facing side was replaced by utilitarian organisation. Various crates and boxes were stacked neatly beside the tent, while two smaller tents served as dressing rooms for the performers.

"Can I help you, ma'am?" a young man asked. He was wearing overalls and a flat cap, and was busy packing something into a box. Marley swallowed.

"I'm looking for the ringmaster," she said.

The man looked her up and down then shrugged, as if deciding she wasn't his problem. "He's gone back to his caravan," he said, gesturing out into the darkness, which was broken only by the small orange flowers of campfires. "It's the red and gold one over to the right. Says 'Joe Fitz' above the door. You can't miss it."

Marley thanked him and set off across the field. She found the caravan easily enough, standing slightly away from the others. She figured the ringmaster liked to maintain his own space, and, perhaps, to remind everyone who was in charge.

People had never really been Marley's strong suit, and after Andrew's death and Sara's disappearance she'd become something of a recluse, at least until Sturm had come along. So she had to screw up her courage, take a deep breath and square her shoulders before she felt brave enough to knock at the door.

There was a light shining through the window, and she could hear someone moving around inside the van, but it took a second knock before the door flew open to reveal the ringmaster in his shirtsleeves. Up close, he looked older than he did in the ring—a function of greasepaint and distance, she supposed—and there were dark circles under his eyes.

"Yes?" he barked. "Who are you, and what do you want?"

Marley felt her hackles rising at his tone, but she took a deep breath and fought down a biting retort. "My name is Marley Cotton, Mr Fitz, sir," she said, hoping she sounded deferential enough. "I wish to join the circus."

Joe Fitz looked her up and down, and Marley could have sworn he rolled his eyes. She wondered if he got a stream of romantics after every show who wanted to run away with the circus.

"I don't think we have anything for you," he said, moving to close the door.

Impulsively, Marley reached out and grabbed it. "You haven't even seen what I can do yet," she said.

The ringmaster sighed in resignation. "All right. You've got five minutes. Get on with it."

Marley glanced around, fighting back a feeling of panic and wishing she'd been better prepared. If only she had her tools with her! But she didn't, so she'd just have to make do.

The ground was damp from recent rain—not really muddy, but soft enough for her purposes. Quickly she scooped up a handful of dirt and began to shape it, her fingers warming to the memory of creation like a virtuoso musician. In a few short moments she had a passable replica of Fitz's caravan and, in another couple of minutes, a little horse to pull it. She set them on the caravan's platform, at the feet of the sceptical ringmaster.

"Move," she whispered, feeling the tingle of magic in her fingertips as she touched them. The horse's legs began to work, and the wheels on the tiny caravan turned. The pair set off across the platform, leaving muddy tracks behind them.

Joe Fitz's mouth dropped open. He closed it with a snap and tried to look nonchalant, but Marley could tell he was impressed.

"How did you do that?" he asked, frowning at the little figures, which were getting dangerously close to the edge of the platform.

"I'm an Architect," Marley said. She scooped up the horse and caravan and turned them around so that they ran back the way they'd come. "It works better with proper clay, but..." she trailed off and shrugged.

"And why do you want to join us? I'll warn you now, there isn't much money in it."

Marley wondered how much of the truth to tell, then threw caution to the wind. "I'm looking for my daughter," she said. "She went missing some years ago, and I believe she may have been taken out of the province. I heard you're crossing the river the day after tomorrow, and I thought I might have a better chance of hearing news of her if I'm with you." She also secretly hoped that some of the circus folk might remember seeing fleeing magicians during and after the Five-Month War—and, really, she didn't have any better ideas.

Joe Fitz was silent for a long moment. "Very well," he said at last, "we'll set you up a spot in the sideshow. You'll have to earn your keep, mind. If your little act here doesn't bring the punters in, you'll be out on your ear, understand?"

Marley nodded. "Thank you, sir."

"Come back tomorrow morning and we'll get you sorted out," he said, then without further comment he went back into his caravan and closed the door. Marley was left standing in the light of the rising moon, excitement and trepidation warring within her.

"Stop," she whispered to the little horse and caravan, which obediently ground to a halt. They were looking rather worse for wear now, mud oozing down their sides and deforming them. Marley gathered them up and squeezed, until she was holding only a muddy ball. She dropped it beside the caravan and wiped her filthy hands on her trousers, then turned back towards the town, wondering what the morrow would bring.

THE NEXT MORNING, MARLEY rose early. She paid her bill and left the dingy little inn without a backward glance. It was something of a relief to have a way forward, even if it had come from such an unexpected quarter.

Shouldering her pack, she set off across the fields in the direction of the circus camp. She quickly realised that she was far too early—nobody could be expected to be up at dawn when they were doing late-night shows. Rather than entering the camp, she detoured around it and went down to the riverbank. She sat on a fallen log and pulled a hunk of bread and a wedge of cheese from her pack as an impromptu breakfast.

The River Ham was wide here, almost at the end of its long journey to the sea. The ferry was further inland, on the other side of the village, where the river was narrower. A cluster of houses on the far shore were visible only as coloured dots. Marley had never left the province before—in fact, she'd never really gone that far beyond Guildthorpe. Andrew had always been the traveller; it was one of the things that had drawn her to him. They'd planned to go travelling together, back when they first married, but her toymaking business had been going so well that she'd been reluctant to leave it, and then Sara had come along and their world had closed in for a time. If she was honest with herself, she knew Andrew had chafed at the enforced domesticity. And then his heart had given out unexpectedly one day, when he was working in the shop like he had all the days before, and by the time she reached him he was almost gone. A smile was the last thing he left her with—that, and their six-year old daughter.

There was one thing to be said for the people of Guildthorpe: after Andrew died, they rallied around her and Sara, and she knew things would have been an awful lot harder without the meals, the childcare, and the shoulders to cry on. They'd helped her raise Sara, which was why it had felt like such a betrayal when the village council had caved before the magicians' onslaught during the war and hadn't fought harder for the children. And she hadn't fought either, not like she should have.

After Sara was taken, Marley had found herself paralysed by a crippling anxiety, compounded by guilt that she should have been out there, moving heaven and earth to find her little girl. It was much easier to blame the village elders, to take her pain and shame out on Guildthorpe. And she probably would still be there, wreaking havoc on the town, if Sturm hadn't turned up on her doorstep late one afternoon, lost and needing a place to stay. She could have sent him down to the pub, of course, but they'd got talking, and it was as if he'd brought a ray of sunlight in to break through her years of gloom. For the first time, it seemed like there might be hope. And then the North Wind had given her a place to start. So she'd dug out Andrew's old pack and tent, locked up the workshop, and left the village for the first time in nearly two decades. George would look after the place while she was gone, and one day, perhaps, she'd return.

She finished her breakfast and removed her cloak, for the sun was higher now and the day was already getting warm. She could hear the circus camp stirring behind her, so she stuffed her cloak into her pack, threw it over her shoulder, and set off.

The first person she saw was Jane of the Jungle, feeding the lion. She looked even younger without her makeup and spangly outfit. Marley had never seen a lion up close before and was in no hurry to start; she gave the cage a wide berth.

She found Joe Fitz talking to a couple of men in dungarees and flat caps, pointing at something on the big top. She waited until they were finished, then coughed to get his attention.

"Ah, yes. Mistress Cotton, isn't it?"

"Marley, please."

"Marley. You're still keen to join our merry band, then?"

"I am, sir."

"Very well. You have your own equipment?"

"I have a tent. I'll just need some clay for my act."

"Very good. You can pitch your tent over there by Granny Winter's wagon. She'll look after you, and remember—what she says goes. Meals are communal and the cost of them will be taken out of your wages. Payday is the first of the month. Any questions?"

"Do you want me to start tonight?"

"Of course. I'll get Harry to fix you up a spot in the sideshow. And don't forget, this is a trial. If you can't pay your way, you're out, got it? We're not a charity."

"Yes, sir. Thank you."

"Go on then, off you go." He turned away, waving at another labourer, and Marley found herself alone. Not knowing what else to do, she set off across the camp to Granny Winter's blue-and-yellow caravan. An old woman was sitting outside it, stirring an enormous pot over a campfire.

"Excuse me," Marley said, "I'm looking for Granny Winter. Mr Fitz sent me."

"Oh, he did, did he?" The old woman asked wryly, looking up. "Another fortune-hunter run off to join the circus, are you?"

"Something like that," Marley said, suppressing a grin. In spite of Granny Winter's gruffness, she found herself drawn to the old lady. Perhaps later she could ask her about the magicians—Granny Winter struck Marley as the sort of person who didn't miss much.

"Hope he doesn't expect you to bunk in with me," Granny Winter grumbled, flicking her long white plait over her shoulder.

"Oh, no," Marley assured her hastily. "I have a tent."

"Good. Pitch it over there, then." She indicated a spot next to the van. "The riffraff won't mess with you if you're camped near me!" She cackled, showing a mouthful of blackened teeth, and Marley grinned along with her. She left the old lady to her cooking, and set to work pitching her tent.

"What's your act, then?" Granny Winter asked, coming up beside Marley as she was stretching her back and surveying her handiwork. She remembered how long it had taken her to figure out the tent on her first night on the road; now she had it down to a fine art.

"I'm an Architect," she said.

Granny Winter sniffed. "Never heard of it," she said.

"I can show you, if you like," Marley said. "Do you have any clay?"

Granny Winter shook her head. "What would I do with clay, girl?" Then she called across to another woman, who was kneading bread. "Hoy, Liza! Bring us a handful of that dough." The woman, apparently unfazed by the odd request, handed Granny Winter a ball of dough, then sat on the caravan steps to watch.

"This do?" Granny Winter asked. It wouldn't, really—it was much too soft—but Marley decided to make the best of it. She fashioned a snake out of the dough, using a stick of charcoal from the fire to detail scales and eyes, then placed it on the caravan platform, bending down close to it.

"Move," she whispered. The snake began to wriggle sinuously, horribly realistically, across the platform. Marley placed a stick in front of it, and the snake reared up to strike. Liza jumped off the steps with a cry of astonishment, and Granny Winter burst out laughing.

"You'll do!" she cackled. "And I thought I'd seen everything. Where's Harry? I'll make sure he's got everything set up for you for tonight. I hope you've got your act worked out!"

Marley gulped. She'd been so caught up in the excitement of joining the circus that she'd given precious little thought to what her act would actually be.

Liza noticed her face and smiled. "Don't you worry," she said, "You come over and sit with me. I'll make you some more dough to practice on."

The rest of the day passed in something of a blur. In the afternoon, a man who introduced himself as Harry came and took her to her booth in the sideshow, where he'd set up a trestle table with a large block of clay wrapped in a damp cloth. A sign above it read 'The Creationist'.

"Don't worry," Harry said, "we'll come up with a better name later." Marley smiled, nervousness beginning to churn in her stomach. She settled down at the table, cutting off a piece of clay and playing with it, running through the routine she'd worked out.

"Ah, a new neighbour," said a voice. Marley looked up to find the ventriloquist, the Double-Bodied Man, watching her. He nodded to the next booth.

"That one's ours," he said. *Ours?* Marley thought, confused, then she realised he meant his dummy, who was sitting on his arm. The man was dressed casually, in rough trousers and a shirt, but the dummy was still in his performance outfit—a formal suit and a sparkly tie.

"I'm sorry," the man continued. "Allow me to introduce myself. I'm Zebedee Hupfnagel." He held out his hand and Marley shook it.

"Is that your real name?" she blurted, before realising how rude it sounded and flushing with embarrassment. But Zebedee just laughed.

"Afraid so," he said. "I had cruel parents. It's Zeb for short."

"Marley Cotton."

"Welcome to the madhouse, Marley Cotton." As if to underline his words, the dummy on his arm cackled maniacally, giving his master a pointed look. "And this is Stanley," Zeb said.

"The brains of the outfit," the dummy said, just as it had in the act, sounding strangely lucid and not at all comical. Marley itched to get a proper look at it. She wondered if Zeb and Stanley always went everywhere together.

This impression was reinforced later, at the pre-show communal dinner, where the ventriloquist turned up with the dummy still firmly attached to his arm, forcing him to eat with one hand. If any of the other circus folk thought this odd, they didn't show it, so Marley tried to shrug it off. But there was something about Stanley that she still found deeply unsettling. Perhaps it was the beady blue eyes, or the manic, fixed smile with its rows of tombstone teeth. Whatever it was, she felt her skin crawl whenever Stanley looked her way.

As the meal progressed, however, she stopped worrying about the ventriloquist and started worrying about her own act. She couldn't believe she was actually going to do it. Animating small clay creatures should be easy—she'd been doing it since she was a child. But what if her magic suddenly failed her? The worries came in to roost, shrieking in her head like a flock of bats, and the food turned to ash in her mouth. And then, before she was even close to ready, it was time.

As it turned out, she needn't have worried. Her first anxiety—that nobody would come to see her act, and that Joe Fitz would turf her out before they'd even left Hamsby—was solved by Harry, the carnival barker, who was adept at drawing people in and relieving them of their money. Her second concern, that they wouldn't like what they saw, was also unfounded. Her act, which involved creating and animating a small village modelled on Hamsby, complete with people, horses and vehicles, was a hit. As she finished up, people started calling out objects for her to create, and soon her trestle was bustling with a clay fishing boat, a crocodile, and a giant cockroach, among other things. The patrons tipped generously, and Harry sported an enormous grin as he shepherded them off to the big top for the main show.

Marley was cleaning up her trestle and rewrapping the clay in its damp cloths when she heard raised voices coming from the neighbouring booth. The sideshow acts were separated only by curtains, so although they were trying to keep their voices low, she had no trouble overhearing. She knew she shouldn't eavesdrop, but nevertheless she paused her packing and stood stock-still, listening intently.

The first voice, she thought, sounded like Zeb, only less wooden than she'd heard him before. There was a liveliness and a human quality to his voice that had been missing in all their previous interactions—she didn't realise just how much until she heard the contrast.

"No!" he was saying, in a low, intense whisper. "I won't do it!"

"Yes, you will," said the second voice, with perfect assurance. There was a familiarity to it that Marley couldn't quite place, and it niggled at her.

"No, I won't. Not that. It would be career suicide."

"Ah, but we'll go on to greater things."

"I don't want your 'greater things'!"

"Then you're a fool. You're nothing without me."

"You can't make me do it." Zeb was almost pleading now.

There was a chilling silence. Then: "Oh, yes I can," said the second voice.

Marley, alarmed, was just about to pull back the curtain and reveal the mysterious speaker, when Harry came bursting into her booth.

"Have you seen Zeb?" he demanded without preamble.

Marley opened her mouth but Harry, not waiting for an answer, barged through the curtain into the neighbouring booth.

"Zeb!" he bellowed. "What are you doing? Get your backside into that tent now! You're on in two minutes!"

Marley watched as the ventriloquist was all but dragged out. There was a pained look in his eyes that she didn't quite understand. As he left, she peered into the booth to see who he'd been arguing with, but to her surprise there was no one there. She chewed her lip for a moment, frowning to herself. Was it possible that Zeb had been arguing with...Stanley? Abandoning her tidying, she hurried towards the big top.

She slipped in through the performers' entrance at the rear, nodding to the one or two people she recognised. Her heart was pounding, and not just from the dash across the field. The overheard argument was fresh in her mind, and trepidation thudded in her chest.

She walked quietly into the wings, which in the big top was a space behind the curtain at the back of the ring where the performers waited to go on. The Aristocratic Acrobats were clustered there, watching, and she ducked in behind them, peering through a crack in the curtain.

Zeb was perched as usual on his stool in the spotlight, Stanley on his lap. From her position behind them, Marley could see the ventriloquist's hand up the puppet's back, but she couldn't help thinking that the motion of movement was all wrong. Whenever Stanley moved or spoke, it was as if the puppet moved first, then the hand. She couldn't explain it.

Zeb's act continued on as normal, and Marley began to relax. Perhaps the argument had been a rehearsal, something for the show. She took a deep breath and let her shoulders drop, for she liked the ventriloquist, despite his oddities, and would have hated to see anything bad happen to him.

She was just thinking about returning to her clean-up when a gasp from one of the acrobats brought her back to the present.

Zeb had left his stool and was walking around the ring, engaging with members of the audience. Marley couldn't hear what he or Stanley was saying, but she caught the crowd's nervous laughter, as if they weren't quite sure what was going on either. Gradually the laughter began to change into something more hostile, until the audience was openly jeering. Marley saw a projectile come flying into the ring, followed by another and another.

"Get him off!" Harry bellowed, barging into the cluster of acrobats. "You're on now! Hurry up!"

The Aristocratic Acrobats lined up and ran into the ring. Somehow—Marley wasn't quite sure how they managed it—they shepherded the rogue ventriloquist from one to the next until they'd spirited him back through the curtain. Joe Fitz, in his ringmaster's gear, followed them on, and Marley could hear him placating the irate crowd. Zeb, who, strangely, was sobbing, pushed past Harry and Marley and hurried out of the tent. Harry moved to follow him but was waylaid by Jane; Marley caught something about an escaped python. No one was paying her any mind, so she slipped out and followed the ventriloquist.

Zeb moved surprisingly quickly, and he was back inside his caravan before Marley could catch him. She was about to go and knock on the door when she heard some indiscriminate yelling and sounds of a scuffle. She ducked behind a nearby van and watched, holding her breath.

A moment later, Zeb emerged alone—the first time Marley had seen him without Stanley. He looked strangely incomplete. He headed for the river, dodging behind the caravans and avoiding anyone who came near. Marley followed, making sure to stay out of sight.

On the riverbank, Zeb paused, gazing out across the expanse. Marley watched from the shelter of a tree, until she saw the ventriloquist scrub a hand across his face, and realised he was crying. She left her hiding place and went over to him, deliberately making enough noise that he wouldn't be startled.

"Zeb, what's wrong?" she asked gently. She could feel her shoulders tensing; other people's emotions made her anxious. But there was no one else around to help, and there was clearly something strange going on.

The ventriloquist wiped his nose on his sleeve and gave a hiccupping approximation of his old laugh. "Nothing. I'm fine."

Marley raised an eyebrow, because even she could tell that was rubbish. "What happened back there?"

Despite Zeb's best efforts, tears began to leak out of the corners of his eyes. "I'm so ashamed," he said. "I said some awful things. I'm going to lose my job and I'll never live it down." He began to sob. "And it's only going to get worse."

Marley perched on a fallen log and patted the space next to her. "Sit down and start from the beginning," she said.

"You won't believe me." But he sat nevertheless.

The toymaker thought about the recent events in her own life and gave a bark of laughter. "Try me. Now, why did you derail your act like that?"

"He made me."

"He? Is someone threatening you?"

"You could say that."

"Who?"

"That's the part you won't believe."

Marley thought back to the fight she'd overheard, and to the way Zeb usually seemed so wooden—so different from how he was now. It sounded crazy, but perhaps...

"Is it your dummy?" she asked. "Is it Stanley?"

Zeb stared at her, his mouth hanging open.

"How did you…?" His eyes darted around in fear, as if he'd let slip a terrible secret.

"Zeb, you know I'm an Architect by birth. But by profession I'm a toymaker, and this sort of thing…well, it's not as rare as you might think."

Although she'd never come across it herself, she remembered reading an article some years ago in *Wood & Tin*, the Toymakers' Guild publication, about enchanted toys gone rogue and how to deal with them.

"You mean…this has happened before?"

Marley nodded. "Tell me about Stanley. How did you become a ventriloquist, and when did you acquire him?"

Zeb plucked at a blade of grass, knotting it between his fingers. "I'm an only child," he said, "and my parents were often busy. We didn't have much money, so they were always working. I didn't have many friends, so as a child I'd talk to my toys. I'd make up things for them to say, and they became as real and as dear to me as any human friends." He shrugged. "I guess I just got really good at it. Then when I was around fifteen, the circus came to town, and I saw a ventriloquist for the first time. I knew then that was what I wanted to be."

"So you ran away with the circus?"

He laughed mirthlessly, twisting the grass compulsively. "Oh no. I wasn't brave enough. And I didn't have an act, not then. I didn't even have a proper dummy, just a couple of old teddy bears."

"So what did you do?"

"I practised. My parents thought I was crazy, but really it was the only thing I was good at. I had to prove to them I could make a go of it. And I *was* good at it—before long, you could have sworn those old bears were talking of their own accord."

"So when did Stanley come along?"

Zeb smiled. "That was one of the proudest days of my life," he said. "I'd started doing small acts with my bears—children's nameday celebrations, that sort of thing. It was the first money I'd ever earned, and Stanley was the first thing I spent it on."

"So you bought him new?" Marley asked, her brain ticking over. Cursed or enchanted toys usually had a history, often a traumatic one; it would be very unusual to find such a problem in a brand-new toy.

"Oh goodness, no!" Zeb exclaimed. "Do you know how much new dummies cost? No, it was sheer dumb luck, really. I'd been performing at a celebration one afternoon in an unfamiliar part of town, and when I was walking home I took a wrong turn. I wound up in a dingy little alley full of decrepit old shops. One of the few that wasn't boarded up was a dusty old antique shop. And Stanley was right there in the window. I knew as soon as I saw him that I had to have him."

Marley glanced across at him; there was the light of obsession in his eyes.

"Let me guess what happened next," she said. "Things got really good for a while, didn't they?"

Zeb nodded sadly. "My luck seemed to change overnight," he said. "People kept booking me until I had more work than I could handle. Then the circus came to town, and I didn't even have to approach them—Joe Fitz himself sought me out. The contract was extremely generous, and I've been here ever since. Only...over the last little while it's started to change."

"How so?"

Zeb shook his head. "At first it was like I was hearing a whisper every now and again," he said. "It was something I couldn't quite catch, and no one else seemed to hear it, so I thought I was just imagining it. Then it gradually grew, so slowly I hardly noticed, until it was an actual voice in my head. By then I was so used to it, I had trouble distinguishing it from my own thoughts."

"What was it saying?"

"Nothing alarming. Observations of things. A running commentary on life, if you will. But then he started making suggestions. And sometimes I'd hear myself saying things that weren't what I intended at all, but I couldn't seem to stop." Tears welled in his eyes again. "The last few weeks have been hell. I don't recognise myself anymore."

Marley remembered how stilted the ventriloquist's manner had seemed, as if he'd been speaking against his will. "And tonight—he made you insult people?"

Zeb nodded. "I know that sounds like I'm just avoiding taking responsibility, but it's true." He shuddered. "I said the most terrible things. I brought the circus into disrepute and I deserve to be punished for it."

Marley scowled. "Why would he get you to do that?" She knew that rogue toys often followed such a pattern, bringing great fortune to their owners before ultimately leading them to destruction, and she had a feeling that Stanley wasn't finished yet.

"I think he wanted to pick a fight with Joe Fitz," Zeb said. "That's not the worst of it, though."

"Go on."

"He wants me to...to kill Joe Fitz and burn the circus to the ground." He began to sob again.

Marley caught her breath. "And are you going to do it?"

"Of course not! I'll kill myself first." He glanced towards the river, and Marley realised why he'd come down there. She fought to keep her demeanour calm, although her heart was thundering in her ears.

"No, Zeb," she said. "That won't be necessary. I can help you fix this."

Hope flared in the ventriloquist's eyes. He gulped and wiped his streaming nose on his sleeve. "You can? You mean I'll finally be free of him?"

Marley nodded, hoping it was true. "Where's Stanley now?" she asked.

"I locked him in a cupboard in my van," Zeb said. "Oh, he's going to be so angry..." He looked terrified. Marley patted his arm in what she hoped was a reassuring manner.

"Don't worry," she said. "I'll be with you. You won't have to face him alone."

Zeb nodded, and together they rose and walked back towards the camp.

When they arrived, they found the place in uproar. Word of Zeb's antics had clearly spread, and as they entered the circle of wagons they were met with a forest of hostile stares. Joe Fitz emerged from the crowd, his face like granite.

"Zebedee," he said coldly. "A word." It wasn't a question. Zeb stared at the ground, quaking in his boots, and Marley realised she needed to step in.

"Mr Fitz, sir," she said, taking the ringmaster by the elbow, a little surprised at her own daring. "Could you come with us? There's something you need to see."

Joe Fitz looked like he might protest, but Zeb looked at him imploringly, his grey eyes huge and liquid, and he relented.

"Back to work!" he barked at the people who had paused in their activities to watch the scene unfold. "What's this all about?" he asked as they made their way across the field to Zeb's caravan.

"There's been a bit of a...problem...with Stanley," Marley said. "We'll explain everything, I promise. But we need to sort him out first."

Joe Fitz's eyebrows shot up, and he looked at them like they were both crazy, but said nothing.

"He's in the cupboard, you said?" Marley asked as they reached the van. Zeb nodded, pulling a small brass key from his pocket and handing it to her. Marley opened the caravan door and ushered the two men inside.

The van's interior looked like a whirlwind had blown through it. Marley knew enough about Zeb to tell that he was usually very neat and house-proud, and she surmised that the destruction must have been a result of the confrontation with Stanley that she'd overheard on her way to the river. Zeb gestured to a cupboard under the bunk, from which there was coming a violent banging and clattering. Marley waved the two men back and slipped the key into the lock. She'd half-expected Stanley to spring out and grab her throat, but when she opened the door the dummy was lying eerily still, his tombstone teeth fixed in a psychotic grin. Marley thought she caught the merest flicker of alarm in the blue glass eyes when he realised Zeb wasn't alone.

"Zebedee, who is this?" the dummy said. Its voice was different from how it sounded in the ring—it was harsher, like a knife scraping on stone, and dripping with menace. Zeb cowered back. Joe Fitz apparently couldn't hear Stanley, for he was glancing around the room in confusion.

"What's going on?" he asked.

Zeb's breath was coming in short gasps; his skin was pale and clammy, and he began to sway. Joe Fitz reached out and grabbed his arm to steady him.

The dummy's eyes slid slowly across, taking in the ringmaster supporting the gasping ventriloquist. "Ah, I see you brought him to me,' he said. "Good man. I may even reconsider your punishment for this outrage."

It was Joe Fitz's turn to gape now, and Marley realised that the physical contact between him and Zeb somehow enabled him to hear Stanley. He looked horrified and revolted, as if he couldn't quite believe the evidence of his senses.

The dummy was struggling to pull himself into a sitting position within the confines of the cupboard, and a glint caught Marley's eye. Her eyebrows shot up as she realised that Stanley was clutching a large knife. Beside her, Zeb moaned.

Marley, for her part, found that she actually felt much calmer than she'd anticipated. Stanley was a nasty piece of work, to be sure, but in the end he was just another toy. Zeb hadn't known how to deal with him, but she had an inkling of how he worked, and she was itching to see if she was right.

The dummy lunged forward, the knife banging against the side of the cupboard. His head swivelled towards Zeb, his beady eyes gleaming maniacally.

"Pick me up!" he demanded. Zeb stepped forward, a look of horror on his face, as if he couldn't control the movement of his legs.

"No, Zeb!" Marley warned, but it was too late—the ventriloquist had hold of the dummy, his hand up Stanley's back, giving him movement and mobility. Stanley motioned forward and Zeb lunged at Marley. She stepped back, wincing as Stanley took a swipe at her and the knife nicked her wrist.

"Joe!" she called over her shoulder, not taking her eyes off the dummy, and she felt rather than saw the ringmaster move so that he was behind Zeb. "On my count!" Marley said, hoping he understood what she needed. "One, two, three!"

Joe Fitz lumbered forward and locked Zeb into a bear hug, trapping his arms at his sides, and Marley took her chance, grabbing Stanley by the scruff of the neck.

"That's a quite enough of that," she said. She pinned his arms and quickly relieved him of the knife as Stanley thrashed around in her grip, shouting all manner of threats and obscenities. Joe Fitz released Zeb, who cowered like a beaten dog. Even the stalwart Joe looked like he wanted to be sick, but Marley was unfazed.

"Oh, stop it," she said, giving the dummy a shake. Stanley glared up at her, violence in his eyes.

Keeping one hand firmly on his neck, Marley slipped her other hand up the dummy's back and into the hollow of his head, where on a normal dummy the ventriloquist would control its movements. Stanley shrieked, a wild, ear-piercing sound, but Marley was unmoved. As Zeb and Joe Fitz clapped their hands over their ears, she felt around in the wooden cavern. She knew vaguely what she was looking for, but it was still a relief when her fingertips closed upon it. She withdrew her hand, clutching a small scrap of paper. Instantly Stanley's screams stopped, and he collapsed lifeless in her arms, once again nothing more than a creature of wood and fabric. Marley laid him down on the bunk and unfurled the paper.

"What...what's that?" Zeb stammered, finding his voice at last.

"It's called a *shem*," Marley said. "It's what gives him life." She used something similar when creating the buildings in her model village; such magic ran in the Cotton family. But she'd never made a golem, although the principle was the same. The potential for things to go wrong was just too great, as Stanley had proved.

Sure enough, the paper was inscribed with a single word. Zeb peered over her shoulder.

"What does it say?" he asked. "It's not a language I'm familiar with."

"*Emet*," Marley said. "It means 'life'. It's a very old spell." The paper made her fingertips tingle; there was so much power in a single word. She took a deep breath and laid her thumb over the first letter. When she removed it, the writing had vanished, leaving only '*met*'— 'dead'.

"He won't be bothering you or anyone else again," Marley said, picking up the lifeless dummy and holding him out to Zeb, but the ventriloquist wouldn't touch him. Marley shrugged, tucking him under her arm.

"Will someone please explain what in the blazes has been going on here?" Joe Fitz had finally recovered from his shock, and his beefy face was growing increasingly red. Marley was half-afraid that steam would start pouring from his ears.

"Of course," she said. "But I think you'd better sit down. It's quite a story."

"WHAT WILL YOU DO NOW?" Marley asked, swinging her legs. She was sitting on the platform of Zeb's caravan in a field beside the ferry, basking in the morning sunlight, a mug of tea in her hand.

"I don't really know," Zeb shrugged. "But I don't think I can stay here, not after everything."

"Joe seemed happy enough for you to stay on."

"I know. But I doubt anyone else will be," he said. "Not when I brought the circus into such disrepute. And Joe saw Stanley with his own eyes. But I don't think the others will believe me." He looked out towards the river, his gaze wistful. "No, it'll do me good to go out on my own, at least for a while. And I need a break from ventriloquism." He'd been unable to even look at Stanley the previous night; eventually, Joe Fitz had taken the dummy, promising to burn it.

"Well, if you ever decide to return to it, come and see me," Marley said. "I'll make you a proper dummy."

Zeb grinned. "I might just do that," he said. "You said you live in Guildthorpe?"

Marley nodded. "I may not be back there for some time, though," she said. "I'm going to stay with the circus for a while and cross the river. I'm not going home until I find out what happened to my daughter." The previous night, she'd told Zeb about Sara and her real reason for joining the circus. After everything that had happened with Stanley, there didn't seem much point in keeping secrets.

"I know it doesn't mean much,' Zeb said, "but I'll keep a lookout. I'll probably travel around for a bit, and, well, two sets of eyes and ears are surely better than one. And if I find her, I promise I'll send her home to you."

"Thank you," Marley said with feeling.

"It's the least I can do. You gave me back my freedom. My life."

The ferry had dropped the first lot of caravans and returned to reload.

"Hoy, lass!" Granny Winter called. "You coming or not?"

"I'd better go," Marley said. "Wouldn't want to miss the boat." They clasped hands, then spontaneously Marley pulled the ventriloquist into an embrace.

"Go well," she said.

"You too."

Marley joined Granny Winter in her van, and stared out across the water to the unknown. She looked back as the ferryman cast off the line and Hamsby began to recede. Zeb's lone caravan stood on the bank, the ventriloquist himself standing beside the horse's head. As Marley watched, he raised his hand in farewell, then took the horse's bridle and turned the caravan away, truly alone for the first time.

The Spellbound House

Zeb Hupfnagel stood in the darkness behind his caravan, listening to the excited murmuring of the crowd on the other side. He took a deep breath, trying to still his racing heart. He realised just how many years it had been since he'd felt this way—really, not since he was a young ventriloquist trying to prove himself worthy of a place in the circus of his dreams. But a month ago he'd stood on a riverbank and watched as that same circus—his home and family of nearly twenty years—had crossed into the unknown without him. The sense of loss had been real and painful, but it was temporary, and it had soon been overtaken by a heady joy in his newfound freedom. His van had been repainted with his new stage name, 'The Extraordinary Hupfnagel', in blue-and-gold letters, and he'd spent every waking moment perfecting his new act, which involved everything from juggling to sleight-of-hand tricks. Everything, that was, except ventriloquism.

Now, finally, he was ready to premiere it, and he couldn't help second-guessing himself. He'd deliberately chosen a small village, hoping for an easier time than in a large town—these people didn't get many travelling shows, so they were more likely to be an appreciative audience. And there'd be fewer of them to talk about it should it all go horribly wrong.

He pushed this last thought from his mind and squared his shoulders. He adjusted his royal blue, gold-lined cloak, enjoying the weight of it, then stepped out from behind the van, swirling it so the golden lining flickered in the firelight.

He had high hopes for the show, and it went even better than he'd envisaged. From the start, the crowd was awestruck, gasping and cheering at every little thing. Zeb realised that, due to its size, the circus had only ever visited larger towns, where the inhabitants were much harder to impress, and he resolved to stick to the small villages from now on. It would mean moving on every couple of days, but if that was what it took to establish a good reputation—and, if he was honest with himself, repair his rather battered ego—then that was what he'd do.

He was just taking his second bow, after giving an encore at the crowd's urging, when he felt the ground begin to rumble beneath his feet. The spectators' cheers of joy took on an alarmed note as a dark shape appeared on the village outskirts. As it loomed nearer—faster than Zeb would have thought possible—the crowd scattered, and he dived for the safety of his caravan. The rumbling intensified as the shape came barrelling across the green, scattering everything in its path and narrowly missing the van. Zeb dashed out onto the platform and stared after it as it disappeared into the darkness at the far end of the village. He shook his head: he could have sworn it was a house. For a second, he wondered if he was going mad, but no—he was sure it was a house. A small brick cottage, running along on a path of bricks that formed itself in front of the house as it went, like the bow wave of a ship. Not so long ago, Zeb would have dismissed the evidence of his eyes as a trick of the light or an overactive imagination, but if his experience with Stanley had taught him anything, it was that just because he couldn't imagine something, it didn't mean it was impossible.

The crowd, which had scattered before the mysterious house, was beginning to re-form, and Zeb was relieved to see that there were no apparent injuries. People huddled in small groups, reliving the ordeal; the air buzzed with speculation. Zeb briefly contemplated trying a few tricks to lighten the mood, but it was no good—the moment had been lost. Gradually the crowd began to trickle away, until at last Zeb was alone. He doused the torches edging the green and returned to his van, but sleep was slow in coming. When he eventually did drop off, his dreams were populated by strange contraptions that he couldn't outrun.

HE WOKE TO THE GREY dawn light and the nip of late autumn in the air. He lit the fire and made himself a cup of tea, which he drank sitting on the caravan steps, the cup steaming between his hands. He'd planned to stay for a couple of days, but after the events of the previous night, moving on seemed to be the best idea. The villagers would be unlikely to come to another show now. It was best to cut his losses. He finished his tea then doused the fire and harnessed his horse, Milly, to the van. Before the village was even properly awake, he was gone.

There was a sense of relief at being on the road again. The house had unsettled him more than he liked to admit—it reminded him a little too much of Stanley, although he couldn't say why—and it felt good to put it behind him. He let Milly plod along at her own pace, for he was in no hurry, and as they went he unfolded a map, looking for likely places to stop. He quickly concluded that they'd probably be spending the night on the road, for out here in the borderlands villages were few and far between.

The day passed in gentle contemplation. It was so different to the travelling he'd done with the circus—all together in a convoy, full of noise and laughter and joking. They'd always gone as fast as possible, for days spent on the road were days they weren't earning money. Zeb reflected that, although his finances had undoubtedly suffered since he'd been on his own, there was a special kind of luxury in having the time to move slowly and notice the world around him.

He stopped for the night as the twilight was deepening from gold to purple and the fireflies were slowly winking to life. In a small clearing that opened up a short way off the road, Zeb unharnessed Milly and let her eat the sweet grass. He built himself a campfire and set his dinner to cook, then lounged beside it, looking up at the slowly emerging stars. *Life doesn't get much better than this*, he thought. He wondered what Marley was doing, and if she'd found her daughter yet.

His reverie was shattered by a rustling in the bushes. He sat up with a start, peering into the trees, but he couldn't make anything out in the deepening gloom.

"Hello?" He called. There was no answer, and as the silence descended once more he lay back again, albeit not as relaxed as before. He took a deep breath to steady himself, breathing in the tang of the wood smoke and the rich scent of damp earth. There were always cracklings and rustlings in the forest, he reminded himself; they were probably just small animals. Nothing to be afraid of.

The pot on the fire was beginning to give out a heady, mouth-watering smell, and Zeb's stomach rumbled as he stirred it. He was just ladling some of its contents into a bowl when Milly started, giving a frightened whinny. Zeb jumped to his feet and went to quieten the horse. When she was calm, he returned to the fire and his dinner—but the bowl was gone.

Zeb shivered. An animal might take his stew, to be sure, but it would have left the bowl. Part of him wanted to pack up and leave right then, but another part, a more curious part, wanted to know who or what was out there. They were just hungry, he reasoned—it didn't mean they were dangerous.

He dug around in his food bag and brought out one of his most precious possessions—a bar of chocolate. He'd bought it on impulse with the last of his circus earnings and he'd been rationing it ever since, for he didn't know when he'd have the means or opportunity to buy another. He broke off a chunk and laid it on a flat rock near the edge of the clearing where he'd heard the rustling in the bushes. Then he got out another bowl and served himself some stew, deliberately sitting with his back to the rock while he ate.

If there was one thing Zeb prided himself on, it was his reflexes. You didn't become a successful conjurer without being able to think and move quickly. So it was that, even with his back turned, he sensed something moving towards the rock. He inched round so slowly as to be almost imperceptible, then at the last minute he turned and confronted the intruder. To his surprise, he found himself face-to-face with a dark-skinned young woman, her eyes wide with shock and what looked almost like guilt as she reached for the chocolate. For a long moment their gazes locked, then Zeb slowly held out his hand.

"Hello there," he said. The words broke the spell; she dropped the chocolate, turned and fled into the forest. Zeb crossed to the rock and picked up the chocolate, staring after her. He briefly contemplated following, but he had no torch, and the last thing he wanted was to get lost in the woods at night. He finished his dinner, cleaned up and went to bed, but he was haunted by the memory of the young woman. For the second night running, he was plagued by strange and unsettling dreams.

The next morning he woke early, just as the first rays of sunlight were beginning to slant through the trees. Unable to go back to sleep, he got up, dressed, and prepared for the day. He knew he should get on the road in reasonable time if he wanted to make it to a town before nightfall, but standing in the clearing, his gaze kept getting drawn to the place where the young woman had appeared. He was beginning to think he'd dreamed her—the product, no doubt, of too much time alone on the road.

On impulse, he crossed the clearing and peered again into the trees. He noticed something he'd missed in the darkness the previous night—the undergrowth was flattened where she must have hidden, watching him. Venturing into the wood, he looked closely at the ground and saw a faint trail of broken sticks and crushed leaves. He began to follow it, trying to be as quiet as possible, although sometimes, despite his best efforts, a stick would break under his boot with a crack like a whip, making him jump. At times the trail almost disappeared, but with careful searching he always managed to find it again. The forest floor was such that only the most experienced woodsman could have passed through without leaving some sign of his presence.

After some time, the trees began to thin out again into another clearing much like the one he'd camped in. Zeb crept to the edge of it, expecting to find a tent or a caravan like his own, or maybe even just a makeshift bed in a pile of leaves if she was really down on her luck. Instead, he peered out from behind a tree and gaped in astonishment.

Before him, looking as if it had been there for years, was the house that had so rudely disrupted his show two nights earlier and set him on the road again. Even though he'd only glimpsed it that night, he would have recognised it anywhere. It was built of a distinctive red mud brick—unusual in this region where the houses were almost universally constructed of grey-blue stone and thatch—and its design was that of a simple cottage, with small windows, a tiled gabled roof, and a brick path leading from the front door straight into the woods. Smoke curled from its chimney, and the whole thing glowed warm and inviting in the early-morning light.

There was no sign of the girl, but Zeb took the smoking chimney as a sign that someone, at least, was home. With a boldness that surprised him, he stepped out from the shelter of the trees and strode along the brick path to the front door. He noticed that the door itself, oddly, was also made of brick, right down to the knocker, which he let fall with a satisfying thud. When there was no answer, he knocked twice more.

He was just about to turn away, when a panel in the door slid open, revealing the young woman who had stolen his dinner the previous night. She looked how Zeb remembered her—including a twinge of familiarity he couldn't quite place—except now her expression was wary, almost hostile.

"Who are you? What do you want?"

Zeb was taken aback. "Uh... my name is Zebedee Hupfnagel. I'm a conjurer. I saw you last night and I just wanted to make sure you're all right."

But at the word 'conjurer' the girl had visibly started.

"Conjurer?" she said. "You mean you're a magician?"

Zeb felt the path shifting under his boots, and looking down, he saw with a jolt of horror that his feet were now encased to the ankle in bricks. He tried lifting one foot, then the other, but he couldn't move.

"I'm not a magician!" he gasped. "I just do tricks. Sleight-of-hand, rabbits out of hats, that sort of thing."

Once upon a time, before the Five-Month War, conjurers like him had sometimes called themselves magicians, despite not actually performing real magic. But after the war and the atrocities committed by actual magicians, the conjuring community had been at pains to distance itself. If it hadn't been for the discomfort in his feet, Zeb would have been offended at being called a magician, but as it was, his focus was on more pressing matters.

"So you don't know any magic?"

"I don't, I swear!"

The young woman shrugged. "We'll see. I find once people have been there or a day or two their true colours come out. You'll release yourself if you're desperate enough."

Zeb's stomach lurched. He'd never be able to release himself from the path, no matter how hard he tried—and even if he could, well, that would just prove he was a magician, and who knew what she'd do to him then? The only weapon he had was his wits.

"What are you going to eat in the meantime?" he asked.

"I'll manage."

"It's a bit tricky, though, isn't it, with me blocking your door?'

"I've got plenty here."

"It's a wonder you needed to steal my dinner, then."

"Oh, be quiet!" she snapped, glowering at him. "You talk far too much!"

Zeb's mouth dropped open, because suddenly he realised what was so familiar about her. The coincidence was almost too extraordinary to be believed, but then not so long ago he would also have scoffed at the idea of a sentient ventriloquist's dummy. There were many things in the world, he was learning, that reached far beyond his understanding.

"Is your name Sara?" he asked, throwing caution to the wind.

A look of shock crossed her face before her mask slipped back into place, and he saw that somehow, impossibly, he was right.

"I don't know what you're talking about. "

"You're not Sara Cotton, from Guildthorpe? Only I met a woman called Marley Cotton not so long ago who was looking for her daughter, and I swear you're the spitting image of her."

"I think you're getting confused." She closed the sliding panel, but there was no sound of her footsteps moving away.

Zeb's shins were beginning to ache. He shifted his weight as much as he could to ease the discomfort, but it was of little help.

"Oh well," he said to the closed door, "since it looks like I'm going to be here for a while, I might as well tell you a story. You probably won't believe it, but when has that ever mattered? Anyway, it all begins with a circus..."

He talked about how he'd found Stanley and joined the circus, and how Marley had saved him when it all went so very wrong. He addressed himself to the closed door, but he'd seen the sliding panel open the tiniest crack, and he knew that she was listening to every word.

"And that was the last I saw of her," he concluded, "as she boarded the ferry to continue her search. But perhaps she should have been looking closer to home."

Zeb stretched his arms and rolled his neck from side to side. The sun was high in the sky now, and his stomach was beginning to rumble. He hoped Milly hadn't got into any mischief. He tried squatting down to make his legs more comfortable, but the bricks made it impossible. Finally he lost patience.

"Look," he said, "I don't mean you any harm. All I want is to go on my way and mind my own business. I'm already going to have to spend an extra night on the road as it is, so if you just let me go, I'll be off and you'll never hear from me again. I promised your mother I'd pass on her message if I saw you, and I have. What you do with it is up to you." He glowered at the door, cursing stubborn youngsters and congratulating himself on never having had any of his own.

Just as his frustration was beginning to turn into despair, the door opened and Sara stood before him. She was dressed simply, in patched brown breeches, a white shirt that showed much evidence of mending, and worn knee-length boots. Her black hair was a mass of thin braids that hung past her shoulders.

"You're really not a magician, are you?"

"I told you that."

"And you really promised to help my mother?"

Zeb shrugged. "For all the good it'll do. It was clear she misses you terribly, and that was hard to see."

"I want to go back to Guildthorpe," Sara said, "but I can't."

"Why not?"

"It's a long story."

Zeb sighed. "I'm a captive audience."

"No, you're not," Sara said, and he felt the bricks around his ankles shift. The relief was blissful, and he immediately sat down on the path and removed his boots, rubbing his swollen joints.

"Sorry," she said.

"I should think so. Do you treat all your visitors this way?"

"I don't get many visitors."

"No wonder." He pulled his boots back on and clambered to his feet. "Now, if you don't mind, I'll be going."

"Wait!"

Zeb turned, staring impassively at her.

"I...need your help." She wouldn't meet his eyes, and Zeb could tell the words didn't come easily to her. Part of him was still angry with her, but she was also not much more than a child—barely eighteen, going by what Marley had told him—and he owed her mother his life.

"What do you need?" he asked, wondering even as the words left his mouth whether it was a good idea.

Sara stood aside, leaving the doorway clear. "Won't you come inside? Like I said, it's a long story, and it's not very hospitable of me to leave you standing on the doorstep." She seemed to have completely changed her tune, and Zeb wasn't entirely sure he trusted it.

"No more traps?" he asked, eyeing her warily. "Promise?"

"I swear on my mother's life."

It would be much safer and much more sensible to just walk away, Zeb reflected. But he'd never really been one to play it safe.

"All right," he said. "No promises, mind. But I'll hear what you've got to say."

He followed Sara into the cottage, gazing around him as he went. On the one hand, it was just like an ordinary cottage, except that the inside was made of the same mud bricks as the outside, rather than the plaster and beams he was used to. He reached out and touched a wall; the brick was pleasantly warm under his fingers, and indeed the whole cottage was much cosier and more homelike than he'd anticipated. But there was also something else, a strange tingling in the air that was both alien and familiar at the same time. It took him a moment to figure out where he'd felt it before, and then he realised—it was the same feeling he used to get around Stanley, before Marley had removed the little scroll that gave him life. He knew Marley had magic, but now he wondered if Sara had inherited more from her mother than just her looks.

She led him into a sitting room with a fire burning merrily in the grate. Zeb started when he looked at the furniture and realised that it too was made of brick.

"Won't you sit down?" Sara asked. Zeb considered refusing, but he couldn't think of a good excuse, and in any case his legs were still aching. He planted himself gingerly into a brick armchair next to the fire, and was shocked to find that it gave beneath him and conformed to his shape more comfortably than any chair he'd ever sat on. Whatever Sara and this house were, they weren't ordinary.

Sara took a seat in an identical armchair opposite, drawing her legs up under her. "Did my mother tell you what happened to me?" she asked without preamble.

Zeb nodded. "She said you were taken by magicians during the war because of your magical talents."

"That's pretty much it." She shrugged. "The details aren't that important, really. But I ended up as a slave to Hugo Sweeney. You know who he is?"

Zeb raised an eyebrow and said nothing. Everyone knew who Hugo Sweeney was. As the brutal head of the magicians' Grand High Council, and the mastermind behind the coup attempt that had started the war, he'd become infamous.

"Of course you do. Sorry. Anyway, I watched and learned. And then I started making things—just little creatures out of mud and straw, mostly. I remembered my early lessons with my mother, and I picked up more along the way. I figured out how to bring them to life. Then I figured out how to make separate things work together. So I started building bricks." She said it like it was nothing, a modest achievement, but even though Zeb knew little of magic, he had the feeling that she was describing something extraordinary.

"I plotted my escape meticulously," she continued. "They didn't suspect a thing. But I didn't have quite the right spell. So the night of my escape, I broke into Sweeney's tower and stole his spellbook. It had what I wanted, so I animated this house and took off. But he caught me just as I was leaving, and he's been chasing me ever since."

Zeb gaped at her. "When was this?"

"Just before the end of the war."

"And you've been running this whole time?"

She nodded.

Zeb ran a hand over his face in disbelief. The war had ended *eight years ago*. Sara had not only done something unheard of, she'd done it when she was just a child. And to have evaded a magician like Sweeney for so long was a feat in itself.

"Why didn't you go home?" Zeb asked.

She shrugged, studying the floor. "I wanted to," she said. "I wanted to so much. But Sweeney was on my tail, and I was terrified of leading him there, of what he'd do to my mother and the village. Nowhere was safe. And then I just got used to running. People think Sweeney is defeated just because he's out of sight. But he's not, and I know what he can do. And as long as I have that spellbook, he'll never rest until he's tracked me down."

There was a long silence.

"I want to help you," Zeb said at last. "I really do. But I honestly don't know what I can do, apart from contacting your mother."

"No!" Sara said. "Leave her out of this. Sweeney will hurt her as leverage against me. I don't know why he hasn't already. I'll go home once the book's destroyed. That's where you come in."

"What do you mean? I don't know anything about destroying spellbooks."

"You don't need to. I just need you to do it for me."

Zeb frowned in confusion. "Why?"

Sara stretched, rolling her shoulders as if to rid herself of a headache. "The thing about powerful spellbooks like this is that they're not just words on pages," she said. "They're sentient, in a way. They protect themselves by binding their owners to them. If you own one of these books, you physically can't destroy it, no matter how much you might want to. And when I stole the book from Sweeney, it decided that I was its new owner. So you see the difficulty I'm in."

"So you want me to destroy it on your behalf?"

She nodded.

"All right then," Zeb said, rubbing his hands. "Let's get on with it. Where is it?" He took the poker from beside the fire and stoked the logs, sending sparks cascading up the chimney.

Sara looked from him to the fire and back again. "If only it were that easy," she said. "Spellbooks can't be destroyed by normal means. You can't burn it, or chop it into pieces or anything like that."

Zeb raised an eyebrow, and Sara stood up. She touched one of the bricks to the side of the fireplace, which warped and melted away, revealing a cupboard-like space within. Removing an ordinary-looking, leather-bound volume, she handed it to Zeb.

"Go on," she said. "Try if you like. See for yourself."

Zeb took the book and threw it into the hottest part of the fire. The flames flared and then died back into a cheerful blaze, but the book remained untouched. Sara let it sit there for a few minutes then pulled it out with the fire tongs. She grabbed the spine with her bare hands and passed it back to Zeb.

"It's all right," she said. "It's quite cool." And indeed it was.

"So how do we destroy it, then?" Zeb asked.

"Good question. There's only one way I can think of."

"Enlighten me."

"All spellbooks—at least, the powerful ones—are made of paper that's created using branches from the Tree of Knowledge. The only way I know of to properly destroy a spellbook is to return it to whence it came by burying it among the roots of the Tree."

"And where's this Tree?"

"Across the river."

"So why aren't you over there?"

"Not much point without someone to destroy it for me."

Zeb sighed. "All right," he said. "I'll come with you to find the Tree. But after we're done, you must go home to your mother. You have to let her know you're all right."

Sara nodded.

"Well then," Zeb said, rising. "I need to go and collect Milly and my caravan. We'll slow you down, but that can't be helped."

"No, you won't," Sara said as they walked towards the door. "You can travel with me. You'll see. If you go back out to the road, you'll be able to find the way into this clearing."

Zeb set a brisk pace back through the woods, and with every step he took away from the cottage, his doubts grew. What had he got himself into now? If Sara had been anyone but Marley's daughter he would have run away as fast as he could, but he'd made a promise and he intended to keep it. And if it also involved thwarting the man who'd caused so much destruction and heartache, then so much the better. Zeb still remembered the circus's first tour back through the province after the end of the war: the sight of burned villages and their shell-shocked inhabitants scratching out an existence in the rubble was something that would never leave him.

Soon the trees began to thin and he glimpsed the blue and gold of his caravan through the waving green leaves. Milly, thankfully, was just where he'd left her, grazing peacefully. She looked up when she heard him and gave a whicker of welcome. Zeb walked over and rubbed her nose affectionately.

"We're going on a bit of an adventure, old girl," he said as he harnessed her to the van. "You have no idea what you're in for."

He returned to the road as Sara had instructed, going back the way he'd come. Even though he was looking closely for a way into the clearing, he almost missed it and had to pull Milly up hard.

"Sorry, old girl," he murmured as they turned onto a rough path through the trees. Zeb was just beginning to wonder if they'd come to the wrong spot when he saw the cottage rising up before him. He frowned; it looked different from when he'd left it. The front was more or less the same, but now there was what looked like a sort of stable attached to the back. Sara appeared at the door and waved at him to go around the side of the house. She met him there and together they backed the caravan into a compartment that appeared to have been purpose-built for it. Milly had a generously proportioned stall next to it. Both were made fully of brick, including the floor. Zeb frowned in confusion.

"Was this here the whole time?"

Sara shrugged. "Not exactly. But we needed it, and now we have it."

"I'm afraid I don't understand."

"No," she said. "Not many people do."

She turned away and, after checking Milly one last time, Zeb followed her into the cottage. It had been a while since he'd felt quite so out of his depth.

Sara had pulled out a map of the provinces and laid it on the large kitchen table.

"I assume we're making for the ferry?" Zeb asked as they pored over it, but she shook her head.

"We'll ford the river here," she said, pointing at an isolated spot a long way between villages.

"Are you sure? It could be quite deep there. Have you done this before?"

"Something similar. It'll be fine."

Zeb bit back his doubts. Sara was young enough to be his daughter, and he had a niggling feeling that he should be the one acting like a sensible adult, but all the same, she seemed to know what she was doing—at least, he hoped she did.

"All right, captain," he said, sweeping a make-believe hat from his head with a theatrical bow. "Lead on."

Sara stood at the front window of the cottage, which looked out over the clearing back towards the road. She placed a hand on the bricks lining the windowsill and took a deep breath.

"You might want to hold onto something," she said.

Zeb grabbed the edge of the brick table, which was fixed to the floor, as the house began to rumble around him. Involuntarily, he cried out.

"It's all right," Sara said, her eyes not leaving the window. "Once we get going you'll hardly feel it."

The house seemed to rise up slightly, as if on short legs, and suddenly they were moving. The gait was ungainly at first, and Zeb felt his stomach lurch, but as they gained momentum it began to smooth out and he was no longer so concerned about being tossed around the room. He hoped Milly was all right—the poor horse must be terrified.

They barrelled out of the woods and towards the road, the house shrinking and expanding around them to fit through the gaps in the trees. After a while, Zeb started to get used to the motion, and slowly loosened his grip on the table. He'd never spent much time on boats, but he supposed this was a little bit like finding one's sea legs.

"Won't people see us if we stay on the road?" he asked, slowly making his way over to where Sara was standing by the window.

"It doesn't really matter if they do," she said. "They won't believe it. Would you?"

Zeb thought back. "I *did* see you," he said. "A few nights ago, when you came crashing through the village green at the end of my show."

Sara looked sheepish. "Sorry about that," she said. "I usually avoid populated places, but one of Sweeney's thugs was on my tail. I had to shake him off." She turned and looked at Zeb. "And what did you think when you saw the house?"

"I thought I was going mad."

"Well, that rather proves my point." She turned back to the view outside the window, occasionally directing the house with a touch of her hand on the sill. Zeb didn't like to interrupt her when she was so clearly concentrating, but the questions kept bubbling up inside him. He retreated to an armchair by the fire and watched the world whizz by through the cottage windows.

"Go on, then," Sara said after some time.

"Go on, what?"

"Ask your questions."

"How do you know I have any?"

She turned round to look at him and raised an eyebrow. "If you don't, you're the least-curious person I've ever met. Most people would have passed out by now with the shock of it all."

"It's not the strangest thing I've seen."

"I find that hard to believe."

Zeb thought of Stanley. "Perhaps, but it's true." Then he relented. "All right. Tell me how you do it. You said you built the house?"

"It's a form of Architecture," Sara said. "It runs in my family, but it comes out slightly differently in each person. My great-grandmother built parts of Guildthorpe, but she also created some of the first golems. My mother, as far as I know, has always just done basic work in the village. But I learned how to combine the two things, and this is the result."

"So the house is essentially a golem? With a...what do you call it? A *shem*?"

Sara frowned. "How do you know about that?"

"Your mother told me. Stanley had one."

"Interesting," she said. "I'd never have thought of animating a toy in that way. We'll have to talk more about that later." She turned back to the window. "Just let me get us over the river first."

Up until then, Zeb had recognised the odd landmark as it had gone sweeping past, but now they turned away from the main road, down a lesser-used track. He was amazed at the house's speed; they'd already covered a swathe of ground that would have taken him the better part of a day in the caravan. He wasn't sure exactly where they were, but at this rate they'd probably be across the river before nightfall, even with the late start. He relaxed back into the chair, and before he knew it the rhythm of the house had lulled him into a doze.

He awoke with a start sometime later, feeling that something had changed, and it took him a few seconds to realise that the house had stopped. He wasn't sure how long he'd been asleep, but the light slanting through the windows had taken on the deeper gold of late afternoon, so it must have been a couple of hours at least. He looked around for Sara and found her in the kitchen.

"Why have we stopped?" he asked, stretching.

"We're at the river," she said, "and I need a break. Unfortunately I haven't figured out a way to make the house travel of its own accord—I have to be directing it the whole time. Besides, I thought you might like to see how we're going to get across."

"Indeed I would. But I want to check on Milly first."

"Of course."

He approached the stable with some trepidation, but to his relief he found Milly standing quite contentedly, nibbling at the hay he'd left for her. She seemed completely unbothered by the strange events of the day. The caravan hadn't fared quite so well—things had jumped off the shelves with the house's motion, but nothing was broken. He took a moment to enjoy the sunshine and stretch, gazing out across the river. It was narrower here than the crossing near Hamsby, but he still couldn't envisage how they were going to ford it. It was an isolated stretch, with no sign of a ferry or any other people.

The front door opened, and Sara peered out.

"There you are," she said. "Are you ready to go? I want to get us across before dark."

Zeb nodded and returned to the house. He stood with Sara at the window as they slowly began to move, inching down the bank towards the water.

"Hold onto something," she said. "It'll be a bit rough for a few minutes."

Zeb grabbed onto the windowsill as the house began to reshape itself around them. The dimensions of the room began to shift, narrowing as bricks moved forward. Zeb jumped as the roof split open, peeling apart like a banana skin, the bricks folding downward and leaving them open to the breeze. Sara glanced across at him.

"Sit down," she said. "You look a bit green. Just close your eyes. It'll be over soon."

Zeb sank to the floor beside the window and buried his head in his hands. The motion became easier to bear with the loss of sight. He stayed there until the lurching subsided, leaving only a gentle bobbing sensation.

"All done," Sara said, and he looked up.

It took him a moment to get his bearings, for the house as he knew it had completely changed. In fact, it was no longer a house at all—he and Sara were now standing on the poop deck of a ship, bobbing gently in the water. Zeb blinked.

"What about Milly?" he asked. His thoughts felt thick.

"She's in the hold, along with the caravan," Sara said. "There's no need to worry."

"And...it floats?" He was still having difficulty coming to terms with a ship made of brick.

"Of course. As long as I'm here, anyway. Shall we get moving?"

Zeb nodded, gripping the deck railing tightly, as if doing so would somehow save them from sinking. The ship had two masts but no sails, and Zeb suspected they were just for show, for a vessel propelled by magic had no need of wind power. There was a steering column but no wheel; Sara simply laid her hands on it and the ship began to move.

They didn't move as fast as the house did on land, but even so, Zeb could tell they'd easily outstrip the ferry. After a few minutes, when it became clear that the ship was in fact buoyant despite its odd construction, he began to relax and enjoy the crossing. It seemed almost no time at all before they were nearing the opposite bank.

"Here we go again," Sara said. Zeb was prepared this time for the terrible lurching, but even so, he found it far more comfortable not to look. When he finally opened his eyes, he was once again back in the cosy living room, as if he'd never been anywhere else. He was beginning to feel like he was caught in a strange dream.

The sun was getting lower now, and Zeb remembered that they had very little left in the way of supplies. "Is there a town nearby?" he asked.

Sara shrugged. "A few villages. Why?"

"I don't know about you, but I'd quite like to eat tonight. And we'll need to get food for the rest of the journey. If we stop for the night not too far from a village, we can take the caravan. It's less...obtrusive."

Sara looked for a minute like she was going to protest, then she nodded.

"All right. I don't like to travel at night anyhow if I can avoid it—it's too hard to see where I'm going."

A short way from the riverbank the woods grew up again, and Sara began to steer them skilfully through the trees. At last they came to a promising-looking clearing, and the house ground to a halt. She pulled out a map and laid it on the table.

"It's hard to be precise," she said, "but I think we're about here." She pointed to a space in the forest. "So that puts us about two miles from this village, here."

"And the Tree of Knowledge?"

She sighed. "That's not quite so easy. It doesn't appear on any map that I know of. It's somewhere in this forest, but that stretches for miles."

"So how do you propose we find it?"

Sara pulled out the spellbook again. "Feel this," she said, patting the cover. Zeb laid his hand on it and was surprised by how warm it was.

"It's hot," he said.

"The theory goes that it gets hotter the closer it gets to the Tree," she said. "Something about like returning to like. It's a woefully imprecise way of navigating, but it's the best we've got."

It would be like looking for a needle in a haystack, Zeb reflected. At this rate, it could take them months. As he went to the stable to get the caravan ready and harness Milly, he resolved to ask some discreet questions in the village.

The village was one of the smallest he'd encountered for a long time; it was little more than a pub, a green and an all-purpose store, and as far as he could tell, it didn't even have a name. They pulled up in front of the shop just as a rotund woman with rosy cheeks and curly brown hair was turning the sign from 'open' to 'closed'.

Sara leapt down from the caravan as Zeb's heart sank.

"Excuse me," she said, "but we were hoping to buy some supplies. Are we too late?"

The woman looked them up and down, taking in the blue caravan with its shining gold letters.

"You're not from round here," she said. Zeb had to stop himself from rolling his eyes, but Sara took it in her stride.

"No indeed," she said, her voice and manner making her seem younger and more innocent than she was. "We've been on the road a goodly time, ma'am, and if we can't replenish our stores we'll be making a hungry few days of it."

The woman softened. "Well now, love, we can't have that, can we?" she said, although privately Zeb wondered whether it was compassion or the prospect of a large sale that motivated her. Either way, he reflected as she held the door open for them, you couldn't argue with the result.

Soon they were well-stocked with bread, cheese, salted meats and even some precious fresh vegetables.

"Won't you stop for a meal in the pub?" the shop owner asked as she finalised the sale—Zeb suspected she'd overcharged them, but there was really nothing to be done about it. "They do the best corn chowder for fifty miles." Sara seemed ready to refuse, but Zeb shot her a look. He was suddenly hankering after a hot meal that he didn't have to cook.

"All right," Sara said. "We can't stay too long, though."

Most of the village's population seemed to have converged on the pub, and the atmosphere was noisy and close. The chowder was indeed excellent, as was the cider, and as they sat among the locals at one of the large communal tables, Zeb felt warm and content.

"What brings you here?" asked an old man to Zeb's left. Sara caught his eye, as if warning him to be careful, but her attention was quickly taken by two women sitting across from her.

"We have a small travelling show," Zeb said, deciding to stick close to the truth.

"Not one of them magicians, are you?"

"No," Zeb said hastily. "Just tricks and showmanship." Then he thought for a moment. "Do you get a lot of magicians through here?"

The man shrugged. "Not as many as we used to. They were a dime a dozen there for a while, what with everything that was going on across the river. We seemed to be on the road to one of their meeting places or something." He made the ward sign of protection. "I never asked too many questions. Some things it's better not to know."

"Aye," another man cut in from across the table, overhearing. "Remember young Toby Whatsit?"

"Jenkins?"

"That's right, Jenkins. He found out more than were good for him."

The two of them chuckled mirthlessly.

"He were too curious about them magicians," the first man said. "So he followed one of their caravans one night. But they found him, took him with them to wherever they were going, and then brought him back as a warning. He ain't spoken a word since."

"That's him over there," the second man said. "Poor beggar." He gestured to a tow-haired young man sitting alone at a small table in the corner, nursing an empty glass.

The conversation moved on to other things, and Zeb nodded along until he was able to excuse himself on the pretext of getting another drink. At the bar he bought two glasses of beer, then carried them over to the young man's table.

"Hello," he said, setting one down in front of him. "I'm Zeb." He held out his hand and the young man shook it, appraising him with bright blue eyes. He pulled out a pad of paper and a pencil from the pocket of his shirt.

Toby, he wrote.

"Nice to meet you, Toby. Mind if I join you?"

Toby nodded, still with a slightly suspicious air, as if he wasn't used to being noticed. But if there was one thing that his time in the circus had taught Zeb, it was how to talk to people. Over the years he'd met every conceivable type of person—young and old, bold and shy—and he'd concluded that, deep down, everyone just wanted to be heard.

It took a while to warm Toby up to conversation, for he seemed unused to it, but once he got going the words began to spill forth. Eventually, after an hour or so, Zeb slowly began to steer things towards the magicians and what had happened to him the night he'd lost his voice.

I don't know where they took me, Toby wrote. *It was beyond the edge of the forest, I think, or maybe just a big clearing. There was an enormous tree. They made me carry something to it—some sort of parcel. Then it was like the world exploded.*

"Why did they take your voice?" Zeb asked.

They thought I was unconscious, Toby wrote, *but I could hear them. One of them said they didn't have to worry because I wouldn't even remember my own name. Then the other one said he wanted to make sure I couldn't speak of it, just in case. Plus he wanted to warn other people not to be so nosey. When I woke up, I couldn't speak, but I did remember. And they were so arrogant, they didn't think to test my recollection, and they never thought I'd be able to communicate any other way.*

Zeb pulled out his pocket map. It wasn't as good as Sara's big one, but it would have to do.

"Can you show me the way they went, before they caught you?"

Toby traced a line eastward with his finger, following the road, then stopped.

"That was where they caught you?"

He nodded.

"And you don't know which way you went after that?"

He shook his head. *They drugged me.*

"Thank you," Zeb said, shaking his hand. "You've been very helpful."

What do you want to know for?

"Oh, nothing special," Zeb said hastily. "I'm trying to write a history of the area and I'm interested in any unusual stories or happenings."

Toby shrugged, seeming to accept the lie. *Another beer?*

"Of course," Zeb said, standing up.

Sara cornered him as he was threading his way back from the bar, drinks in hand. "Making friends, I see?"

"Gathering information."

A look of horror crossed her face. "What have you been saying?"

"Nothing to worry about. Don't look at me like that."

"We have to go. Now."

"I just have to deliver this." Ignoring her protestations, he took the beer to Toby, who was now deep in conversation with another man in a dark travelling cloak. He raised his hand in thanks.

"I have to go," Zeb said, nodding towards Sara. "My friend is getting tired. It was nice to meet you." Toby nodded, smiling, then turned back to his companion. For someone who had appeared to be such a loner, he now seemed rather popular. The thought made Zeb uneasy, although he couldn't say why.

"What did you tell him?" Sara asked as they drove back to the house. The night air was cool, and she wrapped her arms across her chest, scowling.

"Nothing," Zeb said, wondering why she was so defensive. "I asked more than I told. And I think I know where to find the Tree."

Sara glanced around, as if worried they were being followed. "Let's not discuss that here," she said, quickening her pace. Zeb shrugged, but followed her.

When they were safely back inside the house, she turned to him. "Well, what have you found out?"

"Oh, so now you want to know?"

She rolled her eyes. "I still think it was a stupid risk. But it's done now, and hopefully you've got something useful for it."

"As a matter of fact, I think I have." He spread open the large map on the table. "This is where the magicians picked Toby up," he said, pointing. "He doesn't know where they went from there, but he remembers it being in a large field or clearing, perhaps near the edge of the forest. So if they continued in roughly the same direction, that would put the Tree somewhere around here." He traced a loop on the map with his finger. "What do you think?"

Sara stared at the map for a long moment. "It's awfully vague," she said at last, "but it's still the best clue we've got. Get some sleep. We'll leave at dawn."

Some hours later, in the deep watches of the night, Zeb was woken by a faint cracking noise. For a moment he lay there, wondering if he'd imagined it, but then he heard it again. It wasn't an animal; it was more like footsteps, like someone trying to be quiet amid the dry undergrowth.

Zeb bounded out of bed, pulling on a shirt and breeches. He didn't light a lamp for fear of the light showing through the windows, but crept through the kitchen and tapped on Sara's bedroom door. When there was no response, he opened it, approached the bed and shook her shoulder.

"Sara!" he hissed. "Wake up!" She moved faster than he would have thought possible, and suddenly there was a knife at his throat.

"It's all right!" he gasped. "It's me—Zeb! "

"What in the blazes are you doing?"

"I heard someone outside."

"You're sure it wasn't a nightmare?"

"Positive. Listen." They held their breath and, sure enough, the faint cracking came again. Then the front door rattled, as if someone was trying the lock.

Sara leapt up. "Right," she said. "Time to go." Flinging a shawl over her nightdress, she hurried to the living room, the house stirring around her.

"If we run, they'll know we're onto them," Zeb cautioned.

Sara shook her head. "We don't know how many of them there are," she said. "Better to run than to lie here waiting to be murdered in our beds."

Zeb couldn't argue with that. The house rumbled to life, and he instinctively grabbed onto the table as they pitched forward, faster than they'd ever gone before. There was a scream from outside and the house shuddered, as if it had run over something large. Zeb stared at Sara in horror, but her face was impassive.

"You don't want to know what they'll do to us if they catch us," was all she said.

Zeb swallowed and said nothing.

The house continued its headlong dash through the forest, so fast that a number of times he feared they'd crash. Trees reared up alarmingly before the window, ghostly in the moonlight, only to disappear again as the house swerved around or ducked between them.

The night seemed interminable, but eventually the first fingers of dawn light crept over the forest, and Sara finally allowed the house to slow down. Zeb could see that the trees had thinned out a lot—they seemed to have come to the very edge of the woods.

"Where are we?" he asked—the first words either of them had spoken for hours.

"I'm not exactly sure," Sara said, "but we should be about here." She pointed to a place on the pocket map that was lying on the windowsill. It wasn't far from where they'd guessed the Tree of Knowledge must be.

"Cup of tea?" Zeb asked, for her eyes were dark-rimmed and she was swaying where she stood.

Sara smiled tiredly. "Thanks. I think we've shaken them off for now." The house slowed then stopped, and she collapsed into an armchair.

"What happened back there?" Zeb asked, filling the kettle from the water barrel and setting it to boil over the fire. "Who were those people?"

Sara shrugged. "Magicians' goons," she said. "My best guess is your mate Toby put two and two together and sold us down the river."

Zeb felt a dull flush creep up his cheeks. He'd thought he'd been so clever, getting the Tree's location out of Toby, but the lad had been a spy all along. And they'd very nearly paid an enormous price for his foolishness.

"I'm sorry," he said.

Sara sighed. "It's not your fault," she said. "This is what magicians do. They deceive and corrupt people. They would have tracked us down sooner or later."

"Do you think we've lost them?"

"Maybe, but not for long. They know where we're going now, and unlike us, they know where the Tree actually is. So I wouldn't be surprised if they get there before us, although we did slow them down a bit."

"So we'd better keep going, then?" Zeb asked as he poured the tea.

Sara nodded, accepting the cup he handed her. "Afraid so. And we'd better hope we find it soon."

Since they only had Toby's description to go on—that the Tree was somewhere near the eaves of the forest—Sara decided that the easiest way was to simply travel along the edge of the wood until they found it. Zeb declined to point out a whole host of potential problems: they didn't know they were even travelling in the right direction; judging by the map, the wood seemed to stretch on for miles and miles; and Toby had also said it could have been a large clearing, meaning they might be looking in the wrong place altogether. But he bit his tongue and trusted in Sara's intuition. She seemed certain they were going the right way, and he could only hope her confidence wasn't misplaced.

Lunchtime came and went with no sign of the Tree, and as the afternoon wore on, Zeb began to get increasingly anxious. Sara was unusually quiet, staring fixedly out the window, the tightness of her mouth betraying the immense strain she was under. She'd stopped briefly to eat and change out of her nightgown, but that had been some hours ago, and Zeb was beginning to worry that she might collapse from exhaustion.

He'd begun to give it all up for lost when he noticed Sara peering intently through the window; at the same time, the house began to slow down.

"What is it?" he asked, but she didn't answer, just pointed straight ahead. Zeb followed her hand and saw an enormous tree rising up before them. It shimmered like a mirage in the dawn light, and he got the eerie feeling that if he took his eyes off it he'd turn back and find it had vanished.

"Is that it?" he murmured. Sara nodded. The house shuddered to a stop, and all was silent. After a long minute she turned away from the window and gathered up the spellbook.

"Come on," she said, handing it to Zeb. "It's time."

He took hold of the book reluctantly, feeling it thrumming in his fingers; it was almost like it knew the end was nigh, he thought. Slowly, he opened the door and stepped out into the clearing, Sara following.

The Tree loomed up before them, majestic and impossible. It was like nothing Zeb had ever seen: it appeared at once both immense and insubstantial, as if it had been growing for thousands of years yet was barely there at all. The area where the trunk met the ground shimmered and shone such that it was impossible to tell where earth ended and tree began. Other trees straggled out from the edge of the forest to meet it, but they seemed small and dingy by comparison, like pale shadows.

"Go on!" Sara hissed. Zeb took a deep breath and gripped the spellbook tighter. He was torn between a powerful attraction to the tree and an equally powerful repulsion. Just making his feet move forward took an incredible act of willpower, but eventually they obeyed him and he inched, step by careful step, towards the magnificence.

He was perhaps halfway across the clearing when a sudden noise made him turn. From under the eaves of the wood figures were springing, lunging towards Sara, then turning towards him as the realisation hit them.

"Zeb!" Sara screamed. "Run!" He tried with every fibre of his being to obey, willing his legs to carry him forward. The spellbook was a dead weight in his arms, anchoring him to the earth. He could hear the ragged breathing of one of his pursuers behind him, then a shout of glee as the man reached out to snatch his prey. The laugh reminded Zeb so much of Stanley that a jolt of fear ran through him, electrifying his limbs and pushing him forward in a way that no logical thought could have. He slipped free of his pursuer's grasp and, oblivious to the straining of his muscles and the thundering of the blood in his ears, dashed onwards until the Tree loomed up before him.

Stepping beneath its canopy was like stepping out of the world. Instantly Zeb was enveloped in a feeling of great peace. The leaves of the tree fluttered high above him, not just green, but the pink and orange and gold of the sunrise, and a thousand other colours he couldn't name. The Tree itself was enormous; by Zeb's estimation it would take twenty men with their arms outstretched to reach around its girth. Its roots rose up above his head, the spaces between them like great canyons. Gingerly he began to walk down one of the root canyons, the feathery leaves dancing high above.

The spellbook no longer felt heavy in his arms, but it had begun to thrum more strongly, like a longing heartbeat, as if the Tree itself was calling to it. He could no longer see or hear his pursuer, and he found his fear had also vanished. Somehow, he knew that while he held this book in this place, nothing could hurt him.

The canyon seemed to grow longer even as he walked it, and he began to wonder if he'd ever get to the end. At last, however, the great trunk reared up before him. Zeb paused, unsure of what to do next. He felt like there should be some sort of ceremony, or that he should say something, but nothing sprang to mind. After a few moments of indecision, he laid the book in a divot where the roots met the trunk.

"I believe this is yours," he said, blushing at the utter inadequacy of the words. For a long minute nothing happened. Then, slowly, the book began to smoulder, although there was no smell of smoke and no flame. An ether arose from its pages, resolving itself into shapes. Zeb watched in awe as figures appeared in the air before him, acting out a silent pantomime before fading like mist before the sun. Gradually it came to him—this was no ordinary spellbook, a simple collection of magic recipes. This was a storybook, a record of magic across the ages, and these people had lived and breathed it, and in many cases died with or from it. Some of the fleeting stories fluttering before him told of deaths so gruesome he had to look away, or of lives altered beyond recognition, but there was also beauty in it. For the first time, he truly grasped the magnitude of what he'd done, and with it came a sense of loss that tore at his chest and bathed his cheeks with tears. Hugo Sweeney and his ilk had used their knowledge for ill, to be sure, and many of the most painful stories now enacting their final telling before him were due to the rogue magician. But was that enough of a reason to also lose thousands of years of history and advances in knowledge? Was not mankind greater, and the world ultimately better off, as a result of the learning that was vanishing before his eyes?

It was far too late now, and he cursed himself for not thinking things through. He wondered if Sara truly had any inkling of what she'd asked him to do. There was a reason, he now understood, why the spellbook bonded so tightly to its owner. But whoever had set its charms had failed to consider the power of persuasion. It had been so easy for her to convince him, a simple conjurer who knew nothing of great magic except the suffering it had caused people like him. And maybe, after all, it had been the right decision, for what untold chaos would have ensued had the last desperate magicians got hold of such power?

All this flashed through his mind in the blink of an eye. The stories around him whirled faster and faster, making his head spin. He clutched at his eyes, dropping to his knees to try to stop the roiling in his stomach. Then the world went white and he remembered nothing more.

WHEN HE WOKE, HE WAS in his own familiar bed in his caravan. The dim grey twilight of evening seeped through the windows, alighting on objects as well-known as old friends. Zeb propped himself onto his elbows and glanced around, becoming aware as he did so of a pounding in his head. Sara was sitting at the tiny table beneath the window, and appeared to have been there for some time.

"What time is it?" he asked.

"Oh, hello," she said. "It's five o'clock in the evening. You've been out for nearly a whole day."

"What happened? How did I get here?" He remembered the pursuit, and placing the book beneath the tree, and the ghost-like figures that had emerged from it, but he had no recollection of anything else, including what had happened to the men chasing him, or how he'd managed to end up back in his own van.

"It was extraordinary," Sara said, her voice still carrying a hint of awe. "The whole tree lit up—I can't even begin to describe it. Then there was a massive bang—no, more of a *whump*, really—and light radiated out from it like some sort of blast. I was outside its range, but the men who got caught in it...well, it didn't end well for them."

Her face fell.

"For a moment I thought you were dead too. But when the blast cleared, I saw you lying there at the foot of the tree. I knew I couldn't carry you far, so I got Milly and we brought the caravan to you, and brought you back to the house that way. And here we are."

"Where's the Tree?"

"Come and see."

Slowly Zeb swung his feet out of bed, cautiously at first but with growing confidence as he realised his knees wouldn't buckle beneath him. Sara helped him to the caravan's door and together they stood on the top step and looked out. There was a tree there, certainly, but it looked like nothing more than a majestic ancient oak—impressive, but not that out of the ordinary. The gargantuan glowing spectacle that he remembered was gone. He turned to Sara, frowning.

"I know," she said, pre-empting his question. "It's bizarre, isn't it? My theory is that it only shows its true self when the right kind of magic is present."

Zeb shrugged; it was as good an explanation as any.

"What will you do now?" he asked. He was having a hard time meeting her eyes; what he'd seen at the Tree had changed him, and he still wasn't sure if they'd done the right thing. So much irreplaceable knowledge had been lost.

Sara stared into the distance for a long moment, then she shrugged.

"I suppose it's time to go home."

The White Sheep
of the Family

S ara sighed as she followed the path back through the woods. The setting sun arced through the trees, dappling the undergrowth with flecks of gold, but she was immune to its beauty, lost in her thoughts. Her mother had said to be home for supper, so home she was reluctantly going. It had only been a month, but the place that she'd dreamed of almost constantly for eight long years was already stifling her.

Going home had seemed like such a simple concept when its likelihood had been remote. She and her mother would rush joyfully into each other's arms, and things would go back to the way they'd always been, only better.

The reality had been rather more complicated. After destroying Hugo Sweeney's spellbook, she'd taken her enchanted golem house and returned to Guildthorpe, albeit setting a slower pace than her usual breakneck dash. Before they'd parted ways, Zeb had said he'd get a message to her mother, but he'd warned her that it was entirely possible Sara would reach Guildthorpe first.

As it had turned out, this was what had happened. There was no spare key to Marley's cottage that she could find, despite looking in all the usual places and a few unusual ones as well, so in the end she simply transformed her house into a long brick snake, slithered it through the front garden and rebuilt it out the back, in the flat clearing just above the model village.

She knew her presence wouldn't remain secret for long and, sure enough, the following morning brought a visit from old George the innkeeper. His reaction was everything she'd hoped for—he nearly fainted when he saw her—and she began to think that everything would be all right after all.

She was there alone for a week before her mother returned. Early one morning she heard the gate clink, and emerged into the half-light to find Marley standing in the garden, staring open-mouthed at the golem house. Sara stepped out of the front door feeling suddenly shy, anxiety writhing like a snake in her belly. What if her mother wasn't happy to see her? What if she didn't recognise her? But Marley had tears pouring unchecked down her cheeks.

"My darling," she gasped. "My darling, is it really you?"

"It's me, Mama," Sara said. "I'm home."

Marley rushed across the lawn and gathered her into an embrace so fierce that Sara felt the breath whoosh out of her. They held each other for a long time, trying to make up for the lost years. Her mother smelled just the same, Sara realised—like sawdust and wildflowers—and she felt a surge of relief that this, at least, hadn't changed.

Later, the questions had started. Her mother wanted to know everything, from what had happened after she'd been taken, to how she'd built the golem house, to the adventure with Zeb that had finally brought her home. Sara found many of them difficult to answer, and evaded as best she could without it seeming obvious. She wondered a bit at her own hesitation—after all, didn't she want Marley to know what had happened to her, and how much she'd changed? But hanging over it all was her own single burning question: *Why didn't you come looking for me sooner?* She couldn't voice it, for she knew the pain it would cause her mother, and so it hung unspoken, like a pall of smoke over their happy reunion.

While she was captive, Sara had never allowed herself to dream too much about what returning home would be like; it was too painful. And after she finally escaped, day-to-day life on the run was so all-consuming that she didn't have the luxury of wondering. The prospect had always hung before her like a tantalising golden vision of the future that one might find at the end of a fairy tale: *and they all lived happily ever after*. But really, the endings of those adventure stories always remained pleasingly vague: the heroine went out into the world, saved the prince, saved her country, saved herself, and then...what?

Her first week at home was by turns wonderful and excruciating. She'd been a little girl when she was snatched away; now she was a young woman, used to surviving on her own, with thoughts and dreams and opinions that her mother had no frame of reference for. And Marley had changed too. A name kept coming up in her conversation—Sturm, who, she told Sara, was one of the mysterious Weathermen twins who had helped her start her search. She always referred to him as a friend, forgetting that Sara was no longer ten years old. In this house where every corner held a memory of her beloved father, hearing her mother talk with such affection in her voice about another man was jarring. But Sara bit her tongue, trying to be grateful for Marley's happiness.

She was jolted back to the present as the toe of her boot stubbed against a tree root. Below her lay the valley, Guildthorpe nestled in its heart like a collection of toy houses. The setting sun washed the scene in shades of gold and red; it was the very picture of pastoral perfection. Sara knew that many people would give their eye teeth for the privilege of waking up to such a view each morning, but the thought of never seeing another horizon filled her with despair.

The twilight was deepening by the time she made her way through the woods behind the model village and in at the garden gate. Her mother was in her workshop, building toys rather than houses, Sara was glad to see. Old George had told her about Marley's stint of rather heavy-handed Architecture, but since she'd come home her mother hadn't made a single building—much to the villagers' relief, Sara suspected.

"Ah, there you are, love," Marley said, looking up with a smile. "Just in time. Come inside and help me get supper ready."

Sara felt a flash of irritation; she would have spent longer outdoors if she'd known her mother would still be working. But she tamped it down. Her mother was trying hard, she knew. She had a feeling that was half the problem.

"Where did you go today?" Marley asked as they sat down to a simple supper of cold cuts and salad.

Sara shrugged. "Here and there." It was true—she'd just wandered wherever the mood took her through the woods and hills. After so long on the road, she couldn't bear to be cooped up. The autumn was on the verge of giving way to winter, and there was a stark beauty to the last of the dying leaves.

"Have you given any thought to what you're going to do now you're back?" Marley asked, taking a sip of water. "Long-term, I mean. You could learn a trade."

There was a ring of hope in her voice that Sara knew meant, *You could learn* my *trade*. But the thought of being an Architect, or even a toymaker, left her cold. She didn't want to spend the rest of her life stuck in Guildthorpe, slowly destroying and rebuilding a ridiculous little dot of a village that was of no consequence to anyone except those who lived there. Couldn't her mother understand that? Marley wasn't entirely unworldly herself, and she couldn't comprehend how, after seeing all the wonders of the world outside, her mother could be happy stuck in such an out-of-the-way place where nothing interesting ever happened. Sara was too young to have discovered the comforts of smallness and predictability.

"I know you haven't been home that long," Marley pressed, "but you can't just waste your days forever."

Sara rolled her eyes. "What makes you think I'm wasting them?" Anyone who knew her better would have been able to tell from her tone that they were on dangerous ground, but Marley was oblivious—a mark, Sara thought, of how much her mother still saw her as a child.

"Everyone needs a purpose and a skill," Marley said. "If you want to develop your magic, there are people I can speak to about training you…"

"I don't want to develop my magic!" Sara snapped. "Why can't you just leave me be?" She shoved her chair back and stormed out, slamming the door behind her. Not until she was out in the garden did she pause to dash the hot tears from her eyes.

More and more, she was becoming convinced that magic was a curse. It was magic that had torn her from her family in the first place; magic that had forced her to run for so many years; and magic that had very nearly been her undoing at the Tree of Knowledge. She didn't want to cultivate it—if she could have found a way to excise it from herself like a cancer, she would have. But she had no way of explaining this to her mother.

She stayed out until it was fully dark, then snuck back in. Marley was in the sitting room, and she looked up at the sound of the door, but didn't call out or make any move towards her. Standing in the darkened hall, Sara wasn't sure if she wanted her to or not. She hurried upstairs and threw herself into bed, then read until she fell asleep.

The next few days passed in an uneasy truce. Neither of them mentioned the fight or what might have been underpinning it. Sara spent as long as she could each day out of doors, and the two of them generally avoided each other as much as possible, save awkward small talk over meals.

It was at supper on the third day that Marley finally broke the silence. "Would you be upset if I went away for a little while?" she asked.

Sara shrugged. "How long is a little while?"

"Just a week."

"Fine."

"I won't go if you need or want me here. I just thought we could both do with some breathing space."

"Doesn't worry me," Sara said, although in truth she did feel a little abandoned. "Where are you going?"

"To visit a friend."

"Not...Sturm?" She didn't know exactly what had happened between Marley and Sturm, but she could tell from the glow in her mother's eyes and the flush in her cheeks that feelings were running higher than just a simple friendship. Her warring emotions rose up once again within her. On the one hand, Sara was happy for her—it had been many years since her father's death, and Marley deserved to be happy—but on the other, she couldn't quite condone her mother taking up with someone so obviously magical. That way lay only trouble.

"Yes, actually." Marley was challenging her to say something, so Sara bit her tongue and just shrugged again.

"I'll be fine. Stay as long as you want."

MARLEY LEFT EARLY THE next morning, and Sara couldn't help feeling a rush of relief, followed by a surge of guilt. She loved her mother dearly—far more than she showed—and had missed her terribly every single day they'd been apart. But the tension of the last few weeks had become so suffocating that it was like a great weight had lifted.

She ate some breakfast and tidied up, then wandered around the house aimlessly, unsure of what to do with herself. Eventually she did what she'd been doing almost every day since she got home—pulled on her boots and cloak, threw some food into her satchel, shut up the house and went through the little gate at the bottom of the garden into the woods beyond.

Sara had grown up roaming the woods and fields around Guildthorpe with her father, and they were as comfortable and familiar to her as her own back garden. As usual, she walked without any specific destination in mind, just going where the mood took her.

After some time, she left the shelter of the trees and followed a footpath across the fields. The sun was fully risen now, and the day was beginning to warm up. Birds flitted between the bare branches, untroubled by her passing. In the distance, a herd of cows grazed contentedly. Sara inhaled deeply, breathing in the crisp air, feeling the knots in her shoulders begin to loosen. It was good to be out and about again.

The ground began to slope upwards and she leaned into the hill, concentrating on keeping her footing on the rough path, which was now little more than a sheep track. Pausing beside a boulder, she looked back the way she'd come, seeing the dark band of woods stretched out beneath her and, down in the valley, the roofs of Guildthorpe like tiny brown dots. From up here it looked just like her mother's model village.

Her attention was drawn back towards the hill by a shout.

"Hello there!"

Sara turned and saw a young shepherd, about her age, walking expertly along the side of the hill, his sheep fanning out around him. Her face brightened, for this was Tom Brewster, the only person she really counted as a friend, and she'd come this way in the hope of meeting him.

"Morning," she said, scrambling up towards him. "How's things?"

Tom shrugged, and Sara's brow furrowed, for he didn't seem quite his usual happy self. Tom and his mother Polly lived in Guildthorpe, and Sara had known him since childhood. The magicians hadn't looked twice at Tom, for he hadn't a magical bone in his body. His mother was a seamstress and he never talked about his father, but Sara assumed he'd been just as ordinary. And so Tom had been left relatively unscathed by the war that had upended her life so dramatically. Sara had assumed that he'd left the village for better opportunities in a larger town, until she'd bumped into him on one of her ramblings. She would never have thought he'd become a shepherd, but Polly's eyesight had started to fade, making sewing almost impossible, and he'd had to take what work he could. And it seemed to suit him, wandering the countryside with his flock. But today something wasn't quite right.

"What's the matter?" she asked.

Tom sat down on the faded grass and she plopped down next to him. He broke off a piece and chewed it absently.

"Farmer Dawes had a letter from the Governor," he said. "The King's coming to visit."

Farmer Dawes was Tom's employer, a prosperous local farmer whose sheep, by all accounts, produced the finest wool in the land. Sara stared out across the valley, confused.

"The King's coming to Guildthorpe?"

Tom laughed. "Oh no," he said. "Why would he come here? But he's touring the province, and the Governor wants to present him with a cloak made of our wool." He looked downcast.

"But that's great news!" Sara said. "What an honour!"

Tom shook his head. "There's a problem."

"Oh?"

"She wants the cloak to be *white*."

Sara glanced at the sheep strung out around them across the hillside. Some were red, some orange, others yellow, green, blue or purple. There were even two black ones. But not a single one was white.

"Ah," she said.

"You see what I mean?" Tom said. "Where am I going to find a *white* sheep? I mean, whoever heard of such a thing?" He rubbed his face distractedly.

Sara agreed that it was a strange request, and not for the first time she wondered at the whims of powerful people. Dawes sheep were renowned not only for the softness of their wool, but also its vibrant colours. Other flocks produced insipid, pastel-coloured garments—those who could afford it wore only Dawes.

"You could dye it?" she suggested.

"*Dye* Dawes wool?" Tom said scornfully. "It would destroy everything that sets it apart. No, somehow I have to find a white sheep that produces wool as fine as ours, and I have to do it in a week! It's ridiculous!"

"When is the King coming?"

"In a month's time, but we have to leave time for the fleece to be spun and woven. I just don't see how it's possible."

Sara chewed her lip. "I'll help you," she said.

Tom's face brightened. "Will you really?"

"Of course. My mother's gone away for a week, so I've got nothing else to do. And I like a challenge." She patted his shoulder. "Don't worry. We'll figure it out."

But as the morning wore on, she became increasingly worried about how they'd manage it. She spent the day roaming the hills with Tom, and every now and again one of them would voice an idea, each madder than the last. By the time the sun began to sink over the hills and Tom gathered his flock to take them back to the safety of the farm, away from the wild foxes, they were both feeling rather flat.

"Never mind," Sara said, trying to keep her voice cheery. "It's a new day tomorrow. I'll meet you here in the morning. I'm sure we'll come up with something."

Tom nodded, but he didn't seem to share her enthusiasm. They parted ways at the bottom of the hill, Tom turning left towards the farm while Sara headed back through the woods towards Guildthorpe.

Back at the house, she lit the lamps and considered the contents of the larder, but she didn't feel much like cooking. She decided instead to go and see George at The Crossed Keys. He knew everyone and everything in Guildthorpe and the surrounding countryside. If anyone could tell her where to find a white sheep, he could.

She arrived right in the middle of the evening meal service, and the place was bustling. She pulled up a stool at the bar, and Imogen, the barmaid, brought her a plate of stew and a glass of cider. George was run off his feet, so Sara just ate and watched the customers. She wasn't in any hurry. She was glad that she was past the stage now where people stared at her—when she'd first got home, she couldn't come into the village without people glancing at her and whispering. She was the only one of the vanished children to have returned, and consequently all sorts of rumours had abounded. They weren't helped by the fact that neither she nor Marley would talk about what had happened, save to a few trusted friends like George. And so she'd become the local enigma. She'd wanted to stay away from the village as a result, but Marley had encouraged her to keep going.

"If they see you every day, they'll get over it faster," she'd said. And they had.

"Hello, young Sara," George said as the rush died down. "I didn't see you there. What brings you here?"

"Just wanted some company," she said. "By the way, I don't suppose you know anything about sheep?"

The conversation with George proved enlightening. There had been white sheep in the district once, he said, before they were selectively bred for their colours. It was possible some still existed, although they were very rare, which was probably why the Governor wanted one.

"I knew an old shepherd when I was a boy who still had one or two white sheep," George mused, "but I've no idea what happened to them, or to him, for that matter. I doubt he's still alive, but you never know. His name was Sam Shetland, and he lived in a little hut over the back of the hills." He shrugged. "I'm afraid that's the best I can do. Sorry I couldn't be more help." But Sara was pleased; it was a start.

THE NEXT MORNING, SHE told Tom what she'd found out.

"That's good, I guess," he said.

Sara scowled. "Do you have any better ideas?"

"No," Tom said, shaking his head. "Sorry. I didn't mean to sound dismissive. I'll have to get one of the farm lads to watch the sheep for me, and then we'll see if we can track down Mr Shetland or his descendants."

While he went back to the farm, Sara sat on the grass, idly plaiting strands of it into long chains. If Sam Shetland didn't come through for them—or if he was dead and gone—then she wasn't sure what they were going to do. And if Tom couldn't find a white sheep, Farmer Dawes would have to disappoint the Governor. Tom could very well lose his job, and Sara knew that, with his mother unable to work much, he could ill afford to.

Around lunchtime Tom returned with one of the young farm lads in tow. Sara knew there was much more to being a shepherd than just wandering after the sheep, and she hoped the boy could be trusted. But in any case, they'd be back before dark, and Tom would be able to take the flock down the hill himself.

George had given her directions, although they were drawn from decades-old memories and she had no idea how accurate his recollection was or how much the countryside might have changed. Still, it seemed straightforward enough—follow the road out past the Dawes farm, up the valley until it ended, and then continue on along the bank of the stream.

It was a lovely day for an outing—cold but clear—and Sara felt a lightness that she hadn't experienced since returning home. For a while they just walked along in silence, enjoying the sunlight and birdsong. Once they passed the farm, the road became much less busy, with only the odd cart passing them on the way to or from some of the outlying properties. They walked on the wide verge, the frost-burned grass crunching under their boots as they went.

"So your mother's gone away?" Tom asked at last.

Sara nodded, knowing what he was thinking—after such a long separation, why would Marley voluntarily leave her again?

"We needed some time apart," she said. "Things are...well, it's not how I imagined it would be."

"Life rarely is, is it?" Tom said with a little laugh, and for the first time Sara began to really wonder about him. She'd assumed that his life had been so much easier than hers, being allowed to stay with his family, but perhaps that wasn't entirely true.

She stared straight ahead to where the road vanished into the hills. "What was it like for you, during the war?" As soon as the words were out, she wished she could take them back, but it was too late.

Tom said nothing for a long moment. The only sound was the gentle thump of their footsteps and the wind rattling the last of the dying leaves.

"It was awful."

She waited for him to go on, but he didn't.

"I'll tell you about it one day," he said. "I promise. But not today."

Sara nodded, understanding. Some things were just too hard. Some needed to be worked up to. And some she would never tell another living soul.

The road was rougher now, little more than a cart track, with a strip of grass running down the middle. They were heading back into the hills, and the fields around them were becoming rockier and more heavily treed. The lush pastoral country of the dale was giving way to something harsher and less forgiving.

Presently they came to a fork. The main track bent around to the left, with a sign that proclaimed 'Hilldale Farm'. The other branch was so disused as to be almost invisible, but it continued straight up the hill.

"It must be hard work farming here," Sara said, for although she knew little of agriculture, she could tell that the rocky, undulating pastures were rough and inhospitable.

"The hardest," Tom said. "And yet somehow generations of crofters have managed to scratch a living here. But it's a tough life." He paused. "Listen," he said. "Can you hear that?"

Sara listened and, sure enough, she caught the burble of running water.

"That's the way we need to go," Tom said, gesturing to the right-hand track.

"Lead on."

The road joined the stream further up the hill, then petered out shortly afterwards. All that was left of it was a rough path that ran beside the brook, made by animals or perhaps the occasional traveller passing through. It was overgrown with bushes and brambles, the arched branches of trees forming a threadbare tunnel around them.

"Are you sure this is right?" Sara asked.

Tom shrugged. "Not really," he said. "But this is the way George said to come. I guess we'll see."

Sara couldn't imagine why anyone would want to live way out here, so far from civilisation. She was still enjoying being able to buy her food from the village store rather than having to hunt or steal it. Eight years on the run did rather alter one's perspective on these things, but then again, there was no accounting for taste.

She was just beginning to think that George had sent them on a wild goose chase when Tom, who was walking ahead of her, stopped suddenly.

"There," he whispered, pointing through the trees. Sara wasn't quite sure why he was whispering, but she let it go. In front of them was a small wooden hut, smaller even than her golem house, with rough-boarded walls and a shingled roof. She might have thought it abandoned, except for a trickle of smoke that rose from the chimney.

"Do you think that's Sam Shetland's house?" she whispered back.

"Who else's would it be?"

"You never know." There could be a hundred recluses living in these hills for all she knew. But Tom just rolled his eyes and started forward. Sara followed, feeling a twist of apprehension. A man who chose to live all alone up here couldn't be entirely normal, surely.

Tom seemed to have no such worries; he strode up to the house and knocked boldly on the door. As the sound faded away the all-encompassing silence returned, and Sara found she was holding her breath.

Tom had just turned away when the door creaked open. An old man stood there, tall and wiry, with snowy white hair that brushed his shoulders, and a beard down to his waist. He scowled at them, suspicion etched in the lines on his face.

"Who are you?"

"Good afternoon, Mr Shetland," Tom began. "My name is Tom Brewster..."

"Speak up, dammit!" The old man cocked a hand behind his ear and glared.

"My name's Tom Brewster. I'm a shepherd. I wanted to talk to you about sheep."

"You'd best be talking to Dawes down the valley. He's the one to ask about sheep." He went to close the door, but Tom reached out a hand.

"No, sir. I work for Farmer Dawes, and he can't help. I'm looking for a white sheep. I heard you might know something about them."

Sam Shetland's bushy eyebrows shot up. "A white sheep, you say?" He shook his head in disbelief. "You don't want much, do you? Why not try to find a money tree while you're at it?"

"From everything I've heard, they're much the same thing," Sara said before she could stop herself.

Sam stared at her for a long moment, then, quite unexpectedly, burst out laughing.

"That they are," he said, when he'd got his breath back. "And you are?"

"Sara Cotton. I'm a friend of Tom's."

"And why do you need a white sheep?"

"To make a cloak for the King."

"Pah." Sam spat. "What's he ever done for us?"

Sara let that go; she didn't feel up to an argument about politics.

"George Bannister at The Crossed Keys in Guildthorpe told us you once had a white sheep," she said. "It was him that told us where to find you."

The old shepherd smiled. "Ah, young George," he said. "I remember him well. Found him wandering lost on the hillside one day when he was just a lad. He would have made a good shepherd. Sheep are funny creatures, you know. People think they're stupid, but that's only because they don't know them. Loyal like dogs they are, and sensitive, like. They don't take to everyone, sheep don't. More trustworthy than most people, too."

"You're not wrong," Tom said. "I've often thought that."

Sam sighed. "I wish I could help you, I really do. I did have a pair once. White as fine china, their wool was. But it's been many years now since I've kept sheep, white or otherwise. You've had a wasted journey, I'm afraid."

"That's all right," Tom said, putting on a brave face. "Thanks for your time." He turned away and Sara followed, echoing his thanks.

"Good luck!" Sam called, raising his hand in farewell.

They said little as they made their way back down the dale. Tom's shoulders slumped, and Sara guessed he was already fearing what would happen if he failed in his task. For her part, she felt only a steely determination. There must be a way to find a white sheep—but how?

"What do we do now?" Tom asked as they passed the Dawes farm and headed back up the hill to gather the flock.

"We think," Sara said shortly.

And think she did, as Tom called the sheep to him to return to the farm for the night, their rainbow hues taunting them. But nothing sprang to mind, and by the time they were heading back over the hill to Guildthorpe in the twilight, she was cursing the Governor and her ridiculous request, and was becoming rather more sympathetic to Sam's view of authority.

"Why don't you stay for supper?" she suggested as they came down through the woods into the Cottons' back garden. "We can keep working on it."

"I wish I could," Tom said, "but I promised Ma I'd be home. First thing tomorrow, though?"

Sara nodded, and he cut through the garden to the road that wound down into the village. She went in at the back door, pausing to light the lamp in the hallway outside her mother's workshop. On impulse, she tiptoed in. She'd always loved the workshop, and Marley had always welcomed her in there right from when she was small, teaching her how to use the various tools, and other tricks of the trade. There were several half-finished toys on the workbench—a nutcracker, a beautiful little wooden cart, and a wind-up rooster that looked just like the real thing. Stacked on a table against the wall were piles of plaster figurines patiently awaiting painting. Sara picked them up one at a time, turning them over in her hands; there were all sorts of animals, birds, and people, as well as a host of mythical and magical creatures. A memory flashed before her—sitting at her mother's side, aged seven or so, learning to paint these little plaster figures. Their making required little skill, but there was artistry in their decoration, and she remembered how desolate she'd felt seeing her pitiful attempt next to the exquisite detail of her mother's work. But Marley had just smiled and bade her keep trying.

"The beauty is in the creation, not the perfection," she'd said.

Now, as Sara looked at the little white creatures, an idea began to stir. At first, she dismissed it as utterly ridiculous, but the more she thought about it, the less crazy it seemed. She didn't even know if it would be physically possible, but then how else to find out but to try? There were deeper misgivings too: something at the core of her being that revolted at the thought. It would mean going against all the promises she'd made to herself when she got home, and unleashing something she wasn't even certain she could control. The thought terrified her. But then there was Tom. She didn't care about the Governor and her silly white cloak, but Tom was her friend—her *only* friend—and she wanted to help him. That surely counted for something.

Mind made up, she began to dig around in the workshop, trying to find what she'd need. It probably wouldn't work anyway, she told herself. There was no harm in doing a bit of preparation. She could always back out later.

It didn't take long to find what she was looking for: a bucket of plaster dust and a large tub of bandages. She drew water from the well in the garden and returned to the workshop, mixing it with the plaster until she had a grey-white liquid. Then she soaked the bandages and, using another bucket as a frame, began to wrap them to create a rounded, bulbous-looking structure. It wasn't exactly true to life, she reflected, but it was close enough for her purposes.

The hours evaporated as she worked, until she was startled by the hall clock chiming midnight. Stretching her aching back, she stood and surveyed her handiwork. Blowing out the lamp and readying herself for bed, she wondered what Tom would think.

THE NEXT MORNING, SARA woke at dawn, knowing that Tom would be along early. Her head felt thick and fuzzy, and she wanted nothing more than a few more hours of sleep. In the cold light of day, her wild idea of the previous night seemed nothing short of madness. Tom would laugh at it, and it was probably just as well, really, because she wasn't even sure she wanted to go through with it.

She was just finishing her breakfast in the wan early-morning light when there was a knock at the back door, and she opened it to find Tom standing on the step.

"Do you want something to eat?" she asked, ushering him inside. He helped himself to bread and jam, and she sat and watched him eat, her own appetite suddenly gone.

"What's wrong?" he asked between mouthfuls.

"Nothing. Why?"

"You look worried about something."

"No...I'm fine."

He gave her a look that assured her he didn't believe a word of it, but said nothing.

"I've got something to show you," Sara said as he finished eating and took his plate to the sink. "I've had an idea about the sheep. It's bonkers, but, well..." She trailed off, unsure how to finish the sentence. Tom just looked at her quizzically and followed her into the workshop.

"Well, what do you think?" she asked, gesturing towards her creation. Tom stared, his eyes popping.

"It's...a sheep?" he said with a touch of uncertainty.

Sara glared at him. "Of course it's a sheep. You don't think it looks like one?" Perhaps it wouldn't be fit for their purpose after all. The life-sized plaster sheep stood between them, staring at her as if it were mocking her.

"I'm just joking," Tom said. "Of course I can tell it's a sheep. It's actually very lifelike. But why have you made it?"

"It was something Sam Shetland said that got me thinking," Sara said. "He said he had sheep with wool as white as fine china. And it occurred to me that if we couldn't find a white sheep, we could make one. This is only plaster, not china, but I think it'll do in a pinch."

There was a long moment of silence.

"I'm afraid I don't understand," Tom said at last. "It's the fleece that's important, not the sheep itself. I'm not sure how this gets us anywhere."

Sara bit her lip. "What if I made it real?"

Tom stared at her as though she'd proposed running naked down the main street of Guildthorpe. "You can do that?"

"Yes...maybe...I mean, I don't really know."

He looked at her for a long moment. "You don't know if you can, or you don't know if you want to?"

People might think him just a simple shepherd, Sara reflected, but he was really far too perceptive for his own good. She sighed.

"Both."

"You know I'd never ask you to do anything you don't want to do," he said. "It's not worth that. If we can't find a sheep, then so be it."

"Can I ask you something?"

"Of course."

"What do you think about magic?"

Tom sighed ruefully. "Now there's a question," he said. "Not having any myself, I'm not sure I'm qualified to answer it."

"I'd say that makes you more qualified than most."

He pulled out a stool and sat down, his brow furrowed in thought. "If you'd asked me just after the war, I would have told you magic was the root of all evil," he said. "I was just a child, but we were all forced to grow up far too fast. Did you know that out of all the children in the village, I was the only one left behind?"

Sara hadn't known that, although if she'd thought about it she could have deduced it.

"No. What was it like?"

"They hated me," he said simply.

"Who did?"

"Everyone. All those who'd lost children. All those who didn't fight harder to find you and the others. They hated themselves for not standing up to the magicians, but it was easier to resent me for not being magical enough to be taken." He said it without malice, as if this was something he'd come to terms with long ago. "The only one who didn't was your mother. She just hated the village council. There was so much hate." He sighed. "Hugo Sweeney didn't need to burn Guildthorpe to the ground to destroy it. We did that ourselves."

"Is it…is it still like that?" It would explain some of the slightly hostile looks she'd received when she'd arrived back in the village. She'd thought everyone would be happy to see her, but they weren't—probably, she realised now, because their own children were still missing.

"It's a lot better than it was," Tom said. "And the thing is, it was never entirely bad. I was very young, and for a long time I blamed magic as the cause of it all, but it wasn't, not really. I mean, Danica Grey uses magic to heal people, and it was especially effective on those injured during the uprisings. John Blackman makes protection charms for people who want to travel, and Lucy Finch can make your vegetable garden twice as productive. And your mother—I know things went a bit off the rails there for a while, but really she's a one-woman village improvement society."

"Is that enough, though?" Sara asked. "I mean, does all that really make up for all the wicked things caused by magic?" She thought of some of the things she'd seen and done, and shuddered.

Tom sat thoughtfully for a moment, then picked up a hammer from the workbench and handed it to her.

"Tell me," he said, "if you hit your thumb, would you blame the hammer?"

"Of course not," Sara scoffed. "That's just silly."

"Well, the way I see it, magic is no different. It's just a tool. It doesn't have good or evil intent of its own; that's up to the people who wield it. That hammer can be used to build a house, but also to bash someone's skull in. Neither outcome is the choice or fault of the hammer." He shrugged. "It's up to you how you use your magic, not anyone else. It will only do evil if you want it to."

Sara frowned to herself. What Tom said made sense, and it shocked her that she'd never thought of it that way—it seemed so obvious. But were good intentions enough? She'd destroyed Sweeney's spellbook with the best of intentions, but she still wasn't sure the result was the unmitigated good she'd expected. Zeb had intimated as much before they parted, and it still gnawed at her. She could control her magic, yes, but only up to a point. What of the unintended consequences? Would it not be better to forgo magic entirely and thus minimise the risk? But then how many people could she potentially help, but was choosing not to?

Tom seemed to sense her inner anguish, for he reached out and patted her hand.

"What's all this about?" he asked.

Sara bit her lip. "You know I've got a…skill…similar to my mother's?" she said. "I can animate things—like my house. You've seen it. They come alive."

Tom nodded.

"Well, I've never tested it, but it's possible that my abilities might go beyond just being able to make inanimate objects move," she said. "A real golem has a kind of consciousness—not to the level of a human, but it's alive just the same."

"You think you can make the sheep come alive?"

"Maybe."

There was a silence.

"That's terrifying."

"I know."

"I can understand now why you're reluctant to try."

"But you think I should?"

Tom shook his head. "Like I said before, it's not up to me either way. If we don't find a white sheep, Farmer Dawes and I will square it with the Governor. It won't be the end of the world. If you do it, it has to be because you want to."

Sara thought for a long moment, then took a deep breath. "I want to know if I can. But if it works, you have to promise me that you'll keep the sheep. You'll never sell it or give it to anyone, including Farmer Dawes. You can make up some story about how you got it, but its origin has to be our secret. There are still too many magicians out there who would want a piece of it, and of me. Deal?"

"Deal."

"Very well. Sit over there." She gestured to a chair in the far corner of the room, and Tom obeyed. Sara found a small piece of parchment and a pen among her mother's things. She took a deep breath and intoned a short incantation, feeling the power swell within her. She channelled it down through her fingers, into the pen, and through the pen into the single word that flowed from it: *Emet*. Life. Rolling the parchment into a small scroll, she slipped it into the mouth of the plaster sheep.

"Breathe," she whispered.

For a long moment nothing happened, and she began to wonder if there was something wrong with the spell, or if she just didn't have the necessary power after all. Then the sheep started to move. It was so slow at first that it was almost imperceptible, but the round body was moving in and out, in and out. It was still plaster, though—just an animated plaster figure, in much the same way that Zeb had told her Stanley was just a wooden dummy come to life. If she wanted anything more, it would require another, riskier spell.

She took up a knife and made a cut across the ball of her thumb, deep enough that the blood welled. For a second, she wondered if her mother would approve of this kind of magic—she suspected not—but she pushed that thought from her mind. She slipped her bloody thumb into the sheep's mouth, next to the roll of parchment, and felt its plaster tongue licking at her. She whispered another incantation, focusing all her energy on the sheep. She'd seen the magicians do this many times, always for nefarious purposes, and it made her stomach turn to think she was anything like them. But the magic was done now, and there was no taking it back. Her vision swam with a sudden headache: magic always came with a cost.

She first noticed the change in the touch of the sheep's tongue on her fingers. Instead of hard, dry plaster, it was warm, wet and sandpapery, like a real sheep's. She pulled her hand away and noticed that there was a faint sheen of hair on its face, growing thicker even as she watched. Its eyes, too, were soft and wet. Sara ran her hand along the sheep's back and felt curls of wool sprouting under her fingers. She stared at Tom, who was gaping at her, wide-eyed.

"It worked," she said. She couldn't quite believe it. Shock mingled with relief and awe tinged with horror at what she was capable of. If she wanted to, she could raise an army. No one could ever hurt her again. The thought terrified her, for she understood now how easy it would be to become another Hugo Sweeney.

The two of them watched in silence as the sheep continued to grow and change, becoming less and less like a model and more and more like a real sheep. After about fifteen minutes the transformation appeared to be complete; the sheep opened its mouth and let out a surprised "baa" before nosing around the workshop, looking for something to eat. Sara beckoned Tom over and they ran their hands through the wool on its back, which was as white as fine china—as white as plaster. The only indication of its unorthodox origin was a slightly chalky texture.

"She's hungry," Tom said as the sheep baaed again, slightly more forcefully this time. "She can come and graze with the flock. Have you got any rope?"

Sara dug around in the various crates and eventually found a piece of thin rope.

"Will this do?"

"Perfect."

Tom fashioned a crude halter and slipped it over the sheep's head. She gazed up at him uncomplainingly, clearly already trusting him. Sara had noticed that the other sheep in his flock behaved the same way; he seemed to have an instant rapport with animals.

"I think I'll call you Blanca," he said. "What do you think?"

The sheep baaed happily.

"Excellent."

Tom turned to Sara. "I don't really know what to say," he said. "If I hadn't seen it with my own eyes, I wouldn't have believed it. But thank you."

Sara smiled. "What happens now?"

"Blanca and I will pay a visit to Farmer Dawes, and she'll be shorn. The Governor will get her white cloak for the King and everyone will be happy."

"You remember your promise? You won't sell her or give her away?"

"Not on your life." He patted Blanca's head. "You're stuck with me, old girl."

Sara declined to walk over to the farm with them; it just didn't feel right, somehow. Her work was done, and now it was up to Tom. She still wasn't sure if she'd done the right thing. Tom's job would be safe, and she had no doubt that he'd keep his promise and give Blanca a good home. But she didn't know how long the sheep would live, or what quality of life she'd have. Was it irresponsible to have created a life so quickly and unthinkingly under such circumstances? *But if everyone thought that way, nobody would ever be born*, she reasoned. It was done now, and she still felt it had been done for the best. But she wouldn't be doing it again any time soon, of that she was quite certain.

She felt unusually flat for the rest of the week, and deliberately stayed home, not even going into the village. She did wonder from time to time how Tom's meeting with Farmer Dawes had gone, but she couldn't bring herself to make the trek over the hill to find out. She didn't feel like doing much of anything, really.

She was sitting in the garden in the soft evening twilight when her mother came home. Marley looked invigorated despite her journey, with glowing cheeks and smiling eyes, but her brow creased with worry when she saw Sara.

"Hello, my love," she said, embracing her, then pulling back and examining her face. "Is everything all right?"

And Sara, quite unexpectedly, felt the tears welling—not demure, ladylike weeping, but huge racking sobs.

"Oh, my baby girl," Marley said, holding her close. "Tell me what the matter is."

They sat there in the crisp evening air as the twilight faded and the stars began to wink out in the darkening firmament, and Sara talked as she hadn't for eight long years. She told her mother everything that had happened since Hugo Sweeney and his magicians had snatched her away, filling in the gaps of the sparse tale she'd told when she first got home. Sometimes they laughed, and more than once Marley had to wipe away tears. She finished with the story of the previous week, of Tom and Blanca and her newfound power, and all her fears for the future.

"I don't want to be like them," she whispered. "It would be so easy to be cruel, and I don't want to be."

"You won't be, my darling."

"But what if it changes me?"

"Of course it will. But unlike Hugo Sweeney, you have people around you who love you and who will guide you. Magic doesn't have to be evil. Think of all the good you'll be able to do." Marley kissed her damp cheeks. "Why don't you get some rest? I'm sure things will look better in the morning."

Sara nodded and gave her mother a long hug.

"I love you, Mama."

"I love you too, baby girl."

THE NEXT MORNING, SARA woke early but was unable to go back to sleep. After their talk the night before, she felt like a weight had lifted. She rose and washed her face, and, leaving a note for her mother, set off for the village. She wanted to buy some pastries and fruit for breakfast, for she was acutely aware that she'd somewhat neglected the housekeeping during her week alone, and there wasn't much food to be had in the larder.

It was a beautiful morning, and for the first time she could remember, she felt at peace with the world. The people she passed on the road into the village seemed happy to see her; they smiled and tipped their hats, or greeted her warmly. Any resentment that may have been there was now no longer, and she wondered how much had been real, and how much had been simply her own invention because, deep down, she'd still felt herself to be an outsider.

She was standing in line at the newly rebuilt bakery when someone tapped her on the shoulder, and she turned to see Polly Brewster, Tom's mother. Sara had always had a soft spot for rotund, red-cheeked Polly, who was as different physically from her beanpole of a son as it was possible to be, but from whom he got his kindness and his calm. They embraced warmly.

"It's good to see you again, Mrs Brewster," Sara said with feeling. "I hope you're well."

"I am, thank you, love," Polly said. "Truly, I've never been better. I just wanted to thank you for what you did for my Tom."

"I don't know what you mean." She hoped Tom hadn't betrayed her confidence already.

"He said you helped him to track down a white sheep for the Governor," she said. "And that he would never have found one without you. It's been a right boon for us, I can tell you that. Charlie Dawes let him keep the bulk of the fee for the fleece, and the sheep is to be his too. A shearing every year will be enough to keep us very comfortable." She mentioned the price Tom had got for the wool, and Sara's eyebrows shot up. She'd known white sheep were rare and valuable, but she hadn't realised quite how much. But if anyone deserved some good fortune it was Tom and Polly, and she couldn't stop smiling.

"It's my pleasure," she said, with utmost sincerity.

She spent the day in the workshop with her mother, learning some of the tricks of the Architecture trade. Sara couldn't remember the last time they'd spent a whole day in each other's company without bickering, and although she knew it probably wouldn't last, it was a welcome change. In the early evening she went out into the garden, watching the sun sink slowly over Guildthorpe, when a sound from the wood beyond the garden gate made her turn. She smiled as through the trees she glimpsed Tom on his way home—with Blanca trotting along behind him.

The Seven-League Boots

T om Brewster walked home in the twilight, as he did every night, with Blanca the sheep gambolling at his heels. Her wool was beginning to regrow after her recent shearing, giving her an endearing, fluffy appearance. At times she behaved more like a dog than a sheep, running up to him when she saw him coming across the fields and nudging his hand so he'd stroke her soft white head. Tom laughed at her as she darted across in front of him, then cursed as she almost tripped him up. It had only been two months or so since she'd joined their household, but he could no longer remember life without her.

They left the woods and joined the road that dropped down into the valley. Tom always loved this part of the journey, coming down the hill and seeing the village lights laid out before him like clusters of fireflies. For a long time he'd felt like an outsider, even though he'd never lived anywhere else; now, finally, coming back to Guildthorpe felt like coming home.

Blanca's appearance had changed his fortunes in the best of ways: the money he got from her rare white fleece meant that his mother no longer needed to work as a seamstress, and he'd also been able to pay for treatment for her failing eyesight. The treatment had arrested the decline, and although she'd never do fine sewing work again, her eyes were unlikely to get much worse. She now spent her days tending their cottage garden, which was flourishing under her care, and volunteering with the village ladies' society. It lifted Tom's heart to see her so happy after all her years of toil.

When he arrived at the cottage he let Blanca into the back garden, where he'd built her a small sheepfold, and went inside, kicking off his muddy boots at the door. His mother was sitting at the scrubbed kitchen table, holding a letter and looking uncharacteristically pensive.

"What's wrong?" Tom asked, hurrying over. He ran through a mental list of any close relatives who might have died; his grandparents had disowned his mother when she got pregnant with him, and she wasn't in touch with any others that he knew of.

"Oh, hello, love." Polly looked up. "Nothing's wrong. I've just had a letter about...well, it might be best if you see for yourself."

Tom pulled out a chair and sat down next to her, taking the letter.

Dear Mrs Brewster,

My name is Eleanor Darke. You don't know me, but I'm Thorsten Mackinder's apprentice. I'm writing to tell you that Thorsten is gravely ill after a curse we were working on rebounded on him. He has expressed a wish to see his son again, and I'm writing to request that Tom come as soon as possible. I wish I could have brought this news to you personally, but I can't leave him, and he wouldn't permit anyone else to contact you. I know this must be a shock coming out of the blue, and I'm sorry. Thorsten is in the Bloomsville cottage hospital, and I urge Tom to hurry. I honestly don't know how long he has left.

Yours faithfully,

Eleanor Darke

Tom read the letter again, struggling to take it in.

"After all this time," he said at last. "It's been what, eight, ten years? Since before the war."

Polly nodded. "He used to work more round these parts," she said. "But he never was a man who was easy to pin down. He loves you, though. I've never doubted that. He sent me money every month from the moment I told him I was pregnant, did you know that? There were times when we would have been hard-pressed to get by without it. In fact, this month was the first I hadn't heard from him. I suppose this explains why."

"He still left you to do it all on your own," Tom said. His father had never been a big presence in his life, apart from the occasional visit when he was a child. And he'd never felt the loss—he and his mother were a team, and a very good one. No one else was necessary. But at the same time, he didn't much like to think of Thorsten dying. It seemed like such a waste.

He glanced at the letter again. "Do you think I should go?"

Polly shrugged. "That's entirely up to you."

"What about you?"

"You don't need to worry about me. Now that my eyes are better and I don't have to work so hard, I'll manage perfectly well if you go. I'll look after Blanca for you." She smoothed back his hair affectionately. "I know he hasn't been around, and you don't really know him. But I told him from the start that I'd never lie to you about him, and I haven't. You have to decide whether you'll regret it if you don't go. Whether there's anything you'll wish you could have said."

Tom thought for a long moment. "I want to ask him why," he said.

"Why what?"

"Why he never came back, but never really left."

"Well, then," Polly said, "it sounds like you've decided."

"Sounds like I have."

Tom walked over to the bookcase and pulled out his most prized possession—a book of maps of the whole country. When he was a boy, he used to leaf through it incessantly, daydreaming about all the places he'd go when he was grown up. But now he was, and he'd never been to any of them.

"Where is Bloomsville, anyway?" he asked, running his finger down the index.

"Not anywhere near here," Polly said with a shrug.

She was right; Bloomsville was a small town two provinces away. Tom sat down heavily, rubbing his face. "I suppose that's that, then," he said. "It'll take me at least three weeks to get there, even with a fast horse. I doubt I'll make it in time."

"There might be a way..." his mother began, but Tom had already jumped to his feet.

"I won't be long," he said, pulling on his boots.

"Where are you going?"

"To see Sara."

"Wait..."

When he arrived at the Cotton house, it was all in darkness. He knocked anyway, but unsurprisingly got no answer. He cursed under his breath; he'd been hoping to ask Sara if she could take him to Bloomsville in her enchanted house. He knew it could travel much faster than any horse, and he could think of no other way to make it to his father's bedside in time.

Shoulders slumping, he returned home, wracking his brain for another solution. He'd call on Sara again tomorrow, just in case; they might have just gone out for the evening. But his mother dashed even this forlorn hope.

"Marley and Sara have gone away," she said. "I tried to tell you, but you ran out of here so quickly. They're visiting friends and will probably be gone at least a month. I saw Marley this afternoon, just before they left."

"What am I going to do?" Tom said. "There just doesn't seem to be a way." It was funny, he reflected, just how quickly he'd got his heart set on seeing Thorsten. He'd never felt a burning desire to know his father, and had never felt his absence particularly keenly. But now, with the real threat of losing him, he suddenly had a whole lot of things he wanted to ask. He wanted to know exactly how much of who he was came from this man, this mysterious curse-breaker who'd spent his life travelling—or perhaps running. And Thorsten had asked to see him, so perhaps there were things he needed to say and know too.

"Don't worry," Polly said. "I may have something that can help. I just have to find it."

She bustled out, and Tom could hear her climbing the stairs to the attic. She was gone a long time—so long that Tom grew impatient and followed her upstairs. He found her digging through dusty boxes in the small attic, which was full of the detritus of both their lives: discarded furniture; crates of old toys; bags of children's clothes that he'd long since outgrown. His mother glanced up from where she was kneeling, rifling through a large chest by the light of a single lamp.

"I couldn't remember where I'd put them," she said, her voice slightly muffled as she dived back into the chest. "But I think...ah yes, here they are! I knew they were here somewhere!" She arose, dusting off her skirts and triumphantly brandishing a pair of weather-beaten old boots. Tom stared at her, his mouth slightly open, wondering if it was possible that his mother had finally cracked.

It was only downstairs, in the brighter light of the kitchen, that he could properly examine her find. The boots, which seemed to be about his size, were travel-stained and worn, but they still looked to be sturdy, with intact soles and supple leather. On the side of each heel was a scrap of leather cut to look like a wing. It was a strange detail, one that niggled at the back of Tom's mind, but which he couldn't quite place.

"Well?" Polly said, smiling. She looked inordinately proud of herself. "What do you think?"

"I...well, I already have a good pair of boots, Ma," Tom said, hoping he wasn't offending her. "It's a lovely gesture, but I'm not sure I need these as well."

Polly laughed and shook her head.

"Daft lad," she said, ruffling his hair. "You don't know what they are, do you?"

"Ah..." Tom opened his mouth, but no words came. What did she mean? They were just a pair of old shoes.

"They're *seven-league boots*," his mother said. "They'll take you seven leagues in a single step, assuming the magic still works, of course."

Suddenly Tom remembered where he'd seen the wing detail—on a picture in one of the cheap adventure stories he used to buy from a visiting tinker when he was younger. It had been of a famous explorer, and Tom could still see him, posed with one foot up on a boulder as if he were about to stride across the world, the wings on his boots clearly visible. *Digby Myna and his seven-league boots*, he remembered the caption saying.

"Where did you get them?"

"It's a funny coincidence, that. Thorsten gave them to me. For you."

"For me?"

"You would have been too young to remember. On one of his early visits, he told me that one day you'd want to go adventuring, and that these would help you when you did. He said I'd know when the time was right to give them to you." A wistful expression crossed her face. "They were the most valuable thing he owned, and I doubt he was able to get another pair. They're quite rare, you know. It must have made his work harder without them. But he wanted you to have them." She shrugged.

Tom turned the boots over in his hands, looking anew at the intricate details.

"How do they work?"

"Ah," Polly said. "That's the problem. I'm not entirely sure. Thorsten said something about plotting your route and then visualising where you wanted to go. Don't try now!" she added as Tom made to pull on the boots. "You'll want to make sure you're packed and ready to go before you put them on, otherwise you might end up somewhere unintentionally without any provisions or anything!"

That was an uncomfortable thought, especially considering he'd never been further from home than the next valley. "You're right, Ma," he said. "I'll leave it till the morning."

They spent the rest of the evening putting together everything Tom would need, including food, warm clothing and a bedroll in case he got caught in the middle of nowhere. Then they spent quite a bit of time taking out half of it so he could actually lift his pack. At last everything was ready, and Tom, yawning, retired to bed.

HE WAS UP AT DAWN THE next morning, for he had to see Farmer Dawes before he did anything else. Thankfully, the farmer was a reasonable man, and he understood why his best shepherd suddenly needed to go away. He laughed seeing Blanca trailing after Tom—for she followed him everywhere like a dog, and refused to stay with the flock unless he was there too.

"What are you going to do with that one?" the farmer asked. "Take her with you?"

"No," Tom said. "I don't think she'd travel well. She'll stay with Ma." He suspected Polly would like the companionship, although how she planned to keep Blanca from eating the garden he didn't know.

"Well, good luck to you," Farmer Dawes said. "I hope all is well with your father and we'll see you back here before too long."

Tom thanked him and hurried home, Blanca trotting ahead.

Back at the cottage, he and Polly once again pored over the map, tracing a route between Guildthorpe and Bloomsville. They broke it down into seven-league lengths as much as they could, then picked the town or settlement closest to the end of each length. Polly marked these on the map with a red dot.

"That's where you need to aim for," she said. It sounded so easy, but Tom had a feeling the reality would be a bit trickier. How was he supposed to visualise places he'd never been? And what if the boots didn't work at all? He knew Thorsten had some sort of magical affinity—you didn't become a curse-breaker without it—but none of it had passed to him. If the seven-league boots were dependent on the aptitude of their wearer, he was going to be in trouble.

Ultimately, there was only one way to find out. Pocketing the map, he pulled on the boots, hoisted his pack onto his back and kissed his mother. Blanca nudged at his hand for a pat, and he bent down and hugged her.

"Be a good girl," he said. "I'll be back soon."

They went out into the road in front of the cottage, Polly holding tight to the wool on Blanca's neck to keep her from following Tom. He took a deep breath, holding the first waypoint—a small village called Middleton—in his mind, then stepped forward into the unknown.

The world lurched around him, blurring into a nauseating rush of colour and light. When everything slowed down again he found himself on his hands and knees beside a road, and was promptly sick. He pulled his water canteen from his pack and sipped slowly; the swirling in his stomach began to ease, and after a few minutes he felt better. He wasn't sure what he'd thought travelling with the seven-league boots would be like; perhaps the wings had given him the wrong idea. But he hadn't expected it to be like that.

"You all right, mate?" a man called out to him from a cart that was trundling slowly along the road, laden with farm produce.

Tom nodded. "I'm fine, thanks."

"You sure? You don't look it. You're white as a sheet."

"Really, I'm fine."

The farmer shrugged and flicked the horse's reins. "All right, if you say so."

Despite his bravado, however, it was a good half hour before Tom felt able to even contemplate another jump. When he finally did, it had the same effect, although thankfully this time it was less extreme—he was still crippled by nausea, but he managed to keep what was left of his breakfast down. He sat beside the road with his back against a convenient tree, nibbling at bread and cheese while he recovered. Looking at his map, he realised that it was going to take him longer to get to Bloomsville than he'd planned. He and Polly had assumed he'd be able to walk along continuously, like he would normally, just covering far more ground. They hadn't anticipated such strong physical effects or the necessary recovery time.

He managed two more jumps that day, but by the end of the last one he was feeling utterly drained. He landed in the main street of a small town called Hackney Ridge, which, he was relieved to see, was big enough to have an inn. Better still, they had rooms available. He paid upfront for the room and a meal, wolfed down a bowl of soup, and collapsed into bed.

He woke the next morning much relieved to discover that the previous day's nausea had vanished; but all the same, he wasn't looking forward to having to go through it all again. He could only hope it would get easier with experience.

Surprisingly, it did. It was still rough going, but he found he needed less recovery time after each jump. He was able to manage five jumps before stopping for the night, although he misjudged the final one and ended up ten miles from the nearest village. Tired, hungry and unable to face the thought of the walk, he set up camp in a stand of trees not far from the road. Although he'd never been far from home, as a boy he'd spent a lot of time in the countryside around Guildthorpe, and during the summers he'd slept outside more often than in his bed. He hadn't used his small canvas tent in some years, but he found he remembered how to put it up well enough, and he was able to build a campfire and cook himself a passable dinner with relative ease. Crawling into his tent after the meal, he tried not to think about robbers or wild animals or any of the other dangers that could befall a traveller on the road in a strange place, but his sleep was fitful all the same.

And so his days took on a strange kind of rhythm. He never managed more than five jumps in a day, but they did get easier, and by the end of the fourth day he was only one jump and a few miles' walk away from Bloomsville. He spent that night in an inn, deciding to make the jump in the morning when he was fresh, rather than having to camp beside the road again. Lying in bed, he tossed and turned, unable to sleep, wondering what he'd find on the morrow. He only hoped he wasn't too late.

He'd left the shutters open the previous night, and the dawn light woke him. The inn was quiet when he went downstairs, all the previous night's revellers still abed. Rather than trying to rouse someone for breakfast, he decided to eat his own provisions as he walked. Out in the road, he visualised Bloomsville and took a step, the now-familiar blurring sensation engulfing him.

The town was slightly outside the seven-league range, so he wasn't surprised when he found himself on a desolate stretch of road, with only frostbitten fields stretching off in all directions. He took a break and ate some bread and cheese while the spinning in his head subsided, then shouldered his pack and set off in what he hoped was the direction of the town.

Two hours later, he arrived in Bloomsville, which was something between a small town and a large village. He asked a fruit-seller for directions to the cottage hospital, and was soon standing outside a two-storey brick building with several large windows and a gabled roof. He took a deep breath, pushed open the heavy front door and stepped into the entrance hall.

Inside it looked more like a manor house than a hospital, with a black-and-white tiled pattern on the floor and a grand, mahogany-balustraded staircase leading up to the next floor. But the air was bitter with the scent of herbs, and there was a slight tingle in the air that Tom immediately associated with healing magic.

A nurse in a blue gown and white cap was standing behind a desk to the left of the doorway. "May I help you?" she asked. Tom was suddenly acutely aware of how dirty and travel-stained he was.

"I'm looking for Thorsten Mackinder."

"Are you a relative?"

"I'm his son." He realised this was the first time he'd ever said the words out loud.

"Just a moment." She ran her finger down the page of a large ledger. "Room 103. Up the stairs and to the right."

Tom thanked her and climbed the stairs to the first floor. Room 103 was easy to find, its door closed. He paused on the threshold, knowing that the minute he stepped over it, his life was going to change irrevocably. He still wasn't sure what he was doing here, visiting this father he'd never known, but he also knew he couldn't gainsay the wishes of a dying man. Trying to damp down his worries, he raised his hand and knocked softly, then turned the handle and slowly opened the door.

The room was pleasant as hospital rooms went, with a large window and plenty of natural light. A young woman was sitting in a chair by the window, reading, but Tom's eyes were immediately drawn to the bed that dominated the centre of the room. He'd always had the impression from his mother of Thorsten as a fit, wiry man, as befitting someone who spent his life travelling around the country, but the man in the bed was thin and drawn, his shoulder-length black hair spread untidily across the pillow. His eyes were closed and his breathing, though shallow, was even.

The young woman looked up as Tom entered, then recognition flared in her face and she jumped to her feet.

"You must be Thorsten's son!" she exclaimed, then lowered her voice as the man in the bed stirred and then resettled. "I'm so glad you came!"

"I'm Tom," Tom said, holding out his hand. "How did you know I'm his son?"

She smiled. "Why, you're the spitting image of him," she said. "I'm Eleanor Darke, Thorsten's apprentice."

"You're the one who wrote the letter," Tom said in realisation. He hadn't expected her to be so young—a few years younger than him, at a guess. "What happened?"

Eleanor glanced at Thorsten, who stirred again at the sound of their voices.

"Let's talk outside," she said. "It's a bit of a long story and he'll probably be asleep for a couple of hours. Where are you staying?"

"Nowhere, yet."

She led him out of the hospital and to an inn on the main street, The Coach and Four. "I've got a room here," Eleanor said, "although I spend most of my time at the hospital. The landlord is a good man and he'll treat you fairly. Most of the hospital visitors stay here."

She sat at a table in the corner of the taproom while Tom organised a room and carried his things upstairs. He quickly changed his sweat-stained shirt and washed his face and hands before joining her. Two glasses of cider and a large platter of bread, cheese, cured meats and pickles were set out before her, and it was only when his stomach rumbled that he realised how hungry he was.

"Dig in," Eleanor said, handing him a plate. "You must be ravenous after such a long journey. I have to say, I'm surprised you got here so quickly. I thought Guildthorpe was miles away."

"It is," Tom said, swallowing a mouthful of bread and cheese, "but I had a bit of help." He showed her his boots, and Eleanor whistled softly.

"Seven-league boots," she said. "You don't see those very often. Thorsten told me once that he used to have a pair, but he lost them, or gave them away, or something. Where did you get yours?"

"Actually, they're Thorsten's," Tom said. "He left them with my mother to give to me."

"Goodness. Do they work? I mean, obviously they do, since you're here, but...what's it like?"

"Horrible," Tom said, shuddering. "I wouldn't use them unless I had to, that's for certain. Now, tell me what happened to Thorsten."

A shadow crossed Eleanor's face. "I'm still not entirely sure myself," she said, "even though I saw it with my own eyes. He's the best in the business; he doesn't make those sorts of mistakes. He wouldn't have survived all these years if he did." She frowned to herself. "Sorry. I know I'm not making much sense. I'll start at the beginning.

"About six weeks ago, we were engaged by a local farmer to remove a curse from his property. He'd been in a long-running dispute with his neighbour, and it all got a whole lot worse when it turned out his son and the neighbour's daughter had secretly fallen in love. Long story short, they eloped, and the neighbour accused our client of aiding them, which he denied. Next thing our farmer knew, all his crops were dying, and his livestock were failing to thrive. The water in his bores turned brackish and the farm was beset by a series of accidents, one of which seriously injured a farmhand. He was convinced that the neighbour had placed a curse on him, or had paid someone to. And he was right—although not necessarily about who did it, for he's a boorish man who makes enemies easily, and really it could have been anyone. When we got there, we found a series of small curses all interwoven. It was unusual but Thorsten said it wasn't anything he hadn't seen before, and he didn't seem too worried about it."

She paused, taking a sip of cider.

"So over the next week or so we went to work, gradually unpicking the web bit by bit. First, we dealt with the curses on the crops and the livestock, then the water. It was hard work, but it was fascinating how it had been put together. I still don't know if it was done all at once or if it was a series of small misfortunes that various people had invoked over many years, and which happened to all be triggered at the same time—and to a certain extent it didn't really matter.

"Finally, we got to the last and most complex curse: the bringing of accidents. This type of curse is obviously quite dangerous, and not something you want to mess around with if you don't know what you're doing. Thorsten forbade me from working on it and insisted on dealing with it all himself, although he explained to me what he was doing so I'd learn as we went. He's good like that. Anyway, I don't know exactly what happened, but something went wrong. Perhaps he misspoke the unravelling words; I don't know. There are a hundred little traps that an unwary curse-breaker can fall foul of. But the next thing I knew, there was a flash of light and he was lying in the dirt." She shuddered at the memory.

"And now he's constantly beset by accidents. It was a miracle I managed to get him to the hospital in one piece, to be honest. He's in less danger there, but even so, there's been mishaps: incorrect medication, doctors who suddenly got called away as soon as he took a turn, and all sorts of things. He's fighting it, but it's taking its toll, and unless we can find a solution, he won't last much longer. The doctors here are very good, but it seems to be beyond their capacity. And we can't risk moving him to a bigger hospital; I don't think he'd make it. He knows his chances aren't good. That's why he asked me to contact you."

Tom sat back and rubbed his face, trying to take it all in. It was all too much, being reunited with his father under such odd and disturbing circumstances.

"I'm not sure how much help I'll be," he said. "I really don't know what I can do."

"You're not a curse-breaker, are you?" Eleanor said with a smile, but he could tell she was only half-joking.

"No, unfortunately," Tom said. "I take after my mother. I don't have a magical bone in my body."

Eleanor's brow crinkled. "I very much doubt that," she said.

"What do you mean?"

"Well, not everyone can use seven-league boots. You must have some sort of aptitude or they wouldn't have worked for you."

"Really?"

"Of course."

Tom wasn't sure what to say to this. His whole identity had been built around how resolutely *un*magical he was. The only child in the village with no aptitude. The only child left behind by the magicians. A seamstress's son and a simple shepherd. Nothing interesting or extraordinary about him at all. And now this young apprentice whom he'd known all of five minutes was telling him this couldn't possibly be the case.

"What would he need to reverse the curse?" he asked.

"I don't know," Eleanor said, and she suddenly looked very tired. "If I knew I would have tried it."

"Well, we'll just have to ask him then."

"I did. He couldn't—or wouldn't—tell me."

"We'll try again. Maybe he's remembered, or changed his mind."

"I doubt that."

"Do you have any better ideas?"

"No."

"Then I guess we'll see."

They finished their lunch and returned to the hospital. When they got to Thorsten's room, a nurse was just leaving.

"You're just in time," she said. "He's just woken up, and he seems a bit better today."

Tom tried to calm the anxiety that had arisen in his chest, and followed Eleanor into the room. Thorsten was propped up on pillows, looking thin and weak. He wasn't doing anything, just gazing out of the window, but he turned towards them as he heard the door open. He gave Eleanor a tired smile, and then he noticed Tom. An expression of wonder crossed his face, and he lifted his hands from the bedclothes in a weak gesture of welcome. Not knowing what else to do, Tom went over to him.

"My boy," Thorsten rasped, his eyes wet. "You came."

"Hello," Tom said. He wasn't sure what term of address to use; calling him 'Thorsten' or 'Mr Mackinder' sounded so impersonal, but calling him 'Pa' or 'Father' was out of the question. Thorsten seemed to sense his hesitation.

"I'm sorry," he murmured, so softly that Tom had to strain to hear. "You probably don't remember me. I should have visited you and your mother more often. It's my greatest regret. I made the mistake of thinking work was the most important thing..." he trailed off, turning back towards the window.

"It's all right," Tom said. "I've never wanted for anything. I'm glad I can be here now." It sounded stiff and formal to his ears, but he wasn't quite sure how to reassure Thorsten that he'd had a good childhood, without also rubbing it in that he'd never felt the need for a father.

"Tom used your seven-league boots to get here," Eleanor piped up. Tom shot her a look, and she shrugged.

"You did?" Thorsten said, his face lighting up. "I'm so glad your mother kept them." The conversation seemed to be taking its toll, and his eyes drifted closed for a moment.

"Eleanor told me what happened," Tom said. "Surely all curses can be reversed?"

Thorsten was silent for so long that Tom began to think he'd fallen asleep. Then he spoke.

"There is a way," he said.

"What?" Eleanor said, shock written on her face. "Why didn't you tell me?"

Thorsten smiled weakly. "You can't do it. False hope seemed...cruel."

"I know I've still got a lot to learn, but I'm confident I can do it if I try."

"It's not that. It needs...blood."

Even this revelation didn't seem to give Eleanor pause. "Last time I checked, I have some."

Thorsten shook his head against the pillow. "Blood from a relative."

"Oh."

Tom gulped. Was that why Thorsten had asked him here—to use him to save himself? What obligation did he have to this father whom he'd never known?

"It's all right," Thorsten whispered, reaching out a hand. "I'm not asking you for that. I'm at peace with my fate. I just wanted to see my boy once more before I go."

On impulse, Tom took the outstretched hand and squeezed it gently, feeling the bones in the fingers as fine as a bird's. He didn't know what to say, but it didn't matter anyway, for Thorsten had fallen asleep again.

They sat in silence for some time, as the afternoon sun drifted lower, its golden light slanting in through the window and falling across the bedclothes. Tom felt like two halves of himself were at war. One, the practical, self-preserving side, told him that he had no obligation to Thorsten beyond comforting a dying man. Thorsten was technically his father, yes, but really in name only, and Thorsten himself would agree—had already agreed. But the other, more compassionate side protested. If he would jump out into a busy street to save a stranger—which he hoped he would—or walk miles to find a single lost sheep, then surely he could at least explore the possibility of saving Thorsten, without whom, after all, he wouldn't exist.

In all likelihood, he wouldn't be able to do whatever it was he needed to anyway, in spite of his blood. Personally, he thought Eleanor's estimation of his magical aptitude was grossly exaggerated; after all, she hardly knew him. He was no curse-breaker. But if he tried and failed, nobody would be any worse off. Thorsten could go in peace, and Eleanor—and his mother—would know that they'd done everything they could. For his mother was a consideration too. He knew she still cared for Thorsten, and he felt like he'd be letting her down, would be betraying the values she raised him with, if he didn't at least try.

"Do you have any idea what this reversal process could be?" he asked Eleanor at last.

She shook her head. "It's the first time I've had to deal with blood curses," she said. "I'm still quite new at this." She chewed her lip thoughtfully. "I might be able to find out, though."

A nurse came in then to check on Thorsten, and the conversation lapsed as she bustled around. "He'll be sleeping for a good while, I should think," she said gently, once she'd finished taking his pulse and checking his breathing. "You might as well get some rest yourselves. We can send a messenger to The Coach and Four if anything changes."

Tom nodded gratefully and stood up, stretching his stiff neck. A hot meal and a decent sleep wouldn't go astray. Eleanor followed him out and they walked back to the inn in silence, each busy with their own thoughts.

"So how are you going to find out about the counter-curse?" Tom asked as they sat down to supper in the tap-room.

"I'll show you after we're finished," Eleanor said, and he had to be content with that.

When the meal was done, she led him upstairs to her little room, across the landing from his own. Inside it was identical to his, with a bed, a wardrobe and a small wash-stand. Eleanor pulled a haversack out of the wardrobe and carefully removed a thick book. Its leather binding was worn and cracking in places, the gold edging of the pages tarnished. She motioned to Tom to sit on the bed—for there was nowhere else—and sat down beside him, laying the book on her lap.

"What's this?" Tom asked. The title was written in an ornate script in a language he couldn't understand.

"Thorsten calls it the curse-breaker's manual," Eleanor said. She flipped it open, showing intricate, hand-lettered pages in the same indecipherable language.

"Can you read it?" Tom peered at the book. The top of each section was beautifully illuminated and detailed with rather graphic illustrations showing the effects of the various curses.

"Not fluently, but I'm learning. The dialect has all but died out. It only survives by experienced curse-breakers teaching it to their apprentices."

"So this lists all the curses and counter-curses?"

"Not all of them, but most. It's quite rare to discover a wholly new curse—most are variations on the classics. Thorsten makes notes whenever we come across something unusual, just like his master did, and the one before her too." She flipped through the book again, and Tom saw annotations in the margins, written in a variety of hands, but all in the same archaic language.

"Why don't they use modern speech?"

"They don't want it to fall into the wrong hands. As it is, only someone who has studied extensively can hope to understand it. Can you imagine if everyone could read a book of the world's most dangerous curses?"

Tom could, and saw her point. "So where's the part we need?"

"I'm getting to it." She opened the book towards the middle, and started carefully turning the pages. Tom saw that most of the pictures involved people gushing blood from various body parts.

"Here we are," she said at last. "Just let me check something." She pulled a smaller book from her bag and flipped through it. "Dictionary," she said in response to his enquiring glance.

Tom wiggled his toes inside his boots, trying to curb a growing impatience. Of all the images he'd had of curse-breaking, none had involved poring over an ancient text with a dictionary.

"This is definitely it," Eleanor said, looking up. "The bringing of accidents. See, this bit here describes the effect of the curse, and then this is what you need to implement it. This is a very old curse."

"How can you tell?"

"Animal sacrifice. They weren't very subtle back then. You also need hair or blood from the person being cursed."

"Does it list the counter-curse?"

She continued reading. "Sort of."

"What does that mean?"

"So, have you ever cooked from a recipe that didn't include much detail? Where it just says, 'bake until golden-brown' and you have to figure out how hot you need to make the oven and how long it should stay in for?"

"I suppose..."

"Well, it's a bit like that. It gives the basics of what's required, but it's relying on the reader's knowledge to fill in the gaps."

"And can you?"

"Maybe. I'm not sure."

"Oh, well that's great then."

"I'm not experienced enough to know things for sure, but I can take an educated guess. It may work...or it may not."

"And if it doesn't? What will happen—apart from Thorsten dying?"

"Well...the curse could transfer to you. I don't know what else could happen. I doubt any of it would be good."

Tom took a deep breath. This was going to be riskier than he'd thought.

"If it transfers to me, would Thorsten recover?"

"Probably."

"And then he'd be able to free me from it?"

Eleanor stared at him. "That's a huge risk," she said. "He probably could, but there's so many things that could go wrong. Thorsten is an experienced curse-breaker with a lot of magical aptitude—that's why he's been able to fight it for so long. Not everyone could."

"So you're saying it could kill me before he had the chance to free me from it?"

"I'm saying it's possible. Not inevitable, but definitely possible."

Tom thought for a long moment.

"I can't let him die without at least trying to save him," he said at last. "So tell me what I need to do. Do I have to make some obscure magic potion under a full moon?"

Eleanor laughed, cutting the tension. "No," she said. "Thank goodness we don't have to wait around for full moons all the time, or we'd never get anything done. Practically, it's quite simple. Just your blood and his. It's the part that comes next which will be difficult, and I don't know exactly what that will be."

A thought occurred to Tom. "How do you break this curse if the victim has no relatives?"

Eleanor sighed. "You don't. That's what makes it so vile."

Tom was taken aback. Until now, curse-breaking had seemed like a bit of a game—a high-stakes one, to be sure, but a fairly simple equation of good and evil, where good always won, provided you could solve the riddle. It shook him to realise that in some cases there was no solution, and if he'd decided not to visit Thorsten, he would have been condemning him to death.

"Let's get on with it, then," he said, but Eleanor shook her head.

"Get some sleep," she advised. "You'll need it if this is going to work."

"But...what if Thorsten dies overnight?"

"If you attempt this when you're exhausted, you could *both* die."

Tom nodded reluctantly, and stood up. "First thing in the morning, then?"

Eleanor nodded. "Sleep well."

Tom had so much on his mind that he thought he was never going to be able to rest, but as soon as he lay down the exhaustion of the day caught up with him and he fell into a deep slumber, hauled bodily through strange and eerie dreams. He awoke to the dawn light drifting into the room, for he'd deliberately left the shutters open. For a moment he lay there, dazed, trying to remember where he was, then all the pieces fell into place and he sat up with a start. He dressed hurriedly, then dashed across the landing and banged on Eleanor's door.

"All right!" Her voice sounded muffled, as if she'd just woken up, but he didn't have to wait very long before the door opened and she appeared, looking far more composed than he felt.

"Breakfast?" she asked.

"It's too early," he said. "The kitchen staff won't be up. And I just want to get going."

She nodded. "Let's go, then."

When they arrived at the hospital, the big front doors were locked. Tom shook them in frustration while Eleanor rang the bell. It hadn't even occurred to him that it would be too early to visit.

Eventually they heard the soft tap of footsteps in response to their knocking. There was a thunk as a key turned in the lock, and the door cracked open. The matron stood there, glowering at them.

"What's all this about, then?" she asked, frowning. "Visiting hours start at nine."

"Please, ma'am," Tom said, trying his best to be respectful, "we're here to see Thorsten Mackinder. We have something that might help him. I'm his son."

The matron looked them both up and down, then her expression softened.

"Very well," she said. "I wouldn't normally make an exception, but he had a bad night. It's best you see him now. Make sure you're quiet, mind. I won't have anyone else disturbed."

"Yes, ma'am." Tom's shoulders slumped with relief.

The hospital hallways were dim and quiet, with just the odd nurse tapping quietly by on their rounds. The matron led them to Thorsten's room and opened the door.

"Take as much time as you need," she said, ushering them in and closing it behind them.

Tom had thought Thorsten looked bad the previous day, but he'd clearly got worse overnight. His breathing was shallow and sometimes seemed to stop altogether. Eleanor stared at him, horror in her eyes.

"Quickly," she said. "We don't have much time. Give me your hand." She'd explained on the walk over what he needed to do, but now that the time had come, Tom felt his stomach flutter with fear. Nevertheless, he held out his hand as she pulled a small but wickedly sharp knife out of her pocket. She sliced it across his palm so quickly that it was a few seconds before the sting hit. Blood welled along the line of the cut. Then she took Thorsten's hand and did the same to him. He flinched but didn't wake.

Fighting down a wave of nausea, Tom gripped Thorsten's hand palm-to-palm so that their blood mingled and merged. For a long moment, nothing happened, and as his palm grew sticky Tom began to wonder if Eleanor's book could possibly have been wrong. He was just about to turn and ask her, when he was hit by a wave of energy that made him stumble. He felt Thorsten's hand twitch beneath his own. His hair crackled and stood on end, and he squeezed his eyes shut. A series of visions flashed across his eyelids, of disasters and calamities, so fast-moving that he barely had time to comprehend them, but somehow he knew that they were what would result from the curse. He could feel it moving through his body like a physical force, as if it had got into his bloodstream and was turning his veins black. It felt unstoppable, inexorable, and for a moment he was engulfed by a wave of panic.

Then a tiny part of his mind piped up like a bird in a thunderstorm, offering the merest flicker of resistance.

No, his inner voice said, and he felt the force of the curse pause for a minute, as if it had never encountered the word before. Another vision flashed before him, but this time it was of all the things he held dear—Guildthorpe, and his mother, and Blanca. Farmer Dawes and Sara and George were there, and even Eleanor and Thorsten. There were memories of tending the sheep on bright spring days, with wildflowers blooming all around him and the scent of impending summer in the air. He remembered the winter just gone, when the village was blanketed in thick snow for a week, sitting by the fire with his mother in the evening, reading aloud from his favourite childhood stories. With every memory, the curse's power seemed to recede. He delved deeper, back into his childhood—which, for the most part, had been a happy one—remembering the ordinary but sweet days spent wandering woods and fields in the long golden afternoons. His heart ached for home and loved ones, but it was a good ache, and as it swelled, the black mass of the curse finally burst into a thousand pieces and he opened his eyes.

Thorsten was awake and staring at him with eyes like saucers. He still looked thin and drawn, but he was sitting up and lucid. Eleanor's mouth was hanging open. Tom blinked at them.

"What's the matter?" he asked.

Eleanor seemed to be struggling for words.

"What...what on earth was that?" she asked at last.

"What?"

"The curse—it's gone."

Tom furrowed his brow in puzzlement, looking around the room as if he expected to see it lurking in a corner somewhere.

"I suppose it has."

"But...I saw it jump from Thorsten to you. You looked like you were having some sort of fit. That was what happened when it first attached to Thorsten too. But it was...different...with you. It was like you fought back. And then there was this sort of, I don't know, silent *boom*, and then you opened your eyes. I just—I don't understand."

"He's a curse-breaker," Thorsten said, smiling weakly. "My son, through and through. I knew when I left the seven-league boots for you that if you could use them you'd have what it takes."

THORSTEN REMAINED IN hospital for a few days more while they fed him up and got him back on his feet. By the time he left, there was colour in his cheeks and a hint of his old strength in his step, but there was also new grey in his hair and new lines around his eyes.

"I'm getting too old for this," he said as he sat down with Tom and Eleanor in the taproom of The Coach and Four. He said it with a smile, but Tom got the feeling he was only half-joking. Eleanor clearly did too, for she looked up with a start.

"Don't worry," Thorsten said. "I'll keep going until you've finished your apprenticeship. It wouldn't be fair otherwise. But you'll need to start taking on more of the hands-on work, I think."

"Excellent," Eleanor said, seemingly happy with this proposal.

"You know," Thorsten said, turning to Tom, "I could organise an apprenticeship for you, too, if you want it. Not with me, of course—that wouldn't be right—but there are one or two good operators I know who could be persuaded to take you on."

"Me?" Tom said incredulously. "Are you joking?"

"Not at all," Thorsten said with a shrug. "I don't know where you got this idea that you have no magical aptitude, but it's just not true. You could be much more than just a shepherd if you wanted to. It can be a tough life at times, but it has its compensations. You certainly get to see a lot of the world."

Tom bit his lip. "Let me think about it," he said.

"Very well," Thorsten said. "Eleanor and I are leaving tomorrow. Take until then."

"Speaking of which," Eleanor broke in, "you should rest if you're going to be up to travelling." And it was true that Thorsten was starting to look pale and tired. He nodded and rose.

"I'll see you both later," he said.

"Sleep well," Tom replied.

Eleanor rose too. "I should go and pack," she said, then her expression softened. "He means well, you know," she added. She smiled and rolled her eyes. "He's hopeless when it comes to feelings, but he's really very proud of you, even if he doesn't say it. Offering you an apprenticeship is his way of showing how grateful he is for what you did."

Tom shrugged.

"It really is an extraordinary life," she said. "Really consider it. Opportunities like this don't come along every day."

"I will."

True to his word, Tom spent the rest of the day thinking about Thorsten's offer. In the afternoon he went for a walk out through the village and into the woods and fields beyond, not with any intention of getting anywhere but just because he needed space to breathe. If he took up an apprenticeship, this would be his life, he thought—roaming the countryside, working when and where he was needed, never stopping in one place for too long. There was an appeal to it, to be sure: the attraction of an ever-changing vista, of people and places he couldn't even dream of now. But he kept coming back to the day he broke the curse, and wondering. They hadn't discussed it much, but he was beginning to develop a theory about why he'd managed it when Thorsten could not. All those memories, all that love, were far more powerful than any of them could have guessed. And by the time he returned to the village, he'd made his choice.

HE MET THORSTEN AND Eleanor outside the inn early the next morning. He'd half-expected a sleepless night, but once he'd come to his decision, all he felt was an immense sense of relief. The seven-league boots were safely stowed in his pack, replaced with his old non-magical pair, for although it would take longer, he was happy to travel by more sedate means.

"Well?" Thorsten asked after they'd exchanged the usual pleasantries. "Will you be coming along with us?"

Tom paused for a moment, then shook his head. Eleanor nodded; she didn't look surprised. But Thorsten's eyebrows rose until they were almost lost in his hair.

"Whyever not?"

Tom smiled. "I know my life probably seems small and boring to you," he said, "but I like it that way. I like staying in the one place, and building a community with people I care about. I'm good at what I do, and I enjoy it, and dull as it may seem to others, I think it's important. Magical aptitude or not, I know I wouldn't make a good curse-breaker. I'd always be pining for home. It's a very kind offer, but I'm afraid I can't accept it."

He'd expected Thorsten to get angry or to try and convince him to change his mind, but instead he just smiled. And in his eyes was something Tom never thought he'd see—respect.

"You're a smart lad," Thorsten said, clapping him on the shoulder. "Your mother raised you well." He paused, seemingly wrestling with himself.

"I'm very proud of you. I know I haven't been much of a father, but I was wondering—might I visit Guildthorpe sometime? I'd like to see you again, and Polly too, of course."

Tom bit back a smile; from the way he'd said his mother's name, it was clear that Thorsten still carried a torch for her.

"Of course," he said. "You'll always be welcome."

THE SUN WAS SETTING and the clock in the square was striking suppertime when Thorsten Mackinder arrived in the village of Guildthorpe. Candles glittered in the windows of the houses, giving them a warm, homely feel. Thorsten followed a path that his feet remembered, even if his mind did not, until he came to a small cottage set behind a white picket fence, the flowers in its front garden glowing in the twilight. He knocked twice at the sunshine-yellow door, then waited. And when he saw the woman who opened it—older than he remembered her, but no less lovely for that—and, behind her, his own dear boy, he knew that at last he'd come home.

Acknowledgements

Authors often get asked where we get our inspiration from, and most of the time I'm hard-pressed to pinpoint an exact source. In this case, however, there are a few things and people who explicitly inspired this book, and to whom I owe a debt of thanks.

The format of this book is loosely based on a longform improvised theatre technique, 'Follow the Leaver', which I learned from Nick Byrne and the crew at ImproACT. Thanks for taking me out of my comfort zone and helping me reach new creative heights.

Many years ago I heard Australian singer-songwriter Darren Hanlon's lovely song, *Notes on Leaving*, which opens with the beautiful phrase: "In the land of the eternal night-time/There's a single lamppost on a far-off hill/The people go to see if their own shadows/Grow out of their feet and are with them still." Ever since, I've wanted to write a story based on these lyrics, and 'The Light at the Edge of the World' is the result. I hope it does them justice.

My other major source of inspiration is my wonderful husband, Tristan, for whom conversations about time flies, plaster sheep and golem houses are entirely normal. Many of the ideas in these stories originated with him, and many of the plot problems were solved by nutting them out with him over cups of tea. Thanks for helping me find space to write in our day-to-day craziness.

To my darling Anna, thank you for giving me a new perspective on the world. You enrich our lives more than we could have ever imagined, and I can't wait to share even more adventures with you.

To my family—Amanda, Graeme, Esther, Tom, Yelise and Adrian—thanks for always supporting me and taking my creative endeavours seriously.

Thanks also to Grace Weier and Malorie Ralph for friendship and support in a strange place at a strange time, to the Best Mums Group Ever for solidarity in sleep deprivation, and to Catriona Bryce and Shannon Tow for beta reading and all-round confidence-building.

My wonderful editor, Maxine McArthur, was instrumental in helping this weird beast of a book reach its full potential. Thanks for pushing me to take creative risks and for encouraging me to see things differently.

The writing of this book was supported by a grant from the Ipswich Regional Arts Services Network. Huge thanks to Jennifer Hogan and Ant McKenna for encouraging me to apply, and for all the support you give local artists.

I also owe thanks to a large number of people who have welcomed me into the arts scene of my new hometown: Josie Berry, Donna Cavanagh, Debbie Chilton, Jude Covell, Caragh Dickson, EJ Garrett, Nigel Lavender, and Cass Ramsay for cluing me in on what's happening around our region and giving me opportunities to participate; and David Webster and the members of the Blackstone-Ipswich Cambrian Choir for welcoming our family so wholeheartedly.

Thanks also go to Chris Millgate-Smith and the staff and students at Tintern Grammar School and Kilvington Grammar School, whose ongoing support and enthusiasm for my first novel, *Greythorne*, gives me motivation to keep writing. Likewise to local libraries everywhere, but especially the Ipswich Library Service and Libraries ACT. And to my various artistic and writerly friends in Sydney, Canberra, Brisbane, Melbourne, Tasmania and elsewhere, thanks for your ongoing support and inspiration over all these years. Everyone needs their people, and I'm so glad I've found mine.

www.ingramcontent.com/pod-product-compliance
Lightning Source LLC
Chambersburg PA
CBHW050009120726

47903CB00006B/1692